"It's a mes... accident ab... Manny Cordova... looks like the driver lost control."

Nolan listened to the report coming over the police scanner. Since he was the only one on call at the newspaper, it looked as if that "mess" was his responsibility. He loved most things about owning and managing the local newspaper. But stories like this were never fun.

He took a sharp corner slowly, his tires jostling on the poorly maintained pavement. Ahead he spotted the flashing lights of emergency vehicles. Parking behind the police cars, he had a view of the accident. The vehicle—some kind of SUV—had gone off the road and crashed into a rock outcrop.

He'd have to get a photo. About to uncap his camera, Nolan froze. He could just see the rear license plate of the mangled vehicle. And he'd seen that particular pattern before.

And then it hit him.

The SUV belonged to his sister.

Dear Reader,

In our family my husband, Michael, is the one who is usually taking business trips. I stay at home and look after the kids and the house and shovel all the snow (it *always* snows when he goes away). When I found out I was going to be working on a series set in New Mexico, though, I knew that this was my chance. I had never been to New Mexico. Clearly a "business trip" was in order.

So I told my husband, "Honey, I'm going on a business trip to New Mexico." He asked me what I was going to do there. "Oh, go shopping and sightseeing and hang out in the local coffee shops. I'll probably have to take lots of pictures," I added, so it would be clear that I would be working very hard. I think he must have felt sorry for me by this point, because that's when he volunteered to come with me.

Several months after that trip, I sat down at my computer with visions of mountains and deserts and Georgia O'Keeffe paintings filling my imagination. Michael and I had a wonderful time in New Mexico. It's a beautiful place, an enchanting place. The perfect setting—in my opinion— for THE BIRTH PLACE series.

If you've read the earlier BIRTH PLACE books, you'll already have met my hero and heroine. Kim Sherman is the birth center accountant who has come to town for reasons only she knows. And Nolan McKinnon is the local newspaper editor whose world is about to be torn apart by a family tragedy. I hope you enjoy the adventure of their love story. And come back to Enchantment next month to discover the truth behind the legend of the homecoming baby.

Sincerely,

C.J.*Carmichael*

P.S. I'd love to hear from you! Write to #1754-246 Stewart Green, S.W., Calgary, Alberta T3H 3C8. E-mail: cj@cjcarmichael.com.

Leaving Enchantment
C.J. Carmichael

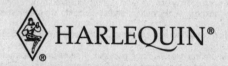

TORONTO • NEW YORK • LONDON
AMSTERDAM • PARIS • SYDNEY • HAMBURG
STOCKHOLM • ATHENS • TOKYO • MILAN • MADRID
PRAGUE • WARSAW • BUDAPEST • AUCKLAND

ISBN 0-373-71170-0

LEAVING ENCHANTMENT

Thanks to all the "Super" authors who made collaborating
on this project so much fun: Darlene Graham,
Brenda Novak, Roxanne Rustand, Kathleen O'Brien,
Marisa Carroll. What a great team of writers to work with!

Special thanks to Anita Cisecki, R.N., ISE,
who works in high-risk obstetrics at the Foothills Hospital
in Calgary, for sharing her amazing experience and
expertise. Lucky for me my brother married your sister!

Books by C.J. Carmichael

HARLEQUIN SUPERROMANCE

CHAPTER ONE

THE SPACIOUS ROOM FELT tranquil and homey—with dim lighting, soothing classical music and the scent of lavender in the air. Steve Davidson rubbed massage oil through the back opening of his wife's favorite flannel nightgown, while Mary crouched on her hands and knees panting softly.

She was ten centimeters dilated.

Lydia Kane, midwife and founder of The Birth Place, observed the young woman thoughtfully. Six years ago, Mary's first delivery had been relatively quick. Lydia had predicted that this second one would be even faster. And yet the baby still hadn't dropped into position in the birth canal.

Across the room, where she was folding the damp towels Mary had used to towel off from a soak in the whirlpool tub earlier, Gina Vaughn, the assisting midwife, was biting her bottom lip. Lydia caught her gaze and gave her a reassuring smile.

Gina was doing wonderfully. Newly certified, a mother of two herself, Gina's passion for the calling reminded Lydia of herself decades ago. Oh, she'd been terribly idealistic at that age. A part of her, she knew, still was.

Even after all these years, every birth Lydia attended gave her the same deep sense of wonder and satisfaction. The belief that she was helping mothers savor the full meaning of their childbirth experience had motivated her to establish The Birth Place in the fairly isolated town of Enchantment, New Mexico, and to keep it running—sometimes overcoming incredible hurdles—for over forty years.

"Excuse me." Steve approached, his eyes creased with concern. "How much longer, do you think? She's really in a lot of pain."

"Let's see how she's doing." Lydia performed a quick examination. The baby hadn't descended into the pelvis yet. *Come on, little guy,* she urged silently. She checked Mary's temperature while Gina assessed the fetal heart rate with a handheld Doppler. Steve and Mary both seemed to relax slightly when they heard the steady rhythm.

"It's 145 to 150 beats per minute," Gina said.

Lydia nodded. "Temperature is normal." She turned back to Steve. "It shouldn't be much longer. Let's wait for a few more contractions. Mary, do you want to try squatting at the side of the bed?"

Maybe a change in position would help bring the baby down.

Lydia knew the Davidson's daughter, Sammy, hoped for a sister. But Lydia suspected Mary was carrying a boy, at least one pound heavier than Sammy had been.

"You're doing beautifully," she told Mary, strok-

ing the petite woman's back, containing her own
growing unease.

"That last contraction was a killer." Mary crawled
awkwardly from the bed, leaning heavily on Steve for
support. She grabbed one of the strong wooden posts,
then squatted, pulling hard on the bed as another contraction swept over her.

"Oh, I need to push!" Mary cried.

Lydia understood the other woman's overwhelming
urge to bear down. In second-stage labor, Mary's entire body was focused on expelling the child from her
womb.

"Good work, Mary," she encouraged.

Gina adjusted Mary's gown so she could get yet
another Doppler reading. Again, the sound of a strong
heartbeat filled the room. Mary and Steve's baby appeared to be coping well.

And yet...

Reserving judgment for a few more minutes, Lydia
considered Steve's worried face. These days, almost
all of Lydia's client's husbands or partners chose to
be present during the birthing experience—sometimes
with siblings and other family members, too. Six years
ago, Steve had been one of those keen father-to-be's.
But in the last, difficult hour of Sammy's delivery,
when Mary had been alternately crying and whim-
pering, he had left the room.

Lydia knew he'd been disappointed later, and so
had Mary. This time Steve was determined to stick it

out—for Mary and for himself. But he already appeared a little woozy.

"This is it!" Mary reached for Lydia's hand as her body surged in one more powerful contraction. "Oh my God, the baby's coming!"

But twenty minutes later, the baby still hadn't descended very much. Lydia checked the time. Almost seven in the evening. More than five hours had passed since the Davidsons had arrived with Mary already in established labor. Lydia didn't know what was wrong. Mary's contractions certainly palpitated strong enough. Baby's heart rate was stable. There was no apparent reason to be concerned and yet Lydia's sixth sense warned that all was not well.

"Something doesn't feel right," she said quietly to Gina.

"Taking a little longer than we expected."

Yes. But why? Lydia looked at the tiny woman who was now back on the bed, exhausted, disheartened. The disparity in size between Mary and her large-framed husband had caused Lydia concern when she'd first met the couple six years ago. But Mary had a proven pelvis. Sammy had weighed in at just over eight pounds.

However, this second child was bigger than the first. Perhaps even bigger than Lydia had estimated.

She made up her mind. "I'm moving them to the hospital."

After a second Gina nodded. "Maybe that's wise."

"I've got the air mattress in the back of my van. Drive it right up to the back door, would you? My keys are in the top drawer of my desk. I'll talk to the Davidsons."

"Is there a problem?" Steve had noticed the two midwives conferring quietly.

"Probably not." Lydia smiled at him, then his wife. "You're doing wonderfully, Mary, and your baby is a real champ, too. But this delivery is taking longer than I expected, and I always play it safe in situations like this. I want to move you to the hospital."

Arroyo County Hospital was just minutes away. Nevertheless, delivery in a bright, modern, bustling hospital was not what the Davidsons had wanted. It wasn't what Lydia wanted for them, either, but she could not take any chances.

"I don't want— Ohhh…" Another contraction hit Mary, sweeping away her objection. Lydia calmly coached her through the pain. When it was over, Lydia performed a quick reexamination to see if the baby's head had dropped. Unfortunately, no progress had been made.

"I'm sorry, Mary, but we have to move you. I know it's going to be uncomfortable, but Gina will ride with you in the back of my van. Steve, do you want to sit up front with me?"

"I'll drive my own vehicle," he decided, his voice taut with anxiety.

"Fine. We'll meet you there. And don't worry. Dr. Ochoa is on duty tonight. He'll take good care of Mary."

DR. OCHOA, AN OBSTETRICIAN at the Arroyo County Hospital, met them in the delivery room. Lydia referred all her high-risk patients to Dr. Ochoa and had unfaltering admiration for the man. His reciprocal respect explained their professional association for over twenty years.

"What's the problem?" he asked, snapping on a new pair of gloves.

Already positioned on the delivery table, pale, exhausted Mary had no energy to speak. Steve, as well, was quiet and tense. Lydia hoped he wasn't going to faint. Gina obviously had the same concern. She was at his side, watching him carefully.

Quickly Lydia filled the doctor in on the patient's case history. "Mary's been at ten centimeters for almost two hours now. The baby still hasn't descended."

The doctor nodded. "Well, let's take a look. Maybe something happened on the drive over." He ambled to the delivery bed. "Hello, Mary, Steve. I'm Dr. Ochoa. How are you doing?"

After a quick examination he noted that the baby was now in position. "But—" he gave Lydia a smile of approval "—I'm glad you brought her in. It's always better to err on the side of caution." He turned back to the anxious parents-to-be. "Shouldn't be long now."

Lydia noticed Steve's shoulders relax a fraction. Did he feel better now that a *real* doctor was in charge? Mary, however, seemed stressed. Lydia took her hand.

Mary's anxious gaze sought hers. "Will you stay until my baby's born?"

"I will."

"You won't leave me?"

"No." She patted Mary's shoulder then glanced at the doctor, who nodded in acceptance.

"And my baby's still okay?"

A nurse had hooked Mary up to an external fetal monitor now and had started an IV, as well. Lydia had only to glance at the machine to see the same fetal heart rate they'd tracked on the Doppler at The Birth Place.

"Your baby is fine, Mary." She smiled across the room at Steve, who was leaning against a wall. "And you're doing great, too, Dad." Steve mustered a small smile in reply.

"Here comes another…" Mary pushed as best she could through the force of the contraction. With legs open and feet resting on the birthing bars, she sat at a fifty-five degree angle, grabbing her thighs.

"Oh-oh-oh…"

"Good work, sweetheart." Steve spoke in an attempt to be reassuring. He couldn't watch anymore, poor man. Lydia was about to suggest he take a breather, when suddenly the baby was crowning.

"The baby's coming, Mary!" the doctor said.

The next contraction came only seconds after the previous. "Keep pushing, Mary," Lydia urged.

Valiantly Mary bore down and the baby's head delivered—large, pink and topped with matted black hair. *Oh, he's beautiful,* but Lydia no sooner had that thought than the head receded partway into the birth canal.

She glanced sharply at the doctor, who frowned in return.

"One more time, Mary," he instructed.

The next contraction should have done it. Mary's face contorted with the effort of pushing. But nothing happened.

Fear, sharp and cold, froze Lydia. Something was terribly wrong here. The baby's shoulders were trapped within the pelvis.

"Heart rate is one hundred," the nurse reported. She put in a call for more help and a second nurse arrived a moment later.

Come on! Come on! Lydia chanted silently as another contraction proved as ineffective as the one before. Lydia slid in next to the doctor.

"Shoulder dystocia?"

Dr. Ochoa nodded.

Lydia had dealt with this complication before and delivered healthy babies every time. Still, she was very relieved that she'd made the decision to transfer the birth to the hospital.

"Why isn't the baby coming?" Steve asked. "Is this normal?"

Far from it. In this position, the baby's supply of oxygen was compromised. Every second counted. But Lydia was trained to project calm, even in moments of crisis. "We're trying, Steve."

"Let's reposition the mother." Dr. Ochoa's tone was becoming more curt by the moment. Lydia did her best to reassure Mary as the bed was lowered to a flat position. Each of the nurses took one of Mary's legs and lifted it up and back toward Mary's ears. The doctor swept his fingers inside the stretched tissue of the perineum.

Seconds ticked by. A minute.

Lydia empathized with Dr. Ochoa as he tried desperately to angle the baby's head down to the floor. But this baby simply would not move. Ochoa was sweating now, trying various maneuvers in increasingly desperate attempts to release one of the baby's shoulders. If he had to, Lydia knew he would break the clavicle. They were running out of time.

"What are you doing?" Mary could barely utter the words through her exhaustion.

"Trying to get the baby out." Lydia glanced at her watch, calculating the time that had already passed. *Come on! Come on!*

"But we didn't—" Another contraction knocked the words out of Mary's mouth. She bore down and Lydia prayed.

"Come on, baby!" His face was turning blue. They *had* to get him out, his heart rate was continuing to drop. Eighty. Now sixty. Blue skin deepened to purple, and Lydia fought to keep calm.

"What's happening?" Steve searched faces anxiously. He and Gina were standing too far back for him to actually see the action.

More personnel flooded into the room. Among them, Lydia recognized Dr. Joanna Weston, an excellent local pediatrician. No one bothered with the pleasantries of a greeting. All eyes focused on Dr. Ochoa and the baby he was trying desperately to bring into the world.

"Try a lateral push." The doctor continued to work at delivering the shoulder, while one of the new nurses applied pressure across Mary's abdomen hoping to dislodge that stubborn shoulder.

"Come on, honey," Lydia urged. "This will be the one that does it."

And it happened. With a grunt of effort, the doctor managed to pull out the anterior shoulder, then the posterior one. The baby was finally out.

Normally Lydia felt relief at this point. But not today. The baby's face was bluish-purple, his body flaccid and blanched.

His. The baby *was* a boy. And big. Lydia's estimate had been correct. He had at least a pound on his sister.

But he wasn't breathing. Lydia watched the doctor check for a pulse. She could tell by Ochoa's furrowed brow that he didn't find one. He clamped and cut the cord, then passed the baby to Dr. Weston. She was the only one who could save this baby now.

Dr. Weston moved quickly and efficiently. She suctioned the baby before beginning to bag him with oxygen.

"Oh, my God. Is my baby okay?" Mary started to weep.

Turning from the resuscitation efforts, Lydia focused on Mary. She smoothed Mary's damp hair and murmured softly. Gina, she noticed, was patting Steve's shoulder.

As she repeated meaningless, comforting phrases, an internal dialogue ran through Lydia's mind, a prayer for the baby lying lifeless under Dr. Weston's care. *Oh, Lord, please let this baby be all right. Please let him be strong and healthy like his sister. Mary and Steve are such good people, excellent parents. Please...*

As Lydia prayed, Mary began to bleed. The flow was too heavy. The doctor inserted his hand into the vagina to see if the placenta was separating.

The next second Mary's eyes rolled back and her body fell limp. She immediately turned blue.

God, no!

"We need oxygen! Fluids!" Dr. Ochoa ordered tersely. "And let's get a second IV going."

Lydia stepped back to give the nurses and doctor better access to Mary. The primary nurse began to bag her with one hundred percent oxygen.

"Code blue to room three-twelve stat."

As the nurse summoned yet more help, Lydia guessed what had happened. Amniotic fluid embolism. She'd seen a few in her career. When the amniotic fluid was sucked into the mother's circulation, the results were instantaneous and often dire.

This whole delivery was turning into the worst obstetrical nightmare anyone could imagine.

Lydia thought of little Sammy, probably sleeping at just this moment. That little girl needed her mother. They couldn't lose Mary tonight. They just couldn't.

While the nurses concentrated on their jobs, Dr. Ochoa delivered a complete placenta. Blood from Mary's uterus flowed freely onto the doctor's shoes, splattering onto the tile floor. The second nurse massaged the uterus frantically, but the bleeding continued.

"Pitocin!" the doctor ordered.

Another nurse, having anticipated this need, got the drug flowing through the second IV. At that moment the crash cart and team arrived and Mary was intubated. The team frantically tried other drugs to try to stop the bleeding.

Lydia stood back, watching the scene helplessly. The average pregnant woman carried about six liters of blood. At the rate Mary was hemorrhaging, she'd lose it all in a matter of minutes.

"We've lost her pulse! She's in cardiac arrest!"

The doctor from the code team began chest compressions. Lydia stepped back to the wall, not wanting to get in anyone's way. Still, her attention remained riveted on her lifeless patient. Mary was too young to die. She had so much to live for.

"Hang on, Mary. Please, please, hang on." Mary couldn't hear, not above the noise level in the room, but Lydia spoke anyway, her words like a prayer.

"How's the baby?" she asked.

Dr. Weston threw her a frustrated look. "Still no respiration or heart rate. He isn't responding…"

Were they going to lose them both? *Oh, God, please no!* "Come on, Mary. You can survive this. Your family needs you."

Family. *Steve.* Lydia scanned the room anxiously but couldn't see Mary's husband. He wasn't in the room anymore. Nor was Gina.

LYDIA HAD PROMISED Mary she wouldn't leave her. And she didn't. The team continued their resuscitation efforts for forty minutes, fifty…an hour. Dr. Weston eventually had to give up on the baby. She squeezed Lydia's shoulder on her way out of the room. Lydia continued to pray for Mary.

But they couldn't bring her back.

At just after nine, two hours after arriving at the hospital with the Davidsons, Lydia stepped out of the birthing room into the cold, wide corridor. A pregnant woman waddled by her, frowning at the blood splatters on Lydia's thick socks and Birkenstock sandals.

"Lydia." Gina approached from the far end of the corridor. Sorrow filled the air between them like a heavy cloud.

"You're still here." Lydia was unable to meet the other woman's gaze.

"I've been with Steve."

"Where is he?"

Gina pointed in the direction she'd come from. "The doctors are talking to him now."

Lydia swallowed. She felt as though she should be the one to bear the awful news, but hospital protocol required that the attending physician announce a client's demise.

"I'll check on him," she told Gina. "You go home now. You need to be with your husband and children."

Gina brushed tears from her eyes. They clearly weren't the first she'd shed that night. They would be far from the last.

Lydia hugged Gina, then forced herself to continue down the hall. She found Steve in a small waiting room, collapsed in one of a dozen poorly upholstered chairs clustered around a vending machine. Dr. Ochoa and Dr. Weston had just left.

"I'm so sorry, Steve." Lydia felt a hundred years old.

He said nothing. Lydia wanted to cradle him in her arms, but he wouldn't even look at her.

Lydia knew there were no words to soften his loss. "Steve, the hospital teams tried their best. They really did."

He didn't seem to hear. "I've lost both of them."

The words tore at her heart.

"Yes."

Finally Steve lifted his head. He stared at her with

outrage, and she could hear what he didn't say. *We trusted you. You said everything would be okay.*

"No."

Lydia held out her arms.

"No!" He rose from his chair and turned, not to her, but to the soda machine. Raising his fists, the big, powerful man started to pound, one fist after another. "No! No! No!"

Each word conveyed crushing disbelief. How could she help him? Lydia was willing to do anything. If only she could take his pain and bear it for him.

She waited for his initial rage to subside, for him to be still. "Steve, let me call someone. How about your mother?"

His chest convulsed and he started to sob. "No!" he cried out once more, then bolted from the room like a panicked child. Once in the corridor he ran past the elevator to the stairs.

"Steve, come back! Let me help!" Lydia tried to follow, but in her sandals, she couldn't keep up. Finally, she skidded to a stop, grasping at the handle of the door to the stairwell. As the door gave, she caught one glimpse of the top of Steve's head.

And that was the last she saw of him.

CHAPTER TWO

HOME LATE FROM THE OFFICE, Nolan McKinnon, editor and owner of the *Arroyo County Bulletin,* was just about to dig into his second slice of pizza when a police call came over the scanner sitting next to his toaster. Nolan recognized the voice of his good friend, Miguel Eiden.

"We've got a 10-45 on Switchback Road. Get an ambulance and backup. Now."

God. It wasn't even ten o'clock. Wasn't it too early for a traffic accident on a Saturday night? Nolan grabbed a notepad and pencil and waited for the details.

"Ten-four, Miguel," said the dispatcher. "How bad is it?"

"It's a mess. Single-vehicle accident about ten miles past Manny Cordova's place. Looks like the driver lost control and ran into a rock wall at speed."

Nolan's full-time reporter, Cooper Lorenzo, had been on call last weekend. Which meant this "mess," as Miguel had put it, was all his. Sighing, Nolan closed the cardboard box over the still-hot pizza and went for his camera.

He loved most things about owning and managing

the local newspaper, but late-night calls, especially for stories like this, were never fun. Still, people expected newspapers to cover these personal tragedies.

Fortunately they didn't occur often in a town of five thousand people.

A minute later, sitting high in the seven-year-old Explorer he'd just bought off an old friend of his father's, Nolan zipped out of his neighborhood, bypassing the commercial heart of Enchantment. Sometime between now and when he'd picked up his pizza it had begun to snow. The white flakes battered his windshield as he left town limits. Switchback Road cut into the sparsely populated Sangre de Cristo Mountains that bordered the northwest side of Enchantment. The narrow, twisting route was picturesque during daylight hours, but it had a checkered history. Every year the townspeople could count on at least one bad accident, most caused by excessive speed.

As a teenager, Nolan had done his share of wild driving. But shortly after he'd begun work full-time at the *Bulletin,* he'd reformed. He'd seen some grisly sights in the past ten years. He really didn't want to experience another. He thought of his pizza cooling on his kitchen counter and the game on TV that was only half over.

Shit. What a life.

Nolan took a sharp corner slowly, his tires jostling on the poorly maintained pavement underneath the fresh snow. Ahead he spotted the flashing lights of emergency vehicles in the dark.

The left-hand side of the road was cordoned off. Without the luxury of wide, paved shoulders, police had done their best to leave a narrow corridor open. Two officers stood at either end of the wreck, directing the sporadic traffic.

Nolan pulled over to the far left, just as an ambulance took off from the scene, sirens blaring.

Once the coast was clear, Nolan inched left again, parking behind one of the police cars. He had a view of the accident now. The vehicle—some kind of SUV—had gone off the road and crashed into a rock outcrop.

He'd have to get a photo.

About to uncap his Nikon, Nolan froze. He could see the rear license plate of the mangled vehicle, illuminated by the headlights from one of the police cars. The numbers taunted him. He'd seen that particular pattern before.

And then it hit him.

This was his sister's vehicle.

His stomach heaved. He dashed from his Explorer and ran for the cover of some scraggly pines. Next thing, he was bringing up that slice of pizza. It was a loud and nasty process and finally drew someone's attention. One of the officers left the others gathering evidence and headed toward him.

A dusting of snow covered Miguel Eiden's dark hair and the shoulders of his uniform. He shook his head unhappily. "I was hoping you wouldn't hear that call, Nolan. I was going to phone you first chance I got."

Nolan dug into the pockets of his jeans and found nothing. So he pulled out the tail of his shirt and used that to wipe his mouth, his chin, his hands.

"That's my sister's SUV." He took a few steps toward the accident scene, but Miguel stopped him.

"I know, Nolan. I'm sorry. She wasn't in the car, though. Just Steve. He's on his way to the hospital now. You must have seen the ambulance."

"What about Sammy? Are you sure she wasn't in the back seat?"

"Yes. Both kiddie seats were empty, thank God for small mercies."

Two car seats? Mary and Steve had just one kid. Nolan closed his eyes, opened them. He couldn't think straight. Couldn't believe this wasn't a crazy dream. Mary and Steve had lived for years in their cozy A-frame about fifteen minutes from here. Steve must have driven this route thousands of times.

"What the hell happened?"

"Don't know for sure. The road is a little icy from the snow, but the skid marks suggest Steve was driving too fast, as well. He went off the road at the beginning of that S-curve. Probably would have dived right down the mountain, except for that hunk of rock at the side of the road."

"And you're sure no one else was in the vehicle?"

"Yeah." Miguel shook his head, scuffed the dirt

with his boots. He looked like he wanted to say something, but in the end only shook his head again.

Nolan swallowed but couldn't rid his mouth of the sour taste of bile. Was his brother-in-law going to be all right? The brief conversation he'd overheard on his scanner hadn't sounded promising. "Was he hurt bad?"

When Miguel didn't answer right away, Nolan compressed his lips and stared at the license plate still visible in the headlights' beam. He felt his good friend pat his arm.

"You better phone your sister, man."

Deliver this awful news? No. He wasn't the right person for that job. He couldn't... Nolan bowed his head, fighting his gut reaction to refuse. Miguel was right. Even though he and Mary hadn't spoken for almost three years, it would be better for her to hear about this from him rather than the cops.

He nodded, then wiped his mouth again. "Maybe I should drive over rather than phone." But what about Steve? "Or should I go straight to the hospital?" God, his brain wasn't functioning.

"Go to the hospital," his friend decided for him. "I'll take you in the Explorer and you can call Mary on your cell phone. Hang on a second."

Miguel jogged back to the accident scene to confer with his fellow officers. Meanwhile, Nolan opened the driver-side door. His mind went blank for a moment. He remembered the last time he'd seen Mary, at their mother's funeral. She'd come close to hating him then, he knew. He didn't want to talk to her now. Not with news like this.

But he had no choice. And he had to hurry. Pulling himself back to the present, he fished the keys from his jeans.

Miguel came up from behind and scooped them from his hands. "I'm driving, buddy."

Nolan nodded in the direction of the wreck. "You've got work to do."

"Officially I'm off duty as of fifteen minutes ago. Hank's going to bring the squad car back to town when they're finished here."

"I'm fine," Nolan protested, but Miguel slid behind the wheel.

"You don't need to do this," Nolan tried to argue again.

Miguel ignored him. He started the engine and waited. Nolan slapped a hand against the closed driver door and gave in. The second he'd slammed his door shut, Miguel had the vehicle in gear. Another cop waved them safely onto the road, and Miguel eased the speed up to the posted limit.

"Do you have your phone?" he asked.

"Yeah." Nolan pulled it out of his jacket.

"Okay. You call Mary. Tell her after I drop you off at the hospital I'm picking up my own car and coming back to get her."

AT THE ARROYO COUNTY HOSPITAL, a nurse ushered Nolan into a special little room and told him the doctor would talk to him shortly. Nolan glanced at a stack of magazines on a table in the corner. The glossy paper gleamed. They'd never been touched. He put a hand to his head and it came away damp. The snow, he remembered.

How was Steve doing? Nolan hung on to hope, despite Miguel's grim expectations.

There'd been no answer when he'd tried calling Mary. She'd always been a deep sleeper, but he'd let the phone ring until the answering machine picked up, and then he'd called again. Still she hadn't answered. Miguel was on his way to her house now. So Nolan wouldn't be the one to tell her about the accident after all.

A deeply-buried regret stirred within him. He never should have let three years pass without making an attempt to reconcile with his sister. His mother had always said he was too damn stubborn for his own good.

The door opened, and Dr. Ochoa came into the room, wearing a clean white lab coat, pen in his hand along with a clipboard. Nolan had consulted with him a few times on various stories for the *Bulletin*. This was the first time he'd spoken to him on a personal level. Mercifully, Dr. Ochoa came straight to the point.

"I'm so sorry," he said to Nolan. "Your sister has died."

Mary? What the hell was he talking about?

"But I spoke to Miguel Eiden at the accident scene.

He said there were no passengers. Just the driver. Just Steve.''

Ochoa sighed. Despite his distress and confusion, Nolan couldn't help but be aware of the older man's intense weariness. ''Mary's death occurred earlier this evening, Nolan. Before the accident.''

''What?''

''I know it's a lot to take in. Let me try to explain. This afternoon your sister and her husband went to The Birth Place. Mary was in labor. After about seven hours the midwife in charge of her birth—Lydia Kane, a very proficient, experienced midwife—decided to transport your sister to our hospital.''

Nolan hadn't even known Mary was pregnant again. He remembered Miguel mentioning two kiddie seats. What the hell was going on?

''On my initial exam, your sister appeared fine and so did her unborn baby. But the situation deteriorated quickly. We lost Mary at nine-oh-three. Her baby was never resuscitated.''

Nolan knew this couldn't be happening. ''Women don't die in childbirth anymore.''

''In very rare cases they do. In this one…''

The doctor recited terms Nolan had never heard before. Shoulder something and amnio something else.

''We tried everything we could to save her. Lydia Kane is to be commended for bringing her to the hospital so quickly. We had all modern medicine to hand, but it wasn't enough. Sometimes it isn't.''

Nolan put both hands to his head. Mary was dead? Gone? *No, please. Let there be some mistake…*

"Mary *Davidson*. You're sure?"

"I'm so sorry."

Even through his shock, Nolan noticed the slight waver of disbelief in the doctor's voice. He hadn't expected to lose this patient.

So why the hell had he?

Nolan forced his teeth together, pressed his lips tight. Don't lash out at the doctor. Not yet. Need to gather all the facts, first. Make sure what Dr. Ochoa said was true, that everything possible had been done.

"Steve was in the room when this happened," the doctor added.

Now, suddenly, Nolan saw the whole picture and all the pieces—the tragic events of this awful night—fell into place. Steve, totally distraught, had tried to drive home after the tragedy. Instead he'd driven off the road. On purpose?

Hell, it was possible. What man who'd just seen his wife die on the delivery bed, who knew that his newborn baby was dead, too, wouldn't have the thought cross his mind?

One quick turn of the steering wheel and it's all over. No more suffering.

It could easily have been an accident, too. Switchback Road was unforgiving at the best of times, requiring every ounce of a driver's attention. The snow had been blinding and Steve had been an emotional mess. Probably his vision had been blurred with tears, as well.

"The ambulance brought him here," Nolan said.

The doctor nodded. "Unfortunately, there was nothing we could do. His head injuries were massive. Again, I'm so sorry."

Nolan didn't know what to say. A family had been wiped out tonight. A mother and father and their new baby. Leaving him and— *Oh, my God.*

"Mary and Steve have a daughter. Six years old…"

Deep sorrow glimmered again in the doctor's eyes.

"Samantha, Sammy for short." Nolan remembered her third birthday. That had been the last happy family gathering before his mother's death and his and Mary's estrangement.

"Someone has to go talk to Samantha," the doctor said "Do you think you could?"

Nolan felt numb. He had to call Miguel, as well. Right now his good friend was probably knocking at the Davidsons' A-frame. Soon he'd realize Mary wasn't home.

"There'll be other family members to notify, too, of course," the doctor continued.

Nolan nodded. He'd have to get in touch with Steve's mother, Irene, before she heard about the accident on the news. Or read his paper.

Shit. He'd have to get Cooper to write something. There was no way he could. Besides, he'd have other

concerns. There'd be obituaries and funerals and…
Oh, hell, this just couldn't be real.

The doctor was consulting his chart again. "Any
other immediate family?"

Steve shook his head. Some aunts and uncles, most
of them out-of-state. He'd have to check with Irene
for the other side of the family. He'd go to her house
now. Maybe Sammy was with her.

Sammy. He couldn't even remember what his niece
looked like anymore. Chubby cheeks and a lisp, he
vaguely recollected. But that had been three years ago.

CHAPTER THREE

KIM SHERMAN KNEW her co-workers at The Birth Place didn't like her. She knew she had a reputation for being ruthless, impersonal, bottom-line oriented. All of which was perfectly true. And why not? Kim hadn't moved to Enchantment almost eight months ago to vie for the local Miss Congeniality award.

Seeking personal admiration of any kind wasn't her style. People either accepted her for what she was— or too bad. For them. *She* didn't care. She never had.

She was good at what she did. Extremely good. Numbers spoke to her. Accounting had been her thing, from the first course she'd taken in high school to her last full credit in college. She'd never encountered a set of books she couldn't balance. A statement of changes she couldn't reconcile.

She was efficient. Organized. A merciless perfectionist.

Some people had a problem with those qualities. Probably because they themselves were incapable of meeting standards that high. Those people tended to avoid Kim, and she was fine with that.

Which was one reason working at night appealed to her so much. She could concentrate without interruption. As an added bonus, she didn't have to listen to the annoying chatter of others who obviously socialized with each other outside of work. Kim checked her Timex and was surprised. She hadn't planned to stay *this* late.

It was past ten. She'd been lost in her analysis of outstanding payables for—what?—almost four hours. The Birth Place was out of money. Again. It was up to her to decide which suppliers they simply had to pay and which could be put off for a few more months.

It was a job many would hate. But Kim didn't mind.

She flicked off the radio by her desk. She'd been listening to a classical station, the sound a comfort in the empty complex. Now, through her open office door, traveled a disquieting noise. Someone laughing quietly… *No, crying.*

Lydia and Gina had been in earlier with a delivery. But she'd heard them leave hours ago. The night janitor had already made his rounds.

Kim shivered and pulled on her gray cardigan, doing up each button, from the bottom to the very top. Grabbing the three-hole punch from her desk and holding it like a baseball bat, she went investigating. The door to the chief administrator's office was shut tight. Since his marriage to Hope Tanner, Parker Reynolds had been taking work home rather than putting in extra hours at the center.

The sound grew louder as she stepped into the main

hall. It seemed to be coming from one of the birthing rooms to her right—definitely someone crying.

No longer concerned about her physical safety, Kim set the three-hole punch on the empty reception desk, next to Trish Linden's silly snow globe of Venice. The middle-aged receptionist had never ventured out of New Mexico. What was she doing with a souvenir of Italy of all places?

Kim followed the hallway around the curving counter. One of the birthing-room doors stood ajar. A faint light slipped out into the hall.

The sobbing was louder now. Raw and unrestrained.

All Kim's instincts told her to walk away. She did not want to get involved with this. But what if the person crying was Lydia? Kim would do anything for Lydia.

Lydia Kane had founded The Birth Place when she was a young mother herself, many decades ago. Though she was now in her early seventies she still worked full-time as a midwife. The only sign she gave of easing up was her recent resignation from the board of directors. Kim guessed she'd made the move under pressure, for reasons Kim could only speculate about.

She peeked through the open crack in the door. Sure enough it was Lydia. She'd changed out of the trousers and shirt she'd been wearing for the labor, earlier. Her long gray hair now hung down the back of a forest-green caftan. Kim watched the older woman pull a beautifully patterned quilt over freshly plumped pillows. As she worked efficiently, briskly, her crying continued.

Lydia's typical self-control and natural dignity made this a most incongruous sight. Again Kim's instincts warned her to back away. But then she inadvertently pushed on the door and the hinges squeaked. Just a little, but enough.

"Who's there?" Lydia straightened and turned to face the door. "Kim?" She wiped away tears with the back of her hand. "What on earth are you doing here?"

"Just some late-night accounting." She didn't share her worries about the finances. It wouldn't be news to Lydia, anyway. They were all used to the center being short of funds, though Kim had been working to rectify the situation since she'd been on board. One of her first projects had been the renegotiation of their contracts with the various health-care providers.

"You work too hard."

Kim stepped into the room. "What about you? Surely this could wait until morning." She knew some of their contracts required the midwives to file notice of a baby's birth within twenty-four hours. But that was paperwork. Why was Lydia cleaning the room?

Lydia compressed her lips and turned away. The old woman's long, lean body shook with the effort of controlling her tears.

"Did something go wrong with the delivery tonight?"

A sob escaped Lydia. A sob filled with deep, wrenching grief.

Oh, God. What was she going to do? There was no one else at the center to deal with this. "Lydia, can I get you something?"

"No. Nothing." She sat on the edge of the bed, and Kim perched beside her.

"Want to talk about what happened?"

"No." She shook her head, then sighed. "Yes. Do you remember Mary Davidson and her husband, Steve?"

Kim nodded. She'd never met the couple, but she'd processed the initial payment from their insurance company. Then Steve had quit his job to start his own company and been taken off the company health plan. Their account had been on her receivables listing ever since.

"I still can't believe it happened. But I lost her tonight, Kim. I lost Mary and the baby. In all my years of midwifing, it's never happened like this before." Lydia's hand trembled as she plucked a tissue from a box on a nearby end table. Kim picked up the entire box and placed it on Lydia's lap.

"I thought I heard some commotion—around seven o'clock?" She'd been heating up soup in the microwave for her dinner when she'd noticed Gina dashing down the hall.

"Yes. We ended up transferring Mary to the hospital. I had a feeling something was going wrong, even though there didn't seem to be a problem. In the beginning Mary progressed so normally, you see. Every indication was that this would be an uncomplicated birth.

"But as labor progressed, I began to feel anxious. Over the years I've learned to trust my instincts. And so I drove Mary to the hospital. Steve followed in his vehicle. Oh my God, if only he'd ridden with me…" Lydia pressed a tissue over her mouth, stifling a ragged sob.

Kim shivered as an awful suspicion prompted her to ask. "Did something happen to Steve?"

Lydia nodded, her hands covering her face again. "After—" She paused for a strengthening breath. "After he heard about Mary and the baby he took off. About an hour later, he was rushed back to the hospital in an ambulance. Dead. Oh, Kim, he had an accident on Switchback Road!"

Kim starred blankly at Lydia, stunned by the massive dimensions of this tragedy. The older midwife continued to take big gulps of air and eventually regained some composure.

"It's all so senseless. Mary Davidson was a healthy woman. She never should have died. As for her baby— I saw his face before the trouble started. He was so dear, so precious. A big baby, a healthy boy."

"Tell me what happened." Kim wasn't keen to hear the details, but it might help Lydia to talk. For sure, the older woman wasn't ready to go home.

Step-by-step Lydia went through the stages of Mary Davidson's disastrous labor and delivery. Kim didn't stop her for explanations of medical terms or procedures that she didn't understand. She just let Lydia talk and talk, second-guessing each decision, going through all the options that had been open at the time.

Finally she fell silent.

"If a similar circumstance presented itself to you tomorrow, you'd make the exact same decisions," Kim said.

Lydia's eyes opened wide, then she allowed her stiff shoulders to slump. "Probably. For the life of me, I can't see where we went wrong. Mary had a proven pelvis. She was healthy and strong. Right up to the end, the baby was doing so well...."

"Lydia, the situation was out of your control."

"It's so difficult to accept. In all my years, I've never lost a baby *and* a mother. Poor Sammy!"

Kim had no idea who Sammy was. Now didn't seem the time to ask. If only she could say something, do something to help. Another person might put an arm around Lydia, murmur comforting words. But for Kim that wasn't possible.

"May I make you some tea, Lydia?"

The older woman shook her head and pulled yet another tissue from the box. She blew her nose and wiped her eyes.

"I'd love to help." Kim felt hopelessly inadequate. If only Trish were here. The receptionist had such a gentle, caring way about her.

"Oh, Kim, I wish…"

Desperate to be of some assistance, Kim leaned forward. "Yes?"

"I'd really like to talk to my granddaughter."

Kim drew in a breath. *What? How?* Then she realized that of course Lydia was referring to Devon Grant in Albuquerque. Devon was in the medical profession, too. And she'd recently joined the board at The Birth Place. In fact, she'd taken her grandmother's position on the board. She would be able to understand Lydia's pain so much better than Kim could.

"Do you know her number? I'll place the call if you'd like."

"Oh, it's too late."

"I'm sure Devon wouldn't mind." In the other woman's shoes, Kim knew she wouldn't. She led Lydia back to the reception area, where she punched in the number Lydia gave her. The phone rang many times. But there was no answer and no message machine, either.

"Devon must be on a night shift."

"Which hospital?" When Lydia told her, Kim dialed directory assistance and soon the line was ringing again.

"May I speak to Devon Grant, please. Her grandmother, Lydia Kane, wishes to speak to her." She passed the receiver to Lydia, then prepared to leave to give Lydia her privacy. Her hand was on the door leading back to the admin area, when she heard the older woman speak softly.

"I see. Okay. I'll try again later."

Kim turned. "What's wrong?"

"Apparently Devon is in the middle of a delivery. She wasn't able to take my call." Lydia was trembling now and struggling not to show it. She hung up the phone, avoiding the younger woman's sympathetic gaze.

"I'm sure she'll call you back soon," Kim said. But she couldn't help wondering if Devon truly had been too busy to take this call. Kim hadn't worked here long, but she was aware of the tension between the two women.

The problem stretched back ten years, to a time when Hope Tanner—then a pregnant teenage girl—had sought refuge at The Birth Place. Hope and Devon had become friends. Then Hope had her baby and left town. Kim didn't know what happened to her baby. Few people did, but Devon was one of them. And she clearly blamed Lydia for *something*.

Up until that time, her grandmother had been Devon's mentor and inspiration. But no longer. Devon had moved to Albuquerque and now the two women rarely spoke.

Kim's sympathies lay one-hundred percent with Lydia. If the older midwife had done something wrong, she must have had a darn good reason. Lydia would have made sure that baby went to a good home.

A good family. If she'd bent a few rules to make that happen, so what?

Devon wouldn't be so quick to judge, Kim thought, if she knew what it was like to be a child who didn't have a family. Or anyplace to call home.

THE NEXT MORNING Lydia Kane resisted the urge to stay in bed. She'd dealt with pain, disappointment and loss many times in her seventy-three years. None had been a reason to neglect her work before and they weren't now, either.

She arrived at The Birth Place fifteen minutes before her appointment with a new couple who'd been referred by an ex-patient. This was their first baby, and Lydia didn't know if she was up to dealing with their excitement, their enthusiasm…their naiveté.

Bringing a new child into this world was a marvelous voyage. That was how Lydia normally felt. But after last night it seemed as if her heart had been replaced with a lead facsimile. The melancholy would fade, she knew from experience. The sense of having failed would not.

She stopped by one of the many collages of photos on display at the birth center. So many tiny faces, proud parents, excited siblings. If only the Davidsons could be among them. Closing her eyes, she composed the picture. Steve standing at the back, a proud hand on Sammy's shoulder, the other wrapped around his wife, who would be holding a bundled baby to her chest.

That's how last night should have ended.

If only… If only…

Lydia turned from the wall and continued to her office, to the sanctuary of her leather chair and old oak desk.

Was there anything she could have done? Any sign she'd missed? It didn't matter that she'd relived every step of the delivery a dozen times last night, and a dozen more this morning. Lydia knew it would take a while for her mind to accept this latest defeat.

Losing a baby happened so rarely. But when the sad circumstance occurred, she was always reminded of the first time she'd lost a baby, her *own* baby, when she was only sixteen.

She'd been so young…too young. Giving her daughter up for adoption had seemed the best option at the time—at least according to her father. Lydia's mother had been dead by then. The child will be happier with a real family, her father had said. And Lydia had prayed for the baby's sake that he was right.

But in her heart, she'd known that she'd let her baby down. She'd devoted her life to mothers and babies ever since. But for all the good she knew that she'd done, cases like the Davidsons made her wonder if the sacrifices she'd made had been worth it after all.

Especially when she considered her own children, the two she'd had after she'd married Ken. Her devotion to her profession had come at a cost, paid in part, she was afraid, by the son she never saw in New

York City and the daughter in San Francisco who only visited sporadically.

Then this past autumn, her second failure as a midwife had been exposed when Hope Tanner came back to town. And now Lydia no longer sat as a member of the board of the birth center she'd founded.

She'd given up everything for The Birth Place. Now she was nothing but an employee. Life could be so ironic.

Noticing Kim Sherman's closed door, Lydia forgot her troubles for a moment. She had no doubt that the accountant had arrived at work at the usual time, despite the long hours she'd put in yesterday.

Kim had been so kind last night. Lydia wondered why the young woman couldn't show that side of her personality more often. It was no secret around here that most people found her abrasive. Her comments were usually brisk and often critical. No one could meet her expectations, it seemed. Even Parker Reynolds, the chief administrator, admitted she was hard to take. But he refused to let her go.

"We need someone like her," he'd told Lydia. "She's renegotiated all our insurance contracts at much better terms. And she's implementing incredible improvements to our billing system."

Lydia changed her trajectory and headed to that firmly closed door.

"Come in."

Lydia was struck by how young Kim appeared, surrounded by the stacks of computer printouts on her desk. The petite woman was only twenty-five, un-married and so pretty. She should be enjoying her youth, not spending every waking hour alone with her numbers. She should revel in her fresh beauty, instead of hiding it behind dowdy sweaters and dark-framed glasses.

"Lydia!" Startled, Kim stood, sending her pen and a sheet of paper to the floor. "Oh!" She gathered the items and returned them to her desk. Waving at the only free seat in the room, she waited until Lydia was comfortable before returning to her own chair.

"Kim, I want to thank you for last night."

"Oh, that was…anyone would have… I mean, are you okay?"

"I'm fine, Kim. But what about you? Working so late last night, then in to the office early this morning. You have to make time for a social life, you know. Not to mention a decent night's sleep."

Kim surveyed the stacks of paper, her expression bordering on the defensive. Lydia had often wondered at the total absence of anything personal in this office. No framed photos or cute magnets. Even Kim's coffee mug was serviceable white ceramic.

Something had to be done about this girl. And Lydia thought she had just the idea.

"I've come to ask you a favor, Kim."

The accountant perked up, as if nothing could have pleased her more.

"At the last board meeting the directors approved a fund-raising event. Parker wants to call it the Mother and Child Reunion, which is a wonderful name, I think. It will be a huge event. We'd like to invite as many of the women who delivered at our center—and their husbands, of course—as we can find. Also, any adult children who were born here will be welcome, too.''

"Lydia. That will be a huge guest list.''

"We won't be able to track them all down. And many will have moved and be unable to attend. At any rate, the board wants us to cap the list at two hundred.''

"Will you be inviting all the staff?''

"Naturally. And board members, too.'' Would her granddaughter come? Devon had attended all business meetings since her appointment. But she might consider this function more social in nature.

"Well, we certainly could use some extra money around here.''

"Yes, we could. Which leads me to that favor I told you I was going to ask. Parker already handles our annual SIDS fund-raiser, so I hate to put another event on his shoulders, too. Would you consider taking on the responsibility?''

"Of course.'' She seemed insulted that Lydia might have entertained any doubt. "I'd be pleased to do it.''

"I don't want you doing all the work. Just the organizing. All the staff will pitch in, including me.'' This would force Kim to interact with her co-workers. Hopefully, over time, some of them would begin to appreciate the young woman's more appealing characteristics—as Lydia did. "This project should be a team effort."

"Oh, don't worry about giving me too much to do. I love to be busy. And I'm a very efficient time manager."

Yes. Maybe too efficient.

"I promise you, this will be the birth center's most successful fund-raising event, ever," Kim continued.

Mindful of her upcoming appointment, Lydia stood. "Let's talk more about this later." On her way out the door, Lydia glanced back at the accountant. Already her head was bent over her papers.

Lydia hoped she hadn't made a terrible mistake. If Kim took on this project without allowing anyone to help, she'd just isolate herself further. Still, even if handing Kim responsibility for the fund-raiser had been a mistake, it wouldn't be the worst one Lydia had ever made.

NOLAN STARED AT THE LAWYER, certain the woman had read incorrectly.

"Executor of the will, I can understand. But Mary and Steve wouldn't have named me guardian of their daughter. That would be Steve's mom, Irene Davidson."

Only fifty-five, Irene was healthy and active. Judging from her home and the car she drove, she had plenty of money, too. Nolan knew she didn't have to work.

Irene had what was needed to raise her granddaughter—time and financial resources. Two things that were lacking in Nolan's life right now.

He'd stretched his credit to the max when he'd bought the *Bulletin* from Charley Graziano several years ago. Between that mortgage and the one for his condo, he had precious little spare cash.

And even less time. Running a newspaper was rewarding but very time-consuming. Then there were all his volunteer commitments.

Yeah, money and time were huge concerns. But the biggest problem of all was this: he and Sammy didn't even know each other.

"When was that will drawn up?"

The lawyer stated a date about six months after Nolan and Mary's mother's funeral. Which made the whole setup even less logical.

He and Mary had said some pretty unforgivable things to each other the day they'd laid their mother to rest. Why would she have turned around, only months later, and done something like this?

"It doesn't make sense."

"There's no mistake, Nolan. You *are* Sammy's legal guardian. She's still staying with the Saramagos. I suggest you pick her up and get her settled before the funeral."

HALF AN HOUR LATER, Nolan was still in shock as he stopped his Explorer in front of the Saramagos' pale pink adobe house. He thought back two days, to the night of Mary's death and Steve's accident. After leaving the hospital he'd driven straight to Irene's. He'd woken her from a deep sleep, sat her on her floral-patterned living room sofa and told her about Mary, the baby, Steve.

She'd reacted with total silence.

He'd repeated the story, adding details this time, getting up to pace, then collapsing into a chair. He'd rubbed the stubble on his face, watching Irene's face turn blanker and blanker.

"I'll make coffee." He'd been in the kitchen, searching for a filter cone, when she'd started to scream.

That had woken Sammy, asleep in the spare room. As he'd assumed, Mary and Steve had dropped her off on their way to The Birth Center.

The little girl had wandered into the kitchen wearing something soft and pink. "Has Mommy had my baby sister yet?" she asked him.

Irene wasn't screaming anymore, but sobbing loudly. Nolan had been stunned by Sammy's question.

Explaining to Sammy what had happened was even harder than telling Irene. The little girl didn't seem to believe him at first. He'd returned to the living room to try to deal with Irene. Unable to calm her down, he'd phoned her doctor.

Teresa Saramago's number had been listed by the phone as one of Irene's emergency contacts, and he'd called her, too. Apparently she had a daughter the same age as Sammy and did some occasional baby-sitting. She agreed to take in the child while he drove Irene to the hospital.

Hard to believe that had happened just two nights ago. Nolan turned off the ignition and sat for a moment, trying to collect his thoughts.

There was a little girl inside that house for whom he was about to become solely responsible. Nolan wasn't married, or engaged, he didn't even have a steady girlfriend. Thirty might be a little old to be living a footloose kind of lifestyle, but it suited him and the demands of his profession.

He wanted to restart his vehicle and drive the hell out of there. Instead, he got out slowly, his reporter's eye ticking off details as he approached the home. A tricycle tipped over near the front step. A red plastic pail tucked into the shrubbery under the front window. Kids lived here, all right. Including, for the moment, his niece.

If only he could leave her here. It was a cowardly thought, but expressed his feelings on the matter exactly.

Nolan stopped in front of the freshly stained wooden door of the well-maintained home. A good mother lived here. She had kids of her own. She'd probably make a perfect surrogate parent for Sammy.

If only he had Steve's mother for support. But Irene had been checked into the hospital and prescribed sedatives. She was still there now. Her friend and neighbor, Mabel Judson, was planning to pick her up tomorrow and keep her at her house until after the funerals. "For as long as she needs," Mabel had said when they'd talked on the phone this morning.

It seemed that as well as inheriting a kid, he was getting his sister's mother-in-law, too. A package deal he could have happily lived without.

Nolan let his knuckles fall against the door. Right away it opened. Teresa Saramago was visibly pregnant, carrying a toddler in her arms. She seemed tired and relieved to see him.

Two little girls stood behind the woman in the hall. One of them had Steve's big eyes, Mary's curly hair.

"Thanks for looking after Sammy," Nolan began.

"We were glad to help," the mother of two, soon to be three, replied. "I wish we could keep her longer, but I'm due myself in a few weeks."

He nodded. "I understand." He wondered if the woman had any idea how panicked he felt right now. How totally unprepared he was for this much responsibility. He felt awkward, standing in the hall, with the mother and two little girls watching him expectantly. What was he supposed to do? Tentatively he held out his hand to his niece.

Sammy started to cry.

"Sammy, you have to go with your uncle now," the woman prompted gently. "You can visit again, soon."

Sammy kept crying and Nolan cringed. This was impossible. Sammy wanted to stay here. *He* wanted Sammy to stay here.

The woman frowned slightly. She set down her toddler, in order to give Sammy a hug, then shot him a look charged with expectation.

He scooped Sammy into his arms, and she stiffened, turning her face away from his. Adjusting his grip awkwardly, he gave another quick thanks to Teresa, then hustled back to his car. As he bent to put his niece in the front passenger seat, the woman shouted from her doorway.

"She's too little to sit in the front—because of the airbags. Put her in the back."

Hell. He should've known that. He'd read articles about airbag injuries to children under the age of twelve. So he settled Sammy in the center of the back seat, making sure to tighten the lap belt securely.

He was in the driver's seat, engine started, ready to head to his condo, when he realized he still hadn't spoken a word to the little girl. He swiveled to face her.

"I'm your Uncle Nolan, Sammy. You probably don't remember me, but I came to visit you the day after you were born. I bought you a teddy bear." '

"The white one?"

Damned if he could remember the color. "Um, I think so."

Her head dropped, and she didn't say anything else. He watched her a moment, then sighed and drove off. Which of them, he wondered, was the most terrified right now?

CHAPTER FOUR

TWO WEEKS LATER, Nolan's spirits weren't any higher. He'd buried his sister, his brother-in-law, his nephew. He grieved for them in the lonely hours of the night, but his days were crammed with activity. Looking after Sammy, meeting with the lawyers, then Steve's accountant. He'd opened an estate bank account and had begun to deal with the financial aftermath of this mind-numbing tragedy.

Unfortunately, his sister's family hadn't been financially stable. They owed a lot on their expensive home and car. And Steve had just taken out an operating loan for his new business.

Add onto that the medical bill he'd just discovered this morning at their house and the whole situation turned very grim. Once the dust settled, Nolan was afraid there would be no nest egg for Sammy and her future education.

Nolan buckled his niece into the back seat of the Explorer and set off for The Birth Place. He might as well take care of this latest problem right away. According to the invoice he'd found, his sister's account was already several months in arrears.

So far, most of Steve and Mary's creditors had been

sympathetic. They had an account with the dry cleaners, the dealership where they serviced their vehicle and several other local businesses. Nolan had met with most of them in the past two days. Everyone had been very kind, assuring him they were happy to wait until the assets had cleared probate before receiving their money.

He'd left Sammy at the *Bulletin* while he'd gone on those appointments, but poor Toni was already strained with the extra work he'd piled on her. Today he'd decided he just couldn't expect her to add child care to her job list—even though she professed herself more than willing to help him out. She was too valuable an employee to abuse in that way. Besides, she wasn't exactly young anymore.

Nolan pulled into the parking lot of The Birth Place. Steve and Mary owed this place more money than all the bills he'd dealt with so far combined. Still, he hoped the accountant here would be as sympathetic to his situation as the other creditors had been.

A MERE TWO WEEKS HAD PASSED since Lydia had put her in charge of the Mother and Child Reunion and already Kim had a venue booked, invitations designed and most of the guest list compiled. A few days ago, Lydia had taken her to lunch. Kim had run through her ideas and Lydia had approved every last one of them.

"Who have you got helping you so far?" she'd asked.

Kim had been vague in her reply. Didn't Lydia think she was capable of handling the project on her own? Well, Kim was certainly going to show her.

A rap at Kim's office door distracted her. Trish Linden apologized immediately for the interruption. "I know you're busy, but someone would like to see you."

People didn't come to see Kim. Kim dealt with all her business over the phone. She frowned at Trish, but before she could ask for more details, Trish had backed out and a tall sandy-haired man strode into the room.

A little girl trailed behind him. Huge, sad eyes. Red, pursed lips. Her denim overalls were stained with something orange and her hair was a tangled mess. In her arms she carried *The Giving Tree,* a Shel Silverstein book.

The man smiled, a full-wattage grin that showcased great teeth and bright, intelligent eyes. He could have been a young college professor with his slightly rumpled jacket and curly hair worn a little too long. The look might be appealing to some women, but Kim didn't trust the charm the man displayed so easily.

"Hope I'm not disturbing you."

"Isn't it obvious that you are? We don't have an appointment, do we?"

His eyes widened. She could tell she'd surprised him with her rudeness, but she didn't care. She'd been hired to work with numbers, not clients.

"I won't take much of your time. I didn't realize I needed to phone ahead."

He tried his smile again, but it faded rapidly when she didn't return it.

"Look, I'll phone ahead next time, okay? But since I'm here and I've already interrupted your very important work…"

She didn't allow herself to react to the slightly sarcastic tone in his voice.

"We might as well settle this thing, don't you think?"

"And what *thing* would that be?"

A ghost of his charming smile returned, and she knew he was going to ask for some sort of concession. He must have brought his daughter along in a sympathy bid. Those tactics disgusted her.

"I have an outstanding invoice to discuss. I'm Nolan McKinnon, by the way. This is my niece, Sammy."

His introduction startled her. "The editor of the *Arroyo County Bulletin?*" She'd been a subscriber for years—ever since she'd read the final report of the private investigator she'd hired with her first paycheck after college. That report had led her from Denver to Enchantment. It was through the classified section of the *Bulletin* that she'd found this job.

She still read the weekly paper with enjoyment—in particular Mr. McKinnon's editorials. In fact, she'd become *addicted* to his editorials.

"Yeah. That's me."

He didn't continue, and suddenly she realized she hadn't introduced herself. "I'm Kim Sherman." She stood to shake his hand. Almost grudging, she added, "I think that teen drop-in center was a real good idea."

He'd spearheaded the organization to start the teen center. And even though she wasn't intending to stay in Enchantment much longer, she'd made a generous contribution—anonymously, of course. She wished that when she'd been in her teens she'd had access to a place like that. A safe meeting ground where kids could gather to chat, do homework and play sports. The Enchantment Teen Center even had counselors available.

"Thank you."

The smile he gave her this time wasn't the charming one. This one was genuine.

"But you're not here to discuss the teen center."

"Afraid not." He pulled a folded sheet of paper out of his jacket pocket. The invoice was stamped with The Birth Place logo.

Kim held out her hand for the paper. On closer examination, she caught her breath. The name in the left corner was Mary Davidson, the mother Lydia had lost two weeks ago.

"I don't want to keep you," he continued. "I just hoped we could settle this. You see, I'm Mary's brother and the executor of her and Steve's estate. Until their assets pass probate, I'm afraid I don't have the funds to cover this."

Kim looked at the little girl again. Was this the Davidson's daughter, then, not Mr. McKinnon's? She remembered Lydia mentioning that name, Sammy. Now the child's quiet demeanor struck Kim in a very intense, personal way. She not only saw, she *felt* the sorrow in the little girl's expression.

For a moment Kim was six again. The neighbor from the apartment down the hall was at her door. A police officer stood behind her, his hat in his hands.

Your mother is gone, Kim. You'll have to come with us.

It had been a long time ago, but Kim hadn't forgotten the overwhelming pain of a child whose world had crashed around her.

Kim had the oddest, most inappropriate impulse. She wanted to hug the little girl, to crush her to her chest.

"I've been trying to put my sister and brother-in-law's affairs in order. I found your invoice in a stack of unpaid bills. It seems their account is over ninety days delinquent, but that can't be right."

She ignored him, looked back at the girl. "That book was one of my favorites when I was little."

Sammy edged closer to Kim's desk. "Do you keep stuff in those drawers?"

Opening the one at the top, Kim found a blue marker and a pad of notepaper. "Would you like these, Sammy?"

The little girl nodded. "I like making pictures."

"Would you like to make one now? How about

you go sit in one of the chairs beside that nice lady who walked you in here?'' If she and Nolan Mc-Kinnon were about to start haggling over the David-sons' invoice, she didn't want Sammy to witness the scene.

She glanced at the uncle. ''Trish will keep a close watch on her.''

''That sounds like a good idea.''

Kim walked the little girl back to reception and stopped to talk with Trish. As she'd expected, the re-ceptionist was only too pleased to help.

Back in her own office, Kim resolved to regain con-trol of the situation. Realizing Nolan McKinnon was the editor of the *Bulletin*, then identifying the little girl as Mary and Steve Davidson's daughter had thrown her a little. But her hands were almost steady once more.

''Okay.'' Kim sat down and leaned over her desk. ''We can discuss your business now.''

Nolan gave her another smile. The sincere kind. ''Wow.''

''Pardon me?''

''Sammy must really like you. She doesn't speak as much in a day to me as she did to you right now. I suppose you're one of those people who is just nat-urally good with kids.''

Heat flooded her cheeks. ''No, I don't think so. I'm not what you'd call a people person.''

She saw him fight back a smile and clenched her

pen tightly. Damn him for laughing at her. Did he think she cared what he thought of her?

McKinnon had taken a seat without an invitation. Now he leaned over his knees and regarded her intently. "You're not from around here, are you?"

"No. I grew up in Denver."

"How long have you been in Enchantment?"

"Almost a year."

"But I haven't run into you anywhere."

"I'm not one for socializing." Her glasses sat perfectly on her nose, but she pushed a finger against the bridge. "Um, I assume you wanted to talk about this invoice?"

The little spark in his eyes disappeared.

She carried on. "It really is more than ninety days delinquent. Our policy is to start charging interest after the third month an invoice is unpaid."

"I see. But surely in special circumstances you'll make an exception? You see, Steve quit his full-time job about six months ago and started his own business. He signed with a new insurance company, but since Mary was already pregnant at the time…"

Kim sat impassively. Over the months she'd worked here, she'd heard all sorts of stories. But here was the bottom line—someone had to pay. If the Davidsons didn't have insurance, then the money would have to come from their estate. And she could not let them get off paying months and months late without an interest penalty.

Eventually Nolan clued in to the fact that she wasn't being swayed.

"Never mind the details. All I'm asking for is a two-month extension with no interest."

She leaned forward slightly. "I'm sorry about your sister, Mr. McKinnon, but we gave her the best care possible."

"Yes. I didn't mean to imply that you hadn't. Believe me, I checked into the full circumstances of her death."

She bet he had. He was a reporter after all. He'd have made certain his sister had received top-notch care, both here, and then, later, at the hospital. She wasn't surprised he hadn't found anything amiss. If it had been humanly possible to save Mary Davidson and her baby, Lydia would have done so.

"The thing is—" Nolan adjusted the invoice on her desk a few inches "—the majority of Mary and Steve's assets are frozen until their wills pass probate. And I still haven't been able to sort through their health insurance papers…"

Nolan let his sentence trail off. Damn, but this was embarrassing. He'd pay the bill himself, but he'd just sunk everything he'd saved for the past year into his annual principal payment to Charley.

He'd been forced to take a loan to pay for the three funerals, and how much of those costs would eventually be covered by insurance was anyone's guess.

Now he had a niece to somehow provide for, including the expense of before- and after-school care.

He did not need Mary and Steve's old bills to worry about, too.

"I don't want to sound heartless, Mr. McKinnon. But since my arrival, I've instigated a new policy. All patients are billed in installments, with the final payment due by the thirty-sixth week of pregnancy. I understand the Davidsons' assets are in probate. But I cannot suspend our interest charges.

"We have salaries to cover here. Overhead. When our patients are late paying their bills it costs us money. Of course, in cases of financial difficulty we make exceptions. Your sister and her husband, however, did not seem to be in that category."

He knew what she referred to. Mary's expensive clothing, the pricey vehicle they'd driven, the area in which they'd lived. No, Mary and Steve had not wanted for much.

"But—"

"One of my policies, Mr. McKinnon—" she removed her glasses and stowed them carefully in a leather container "—is that I make no exceptions."

Did she know she sounded like a ninety-year-old British schoolmarm? Which, given her delicate beauty, was pretty damn incongruous. Kim Sherman looked like one tiny mouse would send her screaming. In actual fact she could probably stare down the entire Internal Revenue Service.

He would be damned, though, before he saw his niece's estate further eroded through additional interest charges. "I'll put the bill on my Visa, then." He pulled his wallet from his back pocket, then slipped out the gold card. The accountant frowned.

"We only accept cash or personal check."

"Oh, for Pete's sake!" He slapped his wallet against her desk.

"I'm sorry, Mr. McKinnon, but that's our—"

"I know, I know. That's your *policy.*"

Kim Sherman spoke quietly. "The reception area isn't far away. Your niece might well be listening as you yell at me. Perhaps you could keep your voice down?"

And perhaps you could try being human for five minutes. He bit back the comment. Losing his temper here wasn't going to solve anything. He peeled a blank check away from his last twenty. He'd cover this later, with a cash advance from his Visa. What did Ms. Sherman care that he'd be the one stuck with an outrageous interest charge as a result?

Kim took a stamp from her desk. Once he'd handed her the check, she pressed a red-inked "Paid" across the face of the invoice and passed it back to him.

He stuffed the invoice into his pocket, feeling exhaustion down to his bones. What he needed was a good nap, but no chance of that now that he had a six-year-old on his hands full-time.

He pushed out of his chair. "Well, I guess I'd better leave you to get back to your policies." Kim Sherman sure was a piece of work. He wondered if anyone ever got the best of this woman.

As he turned to leave, Sammy opened the door and peeked inside.

"I finished my picture."

The grim expression on Ms. Sherman's face vanished. "Can I see?"

Nolan waited impatiently while his niece shyly presented her work to the accountant. When Kim expressed an inordinate amount of pleasure in the picture, Sammy offered it to her.

Kim tacked the stick drawings and doodles onto a small corkboard that held a list of computer codes, as well as other work-related items. Nolan figured she'd crush it into a ball and toss it into the trash once they left.

"Okay, Sam. We'd better get going."

His niece gave him a reluctant look, then turned back to Kim. "Uncle Nolan is looking for a baby-sitter for me. Do you baby-sit?"

Oh, God! Nolan felt like whacking himself in the head. His day couldn't get any worse. Surely he could count on the frigid Ms. Sherman to say no?

"Sometimes I do. In fact, I used to spend a lot of time with children when I was younger."

Somehow Nolan couldn't picture her with children. She wore no rings. And there weren't any photos of family in her office. It appeared she had no strings at all.

But then again, two weeks ago neither had he.

"But your uncle probably has another sitter in mind."

Sammy looked at him expectantly.

"Actually, I don't," he grudgingly admitted. "Sam's grandmother, Irene, is too emotionally distraught. I've thought about advertising."

"I don't want a stranger," Sam said, conveniently forgetting that half an hour ago Kim Sherman had been exactly that. "Please let Kim be my babysitter."

So far his niece hadn't asked him for anything. Not so much as a chocolate-chip cookie.

"Sammy, your uncle doesn't really know me."

"No, I don't. But Sammy seems to like you." Was he crazy to be considering her offer? She had a responsible job. Harming six-year-olds probably wasn't one of her policies.

"I have various volunteer and work activities on week nights. What I need is someone to come by the house on Tuesday and Thursday after dinner. Just for a few hours."

Kim Sherman nodded. "That sounds fine to me. Since today is Thursday, I guess I'll see you later? I presume you want me to come to the address on your check."

"Yeah. Sure."

Sammy clapped her hands, then willingly went to Nolan when he held out his hand. Seeing his niece's happy face, Nolan felt some of the pressure he'd been feeling the past two weeks ease off a little.

Kim Sherman was right. She *wasn't* a people person. But she seemed to be a Sammy person. He hoped that would turn out to be enough.

CHAPTER FIVE

KIM COULDN'T SHUT her office door fast enough. She leaned against the wooden barrier and closed her eyes, torn between equally strong desires. To never see Nolan McKinnon again. And to comfort his poor niece. It was so obvious the man didn't have a clue about children.

Sammy's plight triggered emotions Kim couldn't afford to feel. When she'd moved to Enchantment she'd promised herself two things. She would only stay one year at most, less would be better. And she wouldn't get involved with anyone who lived in Enchantment.

So why had she agreed to baby-sit Sammy? What could she really do to help the little girl? Sure she empathized with losing a mother, losing the only family you'd ever known. But Sammy was Nolan's niece. It was up to him to help the little girl deal with this tragedy.

If only the guy wasn't so hopeless with kids.

Surprising really. So many of his editorials were about helping teenagers. That drop-in center was just one example. Was it only younger children he couldn't relate to then? Because he obviously wasn't relating to his niece.

Kim smoothed her hair, straightened her skirt. She'd committed to the baby-sitting, so no sense fretting over the situation. Maybe she could give Nolan a few pointers on relating to Sammy. Also, she could suggest grief counseling. Celia Brice, a local psychologist who worked part-time at the center, was supposed to be amazing with children. The key was helping Sammy without getting personally involved.

Kim returned to her desk and fished out her glasses, trying not to think about her motives for removing them in the first place. She did *not* care what Nolan McKinnon thought of her looks.

Anxious to put the recent episode behind her, Kim pulled out the binder she'd started for the Mother and Child Reunion. She needed to verify the addresses on her guest list. Some were fifty years old. She hoped she'd be able to trace at least a few of the birth center's original patients. Lydia would like that.

She tried to draw a line under the name next on her list, but the pen wavered so much she had to stop.

When would the shaking stop?

Some herbal tea might help, but she didn't want to face anyone yet. Not Trish, or Parker, or Lydia. One glance at her face and they'd see something was wrong.

Work, her usual solace, would have to pull her through.

She set aside the guest list and began crunching

numbers to figure out if the per plate estimate from a local bistro would be better value than the fixed price deal she'd been given from a caterer in Taos.

But all she could see was the pain emanating from Sammy Davidson's big eyes.

Something in a child's heart died when a parent was lost. In one moment you weren't a child anymore, but you weren't an adult, either. You became...

Nothing.

Kim made fists of her hands and pressed them into her eyes.

Who could love a child the way a mother did? The simple truth was—no one. Not a new foster mother, that was for sure.

And probably not an uncle, either.

WHILE MAKING NOTES on a chart in the room behind the reception counter, Lydia noticed Mary's brother, Nolan, enter the birth center. His niece, Sammy, followed behind him.

What were they doing here?

She heard him ask Trish if he could speak to Kim Sherman.

Some sort of accounting matter, then. If Lydia had her way, they would erase any debt the Davidsons owed to The Birth Place. She'd already spoken to Kim about it, but the accountant was adamant that businesses couldn't be run that way. Unfortunate outcomes did occur now and then: babies born with

Down's syndrome, spina bifida, other less severe genetic deformities that were no fault of the birth center.

Lydia had been forced to accept that the Davidsons' bill had to be paid. But she still didn't like it. She hated worrying about profit and loss and the bottom line. All she wanted, all she'd ever wanted, was to provide top-notch care to mothers and babies. And she wasn't above bending the rules to do so, when the situation called for it. As she had for Hope Tanner's baby.

She'd acted in the best interest of the birth center and the baby that time. And look where that had gotten her—estranged from her beloved granddaughter. Oh, how Lydia missed Devon. She was such a special woman, so caring and intelligent…and stubborn.

Fifteen minutes later, noises out in the hall regained Lydia's attention. She peered out the glass window. Nolan McKinnon was about to leave. His body language screamed frustration, maybe even anger, but he was gentle enough with the child.

Common courtesy required that Lydia step out into the hall and ask how they were doing. She hadn't spoken to either one since the funerals.

But she couldn't.

Not an hour of the day went by that she didn't think of Mary. She couldn't help but imagine how the baby would be growing if he had survived. At two weeks he'd be gaining weight and beginning to settle into a schedule.

Why couldn't even one of them have survived? Then Sammy would have *someone*.

She had her uncle, but Nolan wasn't a natural father. Lydia had noticed how stiffly he held his niece's hand at the funeral and how happily he'd given her up to the pregnant neighbor who'd baby-sat Sammy after the accident.

Of course, a man could *learn* how to be a father. But Sammy needed help *now*.

She had to go out there. But before Lydia managed to do so, a comment from Nolan carried to her.

"Are you happy Ms. Sherman is going to be your new baby-sitter?"

Lydia didn't think she could possibly have heard correctly. She emerged from the back room, a question forming in her mind, but the door had already closed on Nolan and his niece.

Lydia gathered some papers she needed to file. As she walked past the admin area, she noticed Kim's door was shut tight as usual. She considered knocking, then thought better of the impulse and continued to her own office. No sooner had she settled in her squeaky old chair than Trish breezed in with a batch of mail.

"Thanks, Trish." She accepted the bundle, noticing that the top envelope was a pretty blue, the address handwritten rather than computer generated.

Brushing back a strand of her conservatively styled brown hair, the receptionist widened her eyes. "Did you hear what just happened out there?" She gestured in the direction of reception. "It sounds as though Kim Sherman has agreed to help Nolan look after little Sammy. Can you believe it?"

Lydia had already recovered from her own initial surprise. "Actually, I can. I've always thought there was more to that woman than calculators and note-pads."

"I hate to say it, but if that's so, then you're the only one who's seen that side of her. I can't tell you how hard I've worked to befriend that woman. On her first day I brought a cup of coffee to her desk and she told me not to do it again. She didn't even say 'thank you.' She's turned down my every invitation for lunch and she refused to chip in on our wedding gift for Hope and Parker."

"She's not easy, I admit."

"Not easy?" Trish obviously had a better description on the tip of her tongue, but she was too much a lady to utter it. "I'd better get back to the front desk."

Trish was as sweet natured and generous as they came. If she couldn't get along with Kim, then obviously there was a problem.

But Lydia couldn't accept that Kim Sherman was a lost cause. The woman had a heart. And someday everyone in this birthing center would know it.

Lydia had hours of paperwork demanding atten-tion—her least favorite part of her job. In a stalling tactic, she reached for the blue envelope on the top of her stack of mail.

Often Lydia received personal letters from past clients. Expressions of gratitude, snapshots of growing children, progress reports on health issues. She treasured each letter and posted all photographs on one of several corkboards located throughout the building.

Looking forward to the emotional lift she always received from such correspondence, Lydia slit open the envelope and peered inside.

No photo. Just one folded sheet of paper. She pulled it out and smoothed it flat. She began to read, stiffening at the first line, recoiling at what followed.

Lydia Kane
You think you've gotten away with it, don't you?
I know all your secrets. And I'll make you pay.

That was it. No signature. She checked the top corner of the envelope. No return address, either. Who could have sent such an awful thing?

And why?

I know all your secrets. Was this about Hope's baby then? Lydia fingered the pendant around her neck. Hadn't she already paid enough for that mistake? Resigning from the board had almost killed her. And losing Devon's trust and respect...

She gazed with longing at the framed photograph of her granddaughter on her desk. Lydia was approaching her seventy-fourth birthday. She'd never imagined spending her last years like this. Estranged from family. Hands tied here.

This letter was an unbelievable affront. It was also,

probably, a silly prank. That line about making her pay... How could that be possible?

She'd already lost everything that mattered.

AT PRECISELY SIX-THIRTY, Kim Sherman rapped on the front door of Nolan McKinnon's town house. The condominium unit was part of a complex that stretched along Grand Avenue, just a few blocks south of the *Bulletin*'s office on Paseo de Sierra. The attractive adobe building had single carports out front and pretty arched doorways. Kim had left her Camry in the visitor's parking lot.

Nolan answered the door, still dressed in the jeans and sport jacket he'd worn for their meeting. He'd changed his shirt, however. This one was blue, like his eyes.

"I had a feeling you'd be punctual."

Was he making fun of her? "Most people consider punctuality a good quality."

"And I'm one of them. Come on in." He stepped back, making room for her with his body, but his eyes were another story. Kim felt exposed under his steady perusal. Didn't he have anything better to look at?

"Where's Sammy?"

"In the kitchen." He reached over her head to shut the door, making her feel tiny, which, at only five feet two inches and a hundred and ten pounds, she was.

"We just finished dinner," he went on, watching her switch from her street shoes to a pair of soft-soled loafers, his expression bemused. "There's another hot dog if you want one. I made two for Sam, but she didn't even finish her first.''

Kim followed him through to the kitchen. The place was messy, in a masculine way. Newspapers on the sofa in the front room, a sweatshirt on the stair railing leading to upstairs…a basketball on the kitchen table?

Kim plucked the ball off the table. ''There you are, Sammy. I wondered where you were hiding.''

The little girl smiled softly. ''Hi.''

''Hi, sweetheart.'' Kim glanced at the little girl's plate. Half the hot dog sat in a pool of ketchup. The glass next to her plate contained a dark liquid with tiny bubbles floating in it.

''Can I go to the bathroom?'' Sammy looked at Nolan for his approval.

''Of course. You don't have to ask me, Sam.'' He sounded slightly impatient, and Kim guessed this wasn't the first time he'd told her this. That Sam hadn't taken him at his word only proved she didn't feel at home here.

Once the child was out of the room, Kim focused her attention on Nolan. ''You fed her a hot dog and a Coke for dinner?''

Nolan looked a little embarrassed. ''She doesn't eat much. I'm trying to tempt her.''

''Have you asked her what her mother used to cook?'' Kim remembered that had been one of many changes she'd found hard after she'd lost her mom. Her mom had catered to all her special likes and dislikes. And she'd had the best recipe for rice pudding.

"I don't talk about her mother in front of her. It makes her upset."

Oh, he was hopeless. "Don't you think she's upset anyway?"

"I guess so." Nolan's expression was pained. "But she doesn't cry much."

"Probably because she's figured out how uncomfortable that makes you feel."

Nolan said nothing, which made Kim want to shake him. Couldn't he see the harm he was causing? The man needed a lecture in the worst way. But Sammy was already on her way back from the washroom. Was it possible she'd caught a few words of their heated exchange?

"Look, why don't you get going to this meeting of yours," she suggested. They could talk later. They *would* talk later, even though she suspected Nolan wouldn't want to hear what she intended to tell him.

Nolan picked up his wallet from the counter and slid it into his back pocket. His jeans outlined the firm butt and long legs of an athlete. So the basketball hadn't been merely a decorative centerpiece then.

"I won't be too late. I'm meeting the high school newspaper committee at the office. We usually put their weekly together in about two-and-a-half hours."

"Another volunteer project?" she asked as she began to clear the kitchen table. She attempted to close the ketchup bottle, but it was too gummed up. She unscrewed the lid and rinsed it under hot water.

"Why not? Someone's got to keep these kids busy and out of trouble."

She was amused to note he sounded just like one of his editorials.

"That looks good," he said.

"What? Dried ketchup?"

"The smile on your face. You should try it more often."

The personal comment reminded her of all the reasons she'd been foolish to come here. "Just get home on time and I'll be happy." She guessed he was the type of person who was chronically late.

As well as disorganized. The fridge was a hodgepodge. And the dishwasher was loaded haphazardly. "You know there *is* a right way and a wrong way to fill these things."

"There's a right way and a wrong way and then there's *my* way." He picked up one end of Sammy's leftover hot dog. "Sure you don't want any more?"

The little girl shook her head.

"Well, I guess I'll have to eat it then."

To Kim and Sammy's disbelief, he popped the whole ketchup-drenched mess into his mouth.

"Eww," Sammy said.

Nolan grabbed a paper towel and cleaned his face. "Okay, I better run. See you later."

Once he was gone, the kitchen atmosphere turned quiet. Kim finished with the dishes while Sammy sat in her seat.

"Do you like hot dogs, Sammy?"

The little girl shrugged and once more Kim felt her own heart breaking. If ever a child needed a hug… But to Sammy, Kim was little more than a stranger.

Having rearranged the dishes so that the spray from the dishwasher had at least a fighting chance of getting them clean, Kim added detergent, then turned the dial to heavy-duty wash. Some of those plates looked as if they'd been in there about a week.

"How about you show me your room, Sammy?"

The little girl slid out of her chair and obligingly led Kim upstairs. The small town house had two bedrooms and two bathrooms. Kim glimpsed a mass of bedding and clothes in the master suite that prompted her to close the door.

In Sammy's room a small, unmade bed sat in a corner next to the window. An open suitcase lay on the carpet next to a bookshelf stuffed with sporting trophies and various newspaper mementos. Kim picked up one large mug in order to read the printing on the side. For Coach Nolan. Thanks From The U16 Royals.

"Where is your stuff, Sammy?"

The little girl pointed to a stack of boxes at the foot of the bed. One had been opened, and books spilled onto the floor.

"Looks like we need to fix this place up a little." Kim moved to the bed. She was pulling a sheet taut, when it occurred to her that Nolan probably didn't keep a fixed laundry schedule.

"Can you help me take these sheets off the bed,

Sammy? And do you have any dirty clothes? Maybe we can wash a few loads of laundry tonight.''

"In the bathroom.''

Again Kim followed and found a mini disaster zone. Several days' worth of Sammy's clothes were scattered around, along with a couple of damp towels.

"Does your uncle have a washing machine?''

"In the basement.''

Sammy helped Kim carry down the dirty laundry. Kim set the little girl—even lighter than she looked— on the dryer so she could add a scoop of detergent into the washer and press the buttons as directed by Kim.

"Good job.'' Kim lifted the little girl down to the concrete floor. The basement was crowded with sporting gear: a Universal weight machine and a treadmill, parabolic skis, as well as a snowboard, golf clubs and fishing rods, even a yellow dinghy that hadn't been deflated. Kim hoped Sammy had an interest in sports. If not, she and her uncle were in for a very bumpy ride.

Back upstairs, Kim emptied the boxes of Sammy's possessions, then filled them again with Nolan's. She dusted off the shelves, then enlisted Sammy's help in arranging her books and plush animals. In the meantime, Kim emptied out the drawers in a beat-up teak bureau and unpacked Sammy's suitcase.

She took Nolan's framed posters and his college diploma from the wall and stacked them in the basement on her way down to collect dry sheets and towels.

"Do you have any pictures of your mom and dad?" she asked Sammy when she'd returned.

The little girl, cross-legged on the floor amid her collection of Groovy Girls, looked at her blankly. Kim lowered herself onto the floor beside her. "Would you like to have a picture of your family in your room, Sammy?"

A sheen of tears accumulated in the little girl's eyes. She nodded yes, her chin trembling.

"I can't imagine how you must miss them."

Tears fell down Sammy's plump cheeks. Tentatively Kim reached out an arm to console her, but Sammy threw her arms around Kim's neck. Hugging her was the only option.

"I want Mommy. I want Mommy."

"I know, baby." Kim pressed her lips to Sammy's soft hair.

Once started, the little girl could not stop. She cried and cried and called for her mother, and her father, too, over and over and over. Kim had nothing to offer, only her arms and her lap, and it wasn't until she noticed her glasses were fogging that she realized she was crying, too. Almost as hard as Sammy.

NOLAN CAME HOME at nine, and found Kim at the kitchen table, folding a batch of Sammy's laundry.

"I couldn't find your iron."

"That's because I don't own one." Nolan set a

stack of paper on the table and finally she glanced at him. Despite her glasses, he saw right away that her eyes were red and puffy.

Oh no. What had happened?

"You okay?"

"Fine." She lowered her head quickly then smoothed out the wrinkles in a pair of pink overalls.

Big surprise she wouldn't tell him the truth. "Where's Sammy?"

"In bed." Kim's slender chest rose on a deep breath. "She cried herself to sleep."

That didn't sound good. Nolan took the stairs, two at a time, then peered into his niece's room. She was on her back, breathing softly. He went closer and noted that while her cheeks were pink, her skin felt cool.

"She's okay, Nolan. She needed to cry." Kim was at the doorway, watching.

Something felt different. He glanced around, noticed the rows of children's books on his shelves, the toys and animals. Then, on the night table, a framed photograph.

It was a three-year-old snapshot of his sister's family, one that had been enclosed in the last Christmas card she'd sent him.

Ever *would* send him. It was so hard to accept Mary really was gone. With the rush of organizing funerals and dealing with finances and Sammy, sometimes he forgot what had caused all this turmoil.

His big sister was dead.

He rubbed a hand down his face and finally turned to Kim. "I guess I should have done this stuff myself."

"I guess you should have."

Not expecting the rebuke in her voice, he blinked with surprise.

"There are a lot of things you could be doing to help Sammy. Why don't you come downstairs to the living room? We need to have a little talk."

CHAPTER SIX

THE SCHOOLMARM WAS BACK. Nolan followed Kim down the stairs to the family room. She'd cleared away stacks of magazines. And something else was different... She'd dusted? And vacuumed?

She'd gone too far.

"Look, I appreciate you watching Sammy for me, and I'm sure you meant well unpacking her stuff and everything, but this is *my* house and she is *my* niece."

"I'm so glad you understand that. Because, frankly, I was beginning to wonder. How long since the funerals?"

"About a week. So what? I don't see where you get the right to come in here and start rearranging my *house*."

"It's been *over* a week by my count, and Sammy is *still* living out of her suitcase."

Kim stood in the center of the room, hands on her hips. It didn't matter that she was petite. She had the presence of a commander in chief.

But he hadn't enlisted. He didn't have to put up with this. "Okay, so I should have put her clothes in the dresser. Believe me, we've had bigger things to worry about."

"Bigger things than trying to make Sammy feel at home and safe and comfortable?"

"I've *tried,* damn it. I don't know anything about six-year-old girls."

"Well, it's time you learned. I know you lost your sister and I'm truly sorry. But Sammy's a child and she's lost everything. Her mother and father and the baby she'd been so excited about. Can you even imagine what that must feel like to her?"

"I can't give Sammy her family back. I wish I could." He sank into the sofa, tired of the arguing, just…tired. He propped his elbows on his legs and dug his fingers into his hair. Part of him knew Kim had a point. But a man could only do so much.

"What Sammy craves now is the familiar. It doesn't help being uprooted from her home."

"I agree the situation isn't ideal. But what choice do I have? Sammy's family home will have to be sold to pay down the operating loan on Steve's business. Listen, I didn't sign up for this. Not any of it."

Kim was so good at seeing Sammy's side. Could he make her understand what sudden parenthood was like for him?

"I have no experience with little kids. You have to look after them *all the time.* Do you know I can't even go out for a carton of milk without lugging her along?" How did parents deal with all this responsibility? Already it was driving him crazy, he couldn't imagine *years* of living this way.

"I barely know Sammy," he added. "Her mom and I, well, we hadn't talked for over three years."

The pain hit as usual in his chest and gut. He'd been such an obstinate jerk. Too late to change things now.

"Three years?"

"We had a disagreement about our mother. Mary didn't think I spent enough time visiting her. Hell, I probably didn't."

But he couldn't deal with that now. Sammy was his bigger concern. For some reason it seemed important that he make Kim understand how impossible this situation was.

"I have no idea why Mary gave me custody. If I hadn't seen the will myself I would have sworn it was a mistake. Steve's mom was the logical choice."

"But you mentioned earlier she isn't coping very well right now."

"Steve was her only child and his death hit her hard. But she'll recover soon, and when she does I'm sure she'll be desperate to have Sammy. After all, her granddaughter is all Irene has left."

Kim lowered herself into the chair opposite him. "You've got it all figured out, don't you?"

"Hey, I'm not just thinking of my own interests. You said it yourself, this place isn't right for Sammy and neither am I. I'm a single guy with a demanding job and lots of outside commitments. How am I supposed to manage a six-year-old...and a girl to boot! In a few years she'll need a female in her life."

"Maybe you'll marry."

"Right. With Sammy living here, I'm not going to be able to date, let alone find someone to marry."

"I have to admit it sounds hopeless. How do you suppose other single fathers manage?"

He knew she was mocking him. But he didn't care. "I have no idea."

"Well, maybe you can learn."

She wasn't listening to him. This situation was impossible. He wasn't the right man.

"I've made a list for you," she said briskly. "It's on the kitchen table. For one thing, you should be running Sammy's bath for her and helping her wash her hair. She's too little to do it herself."

Really? Nolan recalled handing his niece a couple of towels the first day she'd moved in. He'd had no idea she couldn't handle a shower.

"I've also made a list of the foods her mother used to cook for her. I suspect many of them will be beyond your culinary capabilities, however you should try to keep raw veggies and fresh fruit on hand for her to snack on. And little containers of yogurt. Sammy loves yogurt."

"She doesn't like veggies. She always picks them off the pizza."

"Most kids prefer their vegetables raw. You know, carrot sticks and celery… It's all on the list."

He supposed he could handle fruit, vegetables and yogurt. But how had Kim found out what Sammy liked? "Did you talk about her mother?"

"Of course, I did. And you should, too. Don't force her to grieve in silence, Nolan. It won't be good for her to bottle all those emotions inside."

"I thought you were an accountant. Not a psychologist."

"Let's just say I've had some experience with what Sammy is going through."

She pulled back, averted her head. And suddenly he guessed why she was so quick to sympathize with Sammy's situation. "You lost your parents, too. When you were young."

"I was six when my mother was run over in a pedestrian crosswalk. My father was already dead, I never really knew him."

Far from making a bid for sympathy, Kim spoke as dispassionately as if she was reciting facts from an encyclopedia.

"That must have been tough." He wondered if she'd had any family to take her in. He would have asked, but she was already standing.

"I should be going."

Just as he'd started to feel a measure of sympathy toward the woman, his hackles were raised, again. He didn't know whether to thank her or shove her out the door. She'd been very helpful, but maybe too helpful.

At the foyer, he paused uncomfortably. "I'm new at baby-sitting, like everything else. How much do I owe you?" He reached for his wallet.

"Put that away. I didn't do this for money."

Now he'd offended her again. "Okay… Well, thanks for looking after Sammy."

Her return "you're welcome" didn't sound any more gracious. She exchanged her footwear and retrieved her purse.

Again the incongruity of her delicate looks and her iron-plated personality struck him. She'd just given him one of the worst dressing-downs of his life. Now she looked so pretty and feminine it almost made him want to…

No. He had to be crazy to even be thinking it.

"So…same time on Tuesday?"

He hesitated, but knew he had no alternative. Irene wasn't well and he'd imposed on Toni enough. Most of his friends had their own families to worry about. "That would be great."

He remained in the doorway watching until she was safely in her car. He'd always liked girls who were fun and cheerful and uncomplicated. Kim Sherman was the perfect example why.

AT THE BREAKFAST TABLE the next morning Nolan noticed a new shine in Sammy's hair. For the first time she didn't have circles under her eyes, either.

"Did you sleep well last night?"

She nodded without lifting her gaze from her cereal bowl.

He wondered if she ever had nightmares. When Mary was a kid, she'd often crawled into his bed, shivering after one of her bad dreams.

"I guess maybe we didn't get off to the best start, you and I." Remembering what Kim had said about fruits and vegetables he poured his niece a glass of orange juice and set it beside her bowl.

Again Sammy said nothing, just kept eating. A little slower than before, though.

"I see Kim unpacked some of your stuff last night. I was wondering if you'd like me to move over the furniture from your old room? We could bring the quilt and your pillows." He remembered there'd been a lot of them. "And we could even paint if you want and…" He struggled to recall the details of Sammy's bedroom. He'd only been in it the once, when he'd packed her clothes, books and toys.

Soon he'd have to clean out the house, preparing it for sale. He and Mary had gone through the same process for their mother when she'd moved into the nursing home about a year before she died. That had been pretty unpleasant, but dismantling a young family's home, he knew, would be even worse.

Sammy still hadn't answered his question.

"Would you like your old stuff, Sam?"

She nodded.

"Okay." There was one thing off Kim Sherman's list.

"I'm going to take you to school this morning, okay?" She'd been off these past two weeks, but he felt it was time for her life to return to a regular routine. He'd spoken to the first-grade teacher, a woman he knew. Connie Eckland had suggested they take the

transition slowly and that Sammy come in for a half
day to start. As desperate as Nolan was to get a good
stretch of work in at the office, he had to admit Connie's plan made sense.

Sammy set down her spoon, then guzzled half the
orange juice. She was eating a little better, he noticed.
When he bought groceries today, he'd pick up some
corn bran, which, according to Kim's list, was
Sammy's favorite.

After Sammy brushed her teeth, Nolan thought they
were ready to go. But then she decided she needed to
use the bathroom. They'd almost made it to the car
when she realized she didn't have her favorite book.
Fifteen minutes later than planned, he had her
strapped into her booster seat.

How did parents get anywhere on time?

NOLAN EXPECTED TO FEEL relieved to drop Sammy
off at school. In reality, he found leaving hard. She
looked so small sitting at her desk. The children near
her were watching her curiously.

"You'll call me if she has any trouble?" he asked
Connie Eckland.

"Sammy's going to be just fine."

The red-haired teacher was someone he'd dated off
and on about a year ago. He couldn't remember why
they'd stopped seeing each other. Probably the usual
reason—work. He arranged his dates to accommodate
his erratic schedule and his host of volunteer duties.
He didn't have a lot of spare time in his life.

And that was before he'd inherited Sammy.

"Okay then. You've got my number?"

"I do."

He waved at Sammy one last time, then finally took off. Before he made his way to the office, he'd planned a quick visit with Irene Davidson. With any luck she'd be feeling stronger. He still hoped that eventually Sammy could go and live with her grandmother.

He drove to Mabel's place, two doors down from Irene's impressive bungalow on Copper Avenue. Nolan parked in front of the house and headed up the sidewalk.

Irene's husband had been part owner of a local ski development and had left a pile of money behind when he'd died of a heart attack, not long after Nolan had lost his own mother. Now Irene lived a life of luxury, alternating between her beautiful home in Enchantment and a town house in Maui.

Before he had a chance to knock, the door opened. Mabel was about ten years older than Irene, but still active in the community as the head of the local horticulture society. She wrote a monthly gardening column for the paper and also kept him up-to-date on the society's goings-on.

"Hey, Mabel. How are you keeping? I hope you haven't lost your green thumb. This vine is looking kind of dead." Since it was winter, Mabel smiled at him.

"Oh, Nolan. You're such a tease."

He stepped onto the floral welcome mat and wiped

last night's dusting of snow from his shoes. "Is Irene around?"

"In the living room watching television. I'm afraid she passes too many hours that way."

"Any improvement?"

"A little."

"What does her doctor say?"

"She should continue the Valium for a little while longer. And he said to encourage her to take walks, which I do. She went for over a mile the other day."

"That sounds encouraging."

Mabel led him through the foyer to a large room at the back of the house. Irene sat in a reclining arm chair, an afghan tucked around her feet.

He remembered when Mary and Steve had first married, Irene had been a bit of a problem. A classic overprotective mother, she'd had a hard time letting go of her son and accepting the new woman in his life.

After Sammy's birth, though, she'd mellowed. He knew his sister had used Irene often for baby-sitting.

"Nolan."

He was pleased she recognized him. At the funeral she'd been pretty spaced out.

"How are you doing, Irene?"

Using the remote control, she turned off the program she'd been watching, then raised her chair into an upright position.

"Much better, thank you. I think I'll be ready to go home by the weekend."

"No need to rush." Mabel passed out coffee to

both Nolan and Irene. "You can stay as long as you like."

"You've been a true friend, Mabel. But it's time I returned to my own home." Irene sipped her coffee, then smiled. "And how's my little Sammy doing?"

Nolan shifted his weight on the overstuffed love seat. "Sammy's okay. She started back at school today."

"So soon?"

"Well, everyone says kids need routine. Anyway, she's only attending for the morning. We'll see how it goes."

"She must miss her parents so much." Irene closed her eyes and hid behind her hand. Her frail shoulders trembled.

"You mustn't torture yourself." Mabel looked worried. "The young have an amazing resilience. Sort of like that vine you saw outside, Nolan. I'm sure Sammy is in pain now, but she will bounce back. And so will you, Irene."

Irene shook her head in disagreement.

"But you must," Mabel insisted. "Don't you want to help take care of Sammy?"

Slowly the fog in Irene's eyes lifted. "Of course, I do. Bring her to see me, Nolan, would you?"

"You keep getting better and we'll both come for a visit real soon," he promised. Handing over his empty coffee cup, he went to the chair to give the older woman a hug. Like Sammy, she'd lost nearly everything that awful day in January.

He knew none of them would ever completely heal.

CHAPTER SEVEN

FROM MABEL'S, Nolan drove directly to the old adobe building that housed the *Arroyo County Bulletin*. He'd been working here, off and on, since he was fourteen. Charley Graziano had given him his first job—delivering papers. But Nolan's real interest lay in writing articles.

He submitted his first when he was fifteen. Though it hadn't been printed, Charley had coached him until he produced something worthy of publication.

In high school Nolan had learned to operate Charley's Nikon. He'd covered PTA meetings, varsity sporting events, even school dances. He left Enchantment for a while to study journalism at the University of New Mexico. When he returned, Charley offered him a full-time job, and five years later, the position of editor.

A few more years passed, and somehow Charley had become old. He spent fewer and fewer hours at the office. Eventually he decided to retire. He and his wife wanted to move to Maryland to be close to their daughter and her family. One day, Charley had called Nolan into his office. By now the relationship between the two men approached that of father and son.

"I don't want to leave, Nolan. But since Rosa had the baby, her mother can't stand to be so far apart."

"I understand, Charley." Nolan had assumed he was being let go. He knew the value of the newspaper as a business couldn't possibly match the fair-market value of the building and land. And he'd fully expected his old mentor to cash in and move on.

But Charley had surprised him with an offer. "We'll go into partnership. Pay me ten percent a year. By the time you're forty you'll own everything. What do you think?"

He and Charley had shaken on the deal and then hugged. Nolan was saddened by the idea of losing Charley, but the entrepreneur in him had been excited by the new challenge.

The *Arroyo County Bulletin* had been Charley's passion for decades. Now it was Nolan's. Every time he opened the old oak door with its heavy brass hardware, he thought about his commitment to the community where he lived, and to the man who had taught him so much about journalism. And about life, too.

Charley had been very distressed by Nolan's rift with his sister. During their monthly phone calls, he'd urged Nolan to swallow his pride and make the first move toward reconciliation.

The old man had been right, but Nolan had been too busy—and too damn stubborn—to know it at the time.

"Hey, Nolan. Good to see you." Toni Perez, his right-hand woman, had been working here almost as long as Charley. Despite her arthritis, she could still input copy faster than anyone in the office.

"Good to be here." He opened the door to his office, then wished he hadn't. His desk seemed to bow beneath the stacks and stacks of paperwork.

"Looks worse than it is," Toni called out. "I've been trying to stay on top of the more urgent matters."

"You're amazing," he said, meaning it. The last two editions wouldn't have gone out without Toni putting in major overtime. But she was sixty and couldn't keep working at that pace.

Nolan glanced at his watch. Ten-thirty. He lowered his head and dug in. Next time he noticed the time, it was quarter to twelve. He had to pick Sammy up from school.

"Damn." At this rate he was never going to see the surface of his desk again. He stuffed a folder containing a backlog of letters to the editor into his briefcase. A pale blue envelope slipped out and fell to the floor.

As he stooped to pick it up, the phone rang. He heard Toni answer, then call out to him, "It's for you."

He cursed again, then jabbed the speakerphone button. "McKinnon speaking."

"Dylan Carson here, Mr. McKinnon." Dylan was a volunteer at the teen drop-in center. A while ago he'd been in some trouble himself. Now he was one of their more conscientious helpers, often coming in during school lunch break to assist with administration.

"What's up, Dylan?"

"I'm going over the weekend schedule and I was wondering if you're going to make it for your usual Saturday afternoon?"

Torn by his various responsibilities, Nolan raised his eyes to the ceiling, then wished he hadn't. A discolored patch on one of the tiles suggested a leak in the roof.

"If you can't make it, that's fine," Dylan said. "We understand, man."

"I'd like to, Dylan." He hadn't covered his regular weekly shift since the accident. But who would look after Sammy? Irene was improving, yes, but she couldn't be left with a little girl, yet.

Kim Sherman?

He felt the tug of temptation, then gave himself a mental kick in the rear. His life wasn't complicated enough? She'd only add another twenty items to his to-do list. Probably one of them would be alphabetizing his medicine cabinet.

Which reminded him. She'd told him to make sure he kept all drugs and cleaning products out of reach of the curious little girl. As usual, she was right. He jotted a note to do so as soon as he got home.

Next thing he knew, he was saying something crazy into the phone.

"Dylan, put me down from one until three, okay?" He'd find *someone* to baby-sit. Toni? No, she was already working too hard at the paper. Miguel? He'd do it if he wan't on duty, but Sammy seemed more comfortable with women than men. Perhaps Connie Eckland.

He logged off his computer, then latched his brief-case. On the way out the door he noticed the blue envelope on the floor. Swiftly he scooped it up and shoved it inside his jacket pocket.

"I have to get Sammy from school," he told Toni. "You know how to reach me if something comes up."

Toni nodded at his mess of a desk. "You mean in addition to all that?"

"Yeah. Exactly."

Of course he hit every red light between the office and the elementary school on Desert Valley Road. He was cursing again as he parked on the street across from the main doors.

Sammy sat on the front step. She had a couple of books on her lap. Connie stood behind her, a hand on the little girl's shoulder, obviously miffed that he hadn't shown up on time. He scratched the idea of asking her to baby-sit.

"Sorry I'm late." He dashed across the street, feeling breathless and disorganized. At the foot of the stairs, he paused. "How was your morning, Sam?"

She shrugged. He raised his eyes to Connie.

"Sammy's doing just fine. On Monday she can come for the whole day. We've been talking about that."

Talking. When his niece needed to communicate with him she used mostly gestures. "Is that right, Sam? Do you want to come back for the full day on Monday?"

She nodded.

He tried not to let her lack of words bother him. As he reached out a hand, he was gratified that at least she took it. "Thanks a lot, Connie. Hope you have a good weekend."

"See you on Monday," Connie said brightly to her young pupil. Her gaze was firmer when she settled it on him. "Oh, and Nolan?"

"Yeah."

"We have strict rules against jaywalking at school. You should use the crosswalk. Especially when you're with Sammy." She nodded toward the end of the block.

"Right. Use the crosswalk." He changed direction, Sammy's hand still in his. Who knew there were so many rules involved in looking after children?

He *definitely* was the wrong man for this job.

FRIDAY NIGHT and she was alone. There was absolutely nothing new about this, but tonight Kim felt the loneliness weighing her down like a lingering illness. She did not want to watch the movie she'd rented. The pint of mint chocolate-chip ice cream she'd purchased after work likewise held no appeal.

She wandered her small one-bedroom apartment aimlessly. She'd already taken her run. Every day she did the same forty-minute circuit around town. Lately she'd been thinking about joining a gym. Maybe when she returned to Denver she would do that. It was too late for Enchantment. Already she'd decided that she would give her notice the day after the fund-raiser. Two weeks should be sufficient and then she'd be free to move on.

Drifting out of the kitchen, Kim headed for her bedroom next. The pristine bedspread taunted her. When was the last time she'd had a serious relationship with a man? Wouldn't it be lovely to be getting ready to go on a date right now?

For some strange reason, Nolan McKinnon came to mind.

Kim sat on the edge of the mattress. She knew Nolan, like most of the people in Enchantment, disliked her. She'd given him no reason to do otherwise. She'd been unsympathetic about his predicament with his sister's medical bills and overbearing in her advice on child care.

But that had been on purpose, right? She didn't need to get involved with some man—especially one as attractive and likable as Nolan at this point in her stay in Enchantment. She'd be better off waiting until she'd found a place she could settle before getting back into the dating scene.

Kim had never had a hard time finding men to date, especially when she took the time to make herself up, which she hadn't done in Enchantment. When she styled her hair, put on her contact lenses and a pair of high-heeled shoes, she could definitely turn heads.

But here in Enchantment, a lower profile suited her purposes better.

With a sigh, she stretched, then wandered to the dresser by the window. Outside the sky was already dark. She lowered the blind for privacy, then opened her small jewelry box.

She kept the earrings in a tiny gold box. Now she slid them into her palm and rubbed a finger over the soft pink stones.

Simply touching the beautiful rose onyx brought her peace. The earrings were her only remaining link to her mother.

And to her grandmother.

Lydia Kane wore a pendant, the matching piece to the set. Kim often had to quell the impulse to reach out and stroke the larger stone so like the ones she kept hidden at home.

Seeing that necklace on her grandmother's neck had been the final piece of evidence Kim needed to confirm that she'd found the woman who had given up her mother at birth, over fifty years ago.

Lydia would have been sixteen at the time. She'd left her home in New Mexico to have her baby in Denver, Colorado. Kim had no idea why she hadn't married the father, or considered raising the child on her own. Times had been different then. Kim wasn't here to judge.

She'd just wanted to meet the only relative she had

left in this world. She'd wanted to see where she'd come from. *Who* she'd come from.

And in these regards, she hadn't been disappointed. The color and magic of Enchantment had spoken to her the first day she'd arrived. In her blood, she felt that this was the place of her origin.

As for Lydia, she was so strong and kind. Kim couldn't have asked for a better grandmother. Her one regret was that her mother had never met Lydia. The two women had been so much alike...

The phone rang. Kim felt a moment of disorientation. She so rarely received phone calls at home. A flicker of hope had her rushing to answer. Could it be...

No. Not him. It was probably a telemarketer. Did they work evenings?

Her heart felt as if it were pounding in her head as she went for the call. She dropped the earrings to the counter, then reached for the receiver.

"Hello?"

"Kim? Nolan McKinnon here. I hope this isn't a bad time?"

"Not at all." Fortunately he had no way of knowing how little there was in her life for him to interrupt.

"I was wondering if you might be free to do an extra shift of baby-sitting?"

She'd known this had to be the reason for his call. Still, his words made her heart settle back into its rightful place. "Yes, of course. How *is* Sammy?"

"She's fine. I rented a video for her, but she's paying more attention to the books she borrowed from the school library. Hey—you'll be glad to hear I cleaned out my medicine cabinet and also bought all the food on your list. Yesterday I had Sammy's furniture shipped from her house.''

''That's great news.''

''The thing is, I need to volunteer at the drop-in center tomorrow afternoon from one until three in the afternoon. Is it possible—''

''No problem at all. I'll be at your place by quarter to the hour.''

SAMMY GREETED KIM the next afternoon with a beaming smile, which certainly beat the welcome Kim received from the little girl's uncle as they crossed paths at the door.

''I really appreciate your helping out like this.''

She could tell it almost killed Nolan to say that. With an apology for rushing, he dashed out the door and she locked it behind him.

She walked through to the kitchen, where Sammy was finishing lunch. Her hair was clean but tangled. Her blue T-shirt and green overalls didn't really go together, but they were both stain free. An empty yogurt container, the core of an apple and a milk-coated glass were on the table in front of her. Kim tidied the mess then asked, ''What do you want to do, Sammy?''

''Read books.''

"Are you sure? It's sunny out today. I thought we could walk to the playground."

Sammy shook her head vehemently. "I want books."

Kim remembered the large collection she'd unpacked on Thursday night. Sammy must really love stories. In fact, she'd been carrying a book the first time they met. "Okay, fine, we can do that. How about we give you some pigtails, first?"

They detoured to the bathroom, and Kim took some elastics she'd thought to bring with her out of her pocket. Brushing through Sammy's tangles was a bit of a trick. But the little girl seemed pleased with the end result. She nodded her head and smiled at the way her pigtails bounced.

"Now stories," she demanded when she'd bored of admiring her hair. Sammy tugged Kim's hand and led her to the next room. At the threshold, Kim paused in surprise.

Sammy's old furniture was in place, yes. But the room was a mess of books, toys and clothes. Perhaps, not surprisingly, Sammy's bed was unmade. Her pajamas were two balls of flannel amid a mass of stuffed animals.

"It'll be pretty hard to read in here, Sammy. How about we make the bed?"

Sammy flopped onto the carpet. "Mommy makes my bed."

"I see. And what about your uncle Nolan?"

"He doesn't even make his own bed!"

When Kim laughed, Sammy began giggling, too. "His room is even worse than mine."

"Well, I'll help tidy yours, but your uncle Nolan is going to have to fend for himself." She straightened bedcovers and folded Sammy's pajamas and put them under the pillow.

Sammy sighed, then began picking up books. After about five or six, she held one out to Kim. "Read this, please."

"Sure." Kim cuddled with the little girl and opened the cover. After the first couple of pages, she could tell Sammy wasn't paying attention. When the story ended, the child pulled the book from Kim's hands, then selected another volume at random.

"This one."

They went through the same procedure several times, with Sammy losing interest in each new book shortly after it was begun. After the sixth, Kim tried to resist starting a seventh.

"Why don't we bake cookies?" She wondered if Nolan stocked staples like flour and chocolate chips. "We might have to walk to the grocery store first."

"No cookies. Read another story, please."

"But—" Kim didn't have the heart to resist as Sammy pressed another picture book into her hands. She read it, and the next book and the next.

Closing the cover on that one, she said firmly, "That's enough, Sammy. Let's try—"

But Sammy had fallen asleep. She was a little old

for afternoon naps. The exhaustion of the past few weeks must be catching up to her. Poor, sweet thing.

Kim tucked her into the bed, then reshelved the books and closed the door. According to her watch, it was already quarter after three, the time Nolan had said he'd be home. She heard the front door open and close.

Her heart went crazy again, and Kim put a hand to her chest. When running, she monitored her pulse. Right now she'd put it at something like one hundred and fifty beats per minute.

She forced herself to step deliberately and slowly down the stairs. In the kitchen, Nolan had just poured himself a huge glass of milk. He was whistling and looked carefree and cheerful. His air of well-being crashed the second he saw her.

"Hi there." His tone was reserved.

"Did you have a good time?" He must have. His hair had a healthy, wind-tousled look and color was high on his tanned cheekbones.

"I did. We played some basketball in the gym then went outside to skateboard."

She wasn't surprised to learn he could do that. "You like those kids."

"I do. And it's been a while since I've seen them. I was afraid they'd feel I'd abandoned them."

"But surely they understand about your sister…and everything."

"To a teenager who may be having problems with his parents, or at school, a couple of weeks can feel like forever.'' He lifted his glass and downed all that milk in four swallows.

He set the empty glass on the counter, then wiped the back of his hand across his mouth. "Where's Sam?"

"Sleeping again. I seem to have that effect on her." She resisted the temptation to rinse his glass and place it in the dishwasher. "Um, have you read any books to Sammy?"

He frowned. "Am I supposed to? She's always got a book in front of her face. I thought she could read by herself."

"She can definitely manage some of the simpler books. But even young children who can read on their own sometimes like to be read to."

"I'll add that to my list."

To her surprise he pulled her list from the pocket of a sport jacket hanging on the back of a kitchen chair.

At the same time, a light blue envelope fell to the floor. She picked it up, noticing that it was addressed to the editor of the *Arroyo County Bulletin* and marked "Urgent." She set it on the counter as he jotted down her latest instructions.

"That's great, Nolan," she said. "Reading to Sammy is a good idea, but I raised the subject because I wondered if you've noticed something almost…manic about Sammy's addiction to books."

She hadn't wanted to pass on her observation. She'd guessed he wouldn't be pleased. And he wasn't.

"What do you mean, manic? So the kid likes books. Isn't reading a good thing?"

"Of course it is. Except Sammy seemed so intense when I was reading to her. But only for the first couple pages. Then she'd lose interest until it was time to select the next book."

"So she has a short attention span. She's only six." In an absentminded manner, Nolan picked up the blue envelope on the counter and ripped off a corner, then slit the side open. He pulled out a folded piece of stationery.

"You probably don't want to hear this, but in my opinion it would be a good idea to take Sammy to see a psychologist."

Nolan was so busy reading his letter he didn't seem to hear what she was saying.

"Celia Brice works part-time at The Birth Place. She's a wonderful lady. You should book an appointment for Sammy."

"What?" Nolan glanced up at her, then back at his letter. He read it a second time, then refolded the sheet of paper carefully and returned it to the envelope.

"I was talking about booking an appointment with Celia Brice for Sammy."

"I've heard of Celia." His blue eyes were focused only on her now. "You think Sammy needs to see a psychologist? Because she likes books too much?"

"Not because of the books." Though she still felt there'd been something odd going on in the little girl's head this afternoon. "Because of losing her mother and father." *Stupid,* she wanted to add, but didn't.

"I don't know." He dropped the blue envelope into a basket containing a bunch of other opened mail, then changed his mind and shoved it back into his jacket pocket.

"Nolan, what could it hurt? You said you've heard of Celia. You know she'll be gentle with Sammy." Celia was about Kim's age, but she had the type of warm, caring personality that drew people to her. Kim couldn't think of anyone who'd tried harder to befriend her when she'd first moved to Enchantment than Celia. Except maybe Trish.

But they'd both, eventually, given up.

"I'll think about it."

From his grudging tone, Kim figured that was the most she could hope for.

CHAPTER EIGHT

DAMN IT, Kim Sherman was right. Again. Monday morning Nolan gave up manipulating the tone on the photos he'd just scanned into the computer. An hour ago he'd dropped Sammy off at school, anticipating his first full workday in weeks, but now that he was here, worries about the kid lingered.

Sometime last night, between the time he'd tucked her into bed and woken her for school, she'd removed the picture of her family from its frame and shredded it.

He'd found the pieces this morning in the trash.

Why would she do that?

The obvious answer seemed to be that she was angry. But on the outside she appeared mild, almost placid. He'd never guessed so much could go on inside a six-year-old kid's head.

But that incident wasn't the only sign of a problem. He'd watched her more closely after Kim had left and he'd noticed Sammy's obsession with books *was* a little strange.

Hell. Why was he torturing himself with all this when the answer was obvious? He couldn't deny Sammy the help she needed just because he didn't want to admit Kim Sherman's suggestion had been sound.

He fished the Enchantment phone book out of his bottom desk drawer and looked up Celia Brice's office number. A receptionist told him that the psychologist's first opening was in a week.

Nolan paced. "We can't wait that long. I have a six-year-old niece who's just lost both her parents."

Right away the receptionist realized who he meant. "You're talking about Sammy Davidson?"

Everyone in town knew about the tragedy. Besides the obituaries, there'd been the article, written by Cooper and edited by Toni. He still hadn't been able to bring himself to read it.

"I'm sure Celia will squeeze her in," the receptionist rushed on. "She's at The Birth Place this afternoon. Could you bring Sammy in around four o'clock?"

"That would be perfect." He'd take her straight from school.

Nolan hung up the phone then went to his jacket hanging on a hook on the back of his office door. From the pocket he pulled out the blue envelope and retrieved the letter. When he'd first read this, in front of Kim Sherman, he'd had a hard time keeping his expression neutral.

In his years at the paper, he'd received a wide range of correspondence, but this letter was unusual, even a little disturbing.

For about the tenth time, he read the strange missive.

Dear Editor,
Something must be done to protect the citizens
of our little town. Lydia Kane and her birth cen-
ter are a menace. Someone needs to look out for
all the unborn babies. Please do your job and
reveal this woman for what she is—a baby killer!

No signature at the bottom, just as there'd been no return address or stamp on the envelope.

He scanned the brief message again. Pretty strong words. A crank letter? Maybe. The tone was a little over-the-top. But coming in the wake of Mary's death he couldn't ignore the questions about Lydia Kane's competence and the safety of The Birth Place.

Could this have anything to do with Lydia stepping down from the board of directors? He'd written the story for the *Bulletin* back when it had happened and now he called up the archives to refresh his memory.

He scanned the article quickly. Lydia's grand-daughter, Devon Grant, had been her replacement on the board. The reason given for Lydia's departure was so that she could reduce her workload.

At the time, he'd wondered if there was more to the story. He hadn't probed, assuming the real reasons were personal.

But what if they weren't? What if Lydia *had* behaved with some sort of impropriety? Or worse.

He'd have to investigate. And Sammy's appointment with Celia Brice would provide the perfect opportunity for him to spend some time at The Birth Place without arousing suspicion.

LATER THAT AFTERNOON, Celia Brice met Nolan and Sammy in the busy reception area of the birth center. In a cool green dress, her long blond hair held back in a clip, Celia looked elegant and utterly feminine— the opposite of plain-Jane Kim Sherman. Nolan wondered why he didn't feel the usual pull of attraction at seeing a pretty woman.

Maybe he was just too worried about Sammy.

"Thanks for fitting us into your schedule." He shook Celia's hand.

"No problem. I'm looking forward to getting to know this little lady."

Celia smiled warmly at Sammy, but his niece paid no attention. She was twisting to get a good look at a pregnant woman standing in front of the high reception counter.

Nolan gave the woman an embarrassed smile, trying hard to focus on her pretty face rather than her huge belly.

"Come. I'll show you my office. It's on the second floor."

Nolan tugged Sammy's hand until she stopped gawking. They walked past several exam rooms and offices to the stairwell at the end of the hall. He supposed some comment about not staring at strangers was in order, but at the moment they had a bigger problem in their scope.

"This is the office I usually work out of when I'm here." Celia opened a door and ushered them inside a small room with several comfortable chairs and a coffee table. The view from the window was almost completely blocked by a clump of New Mexico locust.

Nolan stayed in the doorway, feeling awkward.

"Do you know why you're here, Sammy?" Celia crouched to the child's eye level. When the little girl shrugged, Celia glanced up at Nolan.

"I told her we were coming to see a nice lady who wanted to talk to her."

"That's exactly right."

Celia smiled at him warmly, approvingly. What a nice change from Kim's scalding glances.

"And Sammy, you can talk to me, too. About anything you're thinking, anything you're feeling." Celia made eye contact with Nolan again. "Would you like to sit with us? Just to make sure Sammy is comfortable?"

The last thing that would make Sammy comfortable was having him around. "I'll hang out in the hall."

Celia's gaze lingered on him. "I see. Okay then. Sammy, I have some juice boxes if you're thirsty. Do you like fruit punch or lemonade?"

Nolan was pleased to see Sammy follow Celia willingly to a tiny fridge in the corner. No question Celia had a way about her. Her receptionist had told him this appointment would last about an hour—which gave him a reasonable amount of time to start his informal investigation.

Out in the hall, he glanced around, orienting himself. Though he'd lived in Enchantment most of his life, this was only his second time in The Birth Place.

Last time he'd been focused on the problem with Mary's invoice. Today he noticed more of the decor. The main floor had a homey feel with traditional Mexican tiles and lots of big, healthy plants in colorful pottery containers. The whitewashed walls were covered with a hodgepodge collection of Southwestern art, educational posters…and baby pictures. Hell, he'd never seen so many baby pictures.

Up here, though, the decor was plain and serviceable, the atmosphere quiet. Glancing around, he saw several rooms that appeared to be used for storage only.

The sound of footsteps drew his gaze down the hall from Celia's office. Wooden clogs clacked against the floor as a young woman in a dress that looked like a potato sack approached. She had a stethoscope around her neck, so presumably she was a midwife.

"May I help you?" she asked. "Are you looking for your wife?"

Her false assumption gave him an odd feeling in the pit of his stomach. Did he look like the kind of guy who was married and about to become a father? He was definitely the right age.

"I'm just waiting for my niece. She's talking to Celia Brice."

"I see. Well, the reception area is actually that

way.'' She pointed to the stairs. ''You could pour yourself a cup of herbal tea and read a magazine while you wait.''

He could just imagine the kind of magazines they stocked in this place. Even if he hadn't had his own agenda, the suggestion would have held little appeal.

''Actually, I thought I'd drop in to see Kim Sherman while I was here,'' he improvised. ''We have a little accounting matter to settle.''

''In that case, you'll want to follow the hallway at the bottom of the stairs. You'll find the administration area to the right.'' Again the woman pointed toward the stairwell. ''Just past Lydia Kane's office.''

''Thanks.'' He'd been tempted by the large storage room next to Celia's office. Would Mary's records be in there, yet? But the midwife kept watching him until he headed in the direction she'd indicated. He passed another collection of photos and couldn't stop from pausing for just a moment.

His nephew should have been one of those bald, red-faced infants. For the first time Nolan felt the loss of his sister's baby as a physical pain. What would the kid have been like, he wondered. Would he have had Sammy's round eyes? Thick, curly McKinnon hair that was neither brown nor blond?

He rolled his shoulders slightly. The midwife was still watching. He gestured toward the photos. ''Cute.''

She nodded and smiled but wasn't distracted from her vigil.

With a sigh he turned to the stairs, taking them two at a time. Kim Sherman had made a good alibi. But now he thought dropping by to see her wouldn't be a bad idea.

Kim had no compunction about speaking exactly what was on her mind. Perhaps she'd seen something a little off about Lydia Kane. Why not begin his investigation by speaking to her?

As he hit the landing, a crazy possibility occurred to him. Letters like the one he'd received often came from someone who felt like an outsider, someone who'd never managed to fit in....

He hated to entertain the idea after the woman had gone out of her way to help him and Sam. But didn't that description sound a lot like Kim Sherman?

AT QUARTER AFTER FOUR on a Monday afternoon, the last thing Kim expected was a knock on her closed door. She frowned at the interruption. She'd had a productive day so far but had several hours of work remaining on the fund-raiser.

Whoever it was, knocked again.

"Come in," she said, grudgingly. Continuing to input numbers into her Excel work sheet, she didn't see who stood at the doorway. After a few seconds though, the back of her neck began to tingle.

She swiveled to face forward. Then, irrationally, whipped off her glasses.

"Nolan?"

Her pulse began to climb, her skin heated. Why did she always react to his presence this way? She hated the feeling of being out of control. Hated, too, her traitorous wish that he could be here for some reason other than—

"Is Sammy okay?"

"I just dropped her off for a session with Celia."

He wasn't even looking at her. The last time he'd been in her office, they'd been focused on business. Today he was studying the details of her surroundings. She watched him scan her bookshelves, the neat file cabinets, the clear work surfaces. All she had on her desk was a file and a pad of lined paper.

Kim knew her office revealed next to nothing about her personality or background. But she felt nervous anyway. Keeping her distance wasn't working with Sammy Davidson. And she was absolutely hopeless at it where Nolan McKinnon was concerned.

"I think you're doing the right thing taking Sammy to see Celia. Your sister would be very proud of you."

Nolan had pulled an accounting manual from her bookshelf. Now he slid the volume back into place. "Mary, proud? Oh, I doubt that. I'm making every mistake in the book with her kid—as you've had no compunction pointing out to me at every possible opportunity."

He sounded bitter. And Kim felt bad for having given him such a hard time. He was a bit thick when it came to raising children, but he was trying. "It'll get easier. You're doing just fine."

"I bet Sammy wouldn't agree with you. Know what she did last night?" Nolan sat on the corner of her desk.

Too close. Much too close. Kim wheeled her chair back about six inches. "What?"

"She tore up that picture of her family you framed for her."

"Poor Sammy." She remembered going through a similar stage when her mother had died. But her anger hadn't lasted. And neither would Sammy's.

"I just wished I knew why Mary picked me as the guardian. She had to have known I'd be hopeless."

"Why would she think that?"

"Because of the way I treated our mother." He slipped off her desk and prowled to the other end of the office, where he examined the poster of desert horses that had been on the wall when Kim arrived.

It was a photograph Kim admired. She loved the desert, the colors, the sense of freedom she experienced when contemplating the wild horses in their natural setting.

"What does your mother have to do with this?"

"Everything. This whole thing goes way back. Mary was always our mother's favorite and I was Dad's. That worked okay until Dad's heart attack."

"You and Mary were still kids at the time?"

"Yeah. I was twelve, Mary seventeen. I think on some level my mother held me responsible. Maybe she thought I wore him out with all my sports, I don't know. I could never do anything right in her eyes.

Years later she had her stroke, and we only fought worse.''

"Is that when she went into the nursing home?''

He nodded. "Mary visited her twice a week. I managed maybe once a month.'' He looked at Kim as if expecting a shocked rejoinder.

But this time she wasn't prepared to judge.

"I didn't help with anything. Mary took care of all the decisions, shopping and medical visits when Mom was alive. Later, Mary organized the funeral and made burial arrangements. Maybe that's why she threw this guardian thing at me. To even the score.''

Kim refrained from bursting in with a caustic comment. Nolan was just venting. He couldn't really believe Mary would gamble her daughter's future to settle some grudge she may have been holding against her brother.

"But enough about the mess my life has evolved into.'' He tugged at the collar of his shirt and cleared his throat. "I need to talk to you about something else.''

Not Sammy?

What then? A silly, girlish hope tried to flutter in her chest, but she wouldn't let it. Look at the man. He was here about something serious. And even if he wasn't, she had to be the last woman he'd ever want to ask on a date.

NOLAN COULDN'T BELIEVE he'd just unloaded all his family crap on Kim Sherman's shoulders. Talk about an unsympathetic audience. And yet she hadn't given him hell for the way he'd treated his mother.

Maybe because it was too late to do anything about it. Kim probably didn't take any pleasure in yelling at people if she couldn't also provide a ten-point to-do list to solve the problem.

No, that wasn't fair. Kim *was* tough. But she wasn't mean. Looking at her now, in fact, she seemed almost approachable. Her lips were soft…kissable, in fact.

It wasn't the first time he'd felt this urge. Was it possible she felt a hint of the same attraction? Something in her expression made him wonder. He moved closer and placed his hands on her desk. As he leaned forward, she moved backward in her chair.

He'd been wrong. She *didn't* feel it.

As he shifted his gaze from her face, he noticed that Sammy's picture was still posted on her bulletin board. So she hadn't tossed it in the trash. Actually, now that he knew her better, he wasn't surprised.

"Tell me something, Kim. Just how well do you know Lydia Kane?"

A new emotion flashed in Kim's eyes, and he was surprised by the strength of it. She leaned back in her chair and raised that stubborn little chin of hers.

"Why do you ask? Is this about what happened to your sister?"

"Maybe in part." He'd investigated the circumstances of Mary's death and uncovered no wrongdoing. But if Lydia truly was incapable, or worse, had been acting with malicious intent, perhaps she'd covered up her mistake somehow.

"That's crazy, Nolan. Talk to Dr. Ochoa. He'll tell you Lydia did everything by the book. What happened to your sister was terrible. But it wasn't Lydia's fault. In fact…"

Kim slid open the second drawer of her desk. "I have some statistics I've been compiling for an upcoming promotional event. The Birth Place, and Lydia personally, have very high success ratios compared to the national averages. I can copy this for you if you like."

"That would be great." He'd take a look at those numbers. Then try to figure out if they'd been fudged.

Kim excused herself to make the copies. When she came back, she handed him the extra set of papers. She was still a little flustered, and he had to wonder why.

When he'd come in looking for an extension on his sister's account, she'd been cool as an arctic breeze. Then today one question about Lydia Kane had her almost falling over herself to be helpful.

Why?

Did she feel some particular loyalty to Lydia Kane? But Lydia was a midwife and Kim worked in administration—surely their paths rarely crossed.

There had to be another explanation. Could it be guilt? Maybe Kim *had* sent him the letter and now regretted her brash move. But again, why would she do something like that?

Besides, she didn't really seem the type to send an anonymous letter. If Kim had any opinions to air, she'd do so openly.

"Is there anything else?"

He didn't want to leave, but couldn't think of a delaying tactic. "No. I guess not."

"I'll see you Tuesday night then. Will quarter to seven be all right?"

Although her tone was polite, Nolan could tell he was being firmly dismissed. When she stood up to show him the door, though, he couldn't help but note that Kim had great legs. Well, calves, anyway. Her skirt stopped just below her knees, not an attractive length. Combined with her staid gray cardigan, her attire sent out a rather dull message.

And still he had this odd desire to prolong their meeting.

Very odd.

She opened the door. "Thanks for stopping by, Nolan. I'll be sure to send you those itemized lists for the insurance company."

The lie—meant for the man and woman standing by the copier, presumably—came out of Kim's mouth so smoothly he was caught slack jawed. "Um, that would be, um, great."

Her door swung shut, missing the tip of his nose by an inch. Maybe less. He stepped back, patting the breast pocket of his jacket. While scanning her office, he'd spied several samples of her neat, upright penmanship. Nothing like the crude block of printing of this letter.

He checked out the action at the copier. Trish Linden was engaged in deep conversation with Mitchell Dixon, the owner of a local restaurant. As Nolan watched, Mitchell passed Trish a manila envelope. Then he happened to glance in Nolan's direction. He actually blushed when their eyes met.

"Hey, Mitchell."

"Nolan."

Though usually very friendly, Mitchell brushed Nolan off. He turned back to the receptionist, whose cheeks had also pinkened upon realizing she was being observed.

"Guess I'll see you around, Trish."

"Sure." She tucked the large envelope behind her back.

Curious, Nolan lingered in the hall until Mitchell left. With a vague smile in his direction, Trish clutched the envelope close to her chest then rushed off in the opposite direction. He couldn't tell if she was upset or embarrassed. What was in that envelope?

And what was Mitchell Dixon doing hanging around The Birth Place? Not only was he too old to be a prospective father, but his wife had left him about two years ago.

"*Here* you are!"

Celia's musical voice came from the direction of the stairs. Nolan turned as the psychologist and Sammy drew near.

"Katherine told me you wanted to speak to Kim." Celia's gaze swept by the closed door. "I take it you two have finished your business?"

"We have. And you two, also?" He smiled at Sammy, checking out her expression anxiously. "Did it go okay?"

Unsurprisingly, all Nolan got from her was a shrug.

"I really enjoyed getting to know your niece, Nolan. Would it be possible for you to bring her around for another chat? I have an opening Friday."

So soon? Was Sammy really screwed up then? Nolan wished he could ask some questions. But not with Sammy listening.

As if clairvoyant, Trish suddenly appeared at his elbow, no longer carrying the envelope. "I'm on my way back to reception. Would you like to come with me, Sammy? We have some great toys and books in the play center." She touched Nolan's arm briefly. "I'll keep a close eye on her."

"Thanks."

"No problem." The receptionist's skin had returned to its normal color, her emotions clearly once more under control. In fact, she even managed to give Celia an impish grin as she added, "Maybe you can sign on a new member to your 'scratch-and-dent club.'"

"Trish!" It was Celia's turn to blush.

Nolan wished he had the slightest clue as to what was going on here. Once Trish and Sammy were out of the admin area, he asked, "Scratch-and-dent club?"

Celia sighed as she guided him to a quiet corner where they could talk. "It's a long story. Believe me, you don't want to know the details."

"I'm almost always interested in the kinds of stories that make pretty girls blush."

Celia's eyes widened. She thought he was flirting. Well, he was. But not seriously.

"Come on, you can trust me. If it's interesting, the worst I'll do is print it on the front page of the newspaper."

Celia laughed, another musical sound that made him wonder why he didn't find this lovely girl nearly as stirring as the prickly accountant hiding behind her firmly closed door.

"Trish was just teasing me about my taste in men. She thinks I pick guys who make better patients than dates. But we only have a few minutes, so let's talk about Sammy."

"Is she okay?"

"That's a hard question to answer. She's suffered such great losses. I can't offer you a quick fix. But I do have a booklet that deals with helping children grieve. And there's a book list at the back that you could take to the library."

She passed him the materials. Somehow he wanted more.

"What do I do when she won't talk to me?"

"Be patient. She doesn't know you very well."

"But she didn't know you until today. Or Kim Sherman, either, the first time they met. Yet, she took to Kim right away."

"Really?" Celia's gaze drifted to the same door that kept drawing his attention. "I heard Kim volunteered to baby-sit Sammy for you."

He nodded.

"I can't be sure what's going on with your niece, Nolan. Possibly Sammy is more comfortable with women than men. Lots of little girls are at that age."

Yeah. Possibly. Or maybe she'd just figured out what his sister, Mary, hadn't. He wasn't daddy material.

CHAPTER NINE

AT TEN MINUTES AFTER FIVE that afternoon, Kim locked her office for the night. She needed to drop off a check for a security deposit with the manager of the American Legion. Their hall was the only facility in town big enough to host the Mother and Child Reunion, and Kim wanted a signed agreement along with a receipt in hand before she began sending out invitations.

The Birth Place had a quiet, after-hours atmosphere. All the office doors were closed for the night. The reception area was empty of clients and had already been tidied in readiness for the next day.

Kim wasn't alone in the building, though. In the hallway she ran into Lydia. The older woman had on sensible trousers and a cream turtleneck sweater. As always she wore her rose-colored pendant, and Kim did her best not to stare at it as Lydia grasped both of her hands.

"Kim." Lydia sounded delighted to see her.

She always did, had since their initial meeting almost a year ago. At first Kim had wondered if Lydia had somehow found out she was her granddaughter.

But after a period of time she realized that Lydia

spoke warmly to everyone, making them feel like they were the most important person in the world.

Occasionally Kim daydreamed of telling Lydia the truth about her background. But she knew she wouldn't. Lydia had given up her baby and never looked back. She wouldn't want to be reminded of that long-ago mistake.

Lydia squeezed Kim's hands. "I hear you've been helping Nolan McKinnon and Sammy. I'm so glad. How are they making out?"

Kim hesitated to share her concerns about the little girl. She knew Lydia continued to bear some responsibility for Sammy's situation. Still, honesty would not allow her to pretend all was well. "They're adjusting."

The sparkle died in Lydia's kind, gray eyes. "It's a big change for both of them. Sammy barely knew her uncle. Now she's living with him full-time."

Kim nodded. "And Nolan's trying, but he's a novice where children are concerned."

"Even those who plan for children are often surprised at how big an adjustment parenting requires."

"I'm trying to help a little." After her mother's death, Kim had dealt with children of all ages in the various foster homes she'd lived. But Lydia knew none of that.

"I hear you've already been of enormous assistance."

"Hardly. I did suggest to Nolan that he take

Sammy to see Celia Brice. They had their first appointment this afternoon.''

"Excellent. Celia is such a darling. I should have thought of recommending her to Nolan myself. Tell me…'' Finally she released Kim's hands. "How are the plans for the fund-raiser coming?''

"I'm just on my way to sign the contract with the Legion. And I've hired a caterer based on a cost/benefit chart I drew up. I can show you—''

"But, Kim, you're not doing all this on your own, are you? Haven't you organized committees and assigned responsibilities? I've spoken to most of the staff members, and they're all eager to help.''

"Indeed we are.'' Trish Linden appeared, a stack of photocopies in her hands. "In fact, since I'm officially off duty, is there anything I can do right now?''

Kim didn't know what to say. She realized the receptionist and Lydia thought they were being kind. But she *really* wanted to manage this on her own. For her grandmother.

"Kim's on her way to the Legion right now,'' Lydia said. "Maybe you could help her with that and let Kim get home early for a change?''

"Sure I could.''

"No, no.'' Signing up the location was too important a task to let slip out of her control. "Really, the manager is expecting me and the meeting won't take long.''

"Is there something else I could do, then?''

"Maybe. Let me think about it. I'm sorry but I need to leave now. I don't want to be late." Kim brushed past both women, wishing she hadn't seen the slightly hurt expression on Trish's face.

Why couldn't the woman see Kim was doing her a favor? Like all of the birth-center staff, the receptionist worked hard. Shouldn't she be happy to get out of extra volunteer hours?

KIM OPENED HER EYES, disoriented and confused. In the darkness she heard the sound of a key turning in a lock. She felt smooth leather under her cheek and the blanket in her hands had a familiar scent.

Nolan's aftershave.

She was at Nolan McKinnon's house. It was Tuesday evening and she must have fallen asleep. Yawning, she brushed aside the blanket—actually a fleece jacket of Nolan's that had been draped over the back of the sofa—and settled her feet onto the carpeted floor.

She was finger-combing her hair when Nolan entered the family room.

"Fell asleep, did you?"

His low voice sounded intimate in the darkened room. She could see little more than his silhouette against the light from the hall. He had on a leather jacket, and his thick hair fell forward, just above one eye.

"I guess I did." She moved her feet, searching

blindly for her shoes, while she tugged her sweater back into place. "How was the meeting?"

"Ran on too long as usual. I'm sorry I didn't mention the possibility that I'd be late." Standing at the periphery of the room, near the kitchen, he watched her intently, making her feel like she had a button that was undone or that her skirt was riding too high.

She checked both before she identified the problem. Her glasses had fallen off in her sleep. She found them on the floor next to her shoes and slipped them quickly into place.

"How late is it?" Her voice came out hoarse. She cleared her throat.

"After eleven. Would you like a drink?"

She'd been groping for her purse, which was on the coffee table next to the *TV Guide*. She let the handle slip out of her fingers.

A drink at eleven o'clock on a Tuesday evening?

"Sure."

"I'm having a beer, but I've got wine or a liqueur if you'd rather."

"Beer is good. No glass necessary."

While he opened the fridge, she hung his jacket in the closet, catching him just outside the kitchen when she was done. He passed her an open bottle, then put a hand to the small of her back and led her to the sofa.

She sat first, on the far end of the leather cushion, expecting Nolan to take the other end of the sofa, or possibly sit in the reclining chair across the room. But he settled an arm's length from her, angling his body to face her.

Up close she saw sharp interest in his eyes. He wouldn't stop looking at her. And he had a silly half smile on his face. She'd never seen him wear *that* expression while in her company before.

Something strange was going on here. Nolan couldn't like her. She'd given him no reason to. So why this sudden fascination?

IT TOOK NOLAN a few minutes to figure out what he found so appealing about Kim. Being woken unexpectedly had made her momentarily vulnerable. And vulnerability on a strong woman like Kim was—sexy.

Yeah, sexy. He liked the way her hair looked when every strand wasn't in place. He liked the way she blinked a lot when she wasn't wearing her glasses. And he especially liked the way she kept tugging at her sweater and skirt, because that gave him an excuse to look at her tight, graceful body.

Nolan tipped his head back and took a long swallow of beer. Then he leaned forward until only eighteen inches of space separated his head from hers. He could feel Kim's tension as he moved closer. She wasn't at all comfortable. Hell, he wasn't that comfortable, either.

He didn't even like Kim. Why was he so attracted to her?

He warned himself not to rush into something foolish. Didn't he have enough complications in his life right now? He'd had another meeting with the lawyers today, and of course there was Sam to worry about.

There was that anonymous letter, too. He'd phoned a couple of The Birth Place board members, but hadn't been able to find out anything about Lydia's resignation. If there was a secret, no one was talking.

No one except the person who'd written that letter. He'd thought at first it might be Kim, but that didn't make sense. Still, Kim, the outsider at The Birth Place, was in a unique position to tell him things others wouldn't.

On a hunch, he decided to confide in her.

"Turn on that lamp behind you, would you, Kim?"

She looked at him questioningly, but said nothing as she reached under the lamp shade and did as requested. The wattage on the bulb was low, but the light was sufficient to bring out the pattern in her light gray sweater. Oddly, he found the schoolmarmish garment sexy—maybe because it would be so much fun to undo all those buttons....

"I have something I want you to see." He pulled the envelope from his pocket. He could tell she recognized it. She'd picked it up from the floor and passed it to him on Saturday.

"Read it."

She put her glasses back on, then touched the envelope tentatively. "No return address."

She was observant. "That's right."

She slid out the single sheet of stationery and unfolded the two creases. It didn't take long for her to read the short missive.

"How awful! Who sent you this garbage?"

"I wish I knew."

"How could they say these things? Lydia Kane a danger to her community? A *baby* killer?"

Nolan hadn't expected such a volatile reaction. Kim seemed to take the letter personally.

"Those are pretty strong accusations," he agreed. "But are you certain they aren't true?"

"You can't be serious."

"I'm afraid I am." His sister and her baby were dead. Dr. Ochoa seemed confident that she'd had the best possible medical treatment. But if Lydia was up to something underhanded...

Kim guessed what he was thinking. "Nolan, I know you have reason to question the competence of The Birth Place, and Lydia in particular, but take a look at the facts. Your sister's death has been thoroughly investigated by the hospital. They found nothing wrong. And The Birth Place has a solid reputation."

"Yes. You told me that this afternoon."

"Is this why you asked me how well I knew Lydia? Because of this letter?"

He didn't answer, just slipped the envelope back into his pocket.

"I swear to you, no one loves babies more than Lydia. She'd do anything for her patients. Nolan, if that letter was legitimate, don't you think it would have been signed?"

"You have a point. But there could be reasons this person wishes to remain anonymous. If he or she worked for The Birth Place, for instance."

"Impossible. I do the monthly payroll. I could list the names of every one of the full- and part-time employees. No one who works at The Birth Place would send a letter like that."

"You know these people well, do you?"

She grimaced at his obvious jab. "I may not be friends with the people I work with, but I see the commitment on their faces each and every day. They all love Lydia. Harming her is the last thing any of them would do."

"Maybe you're right." He had to admit, the atmosphere she described jibed with his own observations of the birth center.

"But if not a disgruntled employee, then who could have sent that letter?" He stretched his arm out along the back of the sofa. Kim didn't seem to notice. She was lost in thought.

He could tell the moment a new idea occurred to her. She blinked several times, then blurted out, "You don't think it was me, do you?"

"I have to admit I considered the possibility. Even though you've been the accountant for almost a year, you're still a bit of an outsider."

"I have no ax to grind against Lydia."

"Apparently not. In fact, what surprises me is how vehemently you defend her."

His observation unbalanced her, he could tell.

Which made him think he was on to something.
But what?

"Why do you care so much, Kim?"

She raised her chin. "I don't like to see good people suffer. Lydia *is* a good person. Please tell me you
aren't going to print that disgusting letter in your paper."

"Well, not without any substantiation I won't."

She pulled her sweater in tightly. "That's what you
were doing at the birth center today—looking for cor-
roborative evidence."

"Don't take this personally, Kim. A letter like this
shows up in my mailbox, I can't simply ignore it."

"Why not?"

Nolan removed his jacket and set aside his unfinished beer, while he considered Kim's question. *Why
not?* To him the answer was obvious. Kim couldn't
be serious. And yet, wasn't she always?

"A newspaper editor has a certain responsibility to
his community," he began.

"I don't need a lecture about freedom of the press.
What I'm concerned about is responsible journalism.
That letter contains nothing but a bunch of libelous
trash."

"Kim." He put his hand over hers. The move had
the desired effect of shutting her up. "I've already
told you I won't print the letter unless there really is
a story behind it."

"But I'm telling you there isn't. Lydia is above
reproach."

If that was true, then why wouldn't Kim look him in the eyes? She was hiding something. And that bugged Nolan for more reasons than one.

So far Lydia was the second person he'd seen Kim show any concern or liking for. The first had been Sammy.

Was Nolan a total fool for wishing *he* could be one of the people Kim cared about? He'd thought he didn't like Kim. But now he realized that simply wasn't true.

Nolan wasn't often confused about his own emotions. Usually they weren't that complicated. But Kim had him completely off balance. His easy charm didn't work on her. She forced him to dig deeper. And he didn't even know why he was so attracted to her. Look at her clothes, for Pete's sake. His *mother* had dressed with more style.

Yet, the body beneath those clothes sparked his interest. When she'd pulled her sweater tight he'd seen curves a guy wouldn't expect on such a petite woman. And her legs—well, he'd already established that they were pretty fabulous.

"Kim?"

"Yeah?"

"Are you finished with your drink? Because I could take that bottle out of your hands." He was going to kiss her. Trying to fight this attraction was just plain stupid. If he kissed her he could find out if there was any basis to these feelings he had around her.

And he could also find out how many layers of permafrost covered her heart. If, indeed, she had one.

"I'm done." She let him take the bottle even though it was full.

He set it on the coffee table next to his, then slid over until only inches spanned the distance between his thigh and hers.

"Kim, you've intrigued me from the start. I don't know why. You obviously don't think I can do anything right."

She swallowed. He suspected she knew what he wanted to do and that she was nervous. She didn't seem unwilling, though.

Slowly he reached out and took hold of her glasses. She closed her eyes as he eased them off her face and placed them on the table next to their bottles.

"Kim." He cupped her delicate face with both hands. Her gray eyes seemed huge now, her mouth soft and inviting. Could it be possible she wanted this kiss as much as he did?

He touched his lips to hers. No ice here. Only sweet, warm woman. He moved closer, his body next to hers. He pressed harder with his mouth and hers opened willingly.

He felt her reluctance slowly melt away. She put a hand to his shoulder. The other crept around his neck.

Why had he expected a tepid reaction from her? This woman responded to his kiss the way she responded to a verbal challenge. With verve and passion. She caught his bottom lip between her teeth and nipped gently. His desire flamed higher.

Lord help him, his experiment was now totally out of control. He felt like a teenager as he kissed her, and kissed her, and kissed her.

Kim's moans were deliciously encouraging. Ice? Why had he ever associated the word with this woman? He dragged his fingers through her luscious hair. It felt thicker than he'd expected. And softer.

"Oh, Kim." He hadn't had enough of kissing her, yet it was impossible to keep his hands off her. He touched the first button of her cardigan, expecting her to nod approval. But she surprised him by pulling back.

"Don't."

He withdrew his hands, confused. "What's wrong?"

"I can't get involved with you."

"What do you mean?" She hadn't kissed him like a woman who wasn't intending to get involved.

"I'm not going to be in Enchantment much longer."

"Why?"

"I'm planning to hand in my resignation after the fund-raiser I've been organizing. In about a month." She put her glasses back on and patted her hair.

"Aren't you happy here?"

"That isn't the point."

"I don't get it. If you weren't interested in me, why did you just spend fifteen minutes kissing me?"

"Look, it was a test, all right? You wanted to know what it would be like and I—well, I admit it. I've been kind of curious, too."

Even though she was correct, he found that he resented her thinking of their kiss as nothing but a test. It sounded so clinical. But she hadn't *felt* clinical in his arms.

"Okay, maybe I went about this wrong. Jumping into necking on the couch before we've even had our first date."

"You don't get it. I don't want to date you. I don't want to get involved, period."

Again she wouldn't meet his eyes. Something wasn't adding up here. He watched silently as she continued to put herself back together. But no matter how hard she tried, she couldn't tame her hair. It framed her face in a luxurious mass that he longed to bury his face in.

She found her purse and reclaimed her shoes for the second time that night. As she went to the closet for her coat, he followed.

He wished he could get inside her head. "So you just want to forget that this evening ever happened?"

"That sounds like a good start."

He put a hand on her shoulder, forcing her to meet his gaze. With satisfaction he saw that she wasn't nearly as calm and settled as she was trying to appear.

"Sorry, Kim, but I'm not going to forget what it was like to kiss you. And I'm willing to bet you won't forget, either."

CHAPTER TEN

SITTING IN HIS OFFICE two days later, Nolan pulled out the fact sheet Kim had given him on Monday. He scanned the opening paragraphs explaining the overall philosophy of midwifery: that pregnancy and child-birth are a normal part of a woman's life and that women have the right to be equal partners in the pro-cess.

Following some feel-good mumbo jumbo were the hard facts he craved. The majority of births took place at the mother's home, with a smaller percentage at The Birth Place and just over ten percent ending up at the local hospital.

The report emphasized the high percentage of women experiencing spontaneous vaginal births rather than cesarean sections. It highlighted steadily declin-ing perinatal mortality and morbidity rates. Hell, they even monitored the breastfeeding rate on discharge. In the past year this rate was 95.3%, up .5% from five years ago.

He had to admit the numbers painted a picture of a very successful birthing center. But where did his sister's experience fit in all this data? Since Lydia had transferred her to the hospital, would the mortality of mother and baby even show up on The Birth Place's records?

Probably not. In which case, wasn't it possible there were other deaths that weren't included on Kim's fact sheet?

Nolan decided to call Dr. Ochoa. He left a message with the physician's receptionist, indicating that he was researching a possible story for the local paper. Fifteen minutes later, Ochoa called him back.

"Nolan, what's up?" A note of caution sounded in the doctor's voice.

"I'm not calling about Mary this time," Nolan reassured him. Ochoa had already been very patient about answering all his questions regarding that awful night. "I'm considering an article on The Birth Place. I understand they refer all their high-risk cases to you."

"That's right. I've worked with Lydia Kane and her staff for over twenty years."

"And your experience has been..." Nolan reached for his pen and notepaper.

"Overwhelmingly positive. While naturally I favor hospital deliveries for women, I must admit that The Birth Place offers an excellent alternative for a healthy expectant mother."

"And what happened to my sister...you said that was rare?"

"The first case I've seen since I've been practicing in Enchantment. Once, in my residency days, we lost a mother in a similar situation. But we were able to save the baby. Nolan, even if your sister had been admitted to the hospital at the first sign of labor, the outcome would have been the same.''

Nolan closed his eyes. Composed his thoughts. This wasn't about Mary.

''So in the twenty years you've worked in the Arroyo County Hospital, my sister was the only mortality due to childbirth?''

''Yes.''

Out of thousands of deliveries in twenty years, why Mary? Why had his sister been the unlucky one?

Even as the thoughts spiraled in his brain, Nolan realized he was losing his focus again. Was The Birth Place safe? Was Lydia Kane a responsible midwife? These were the questions he needed to address.

''What about babies? Are the ones born at The Birth Place as healthy as the ones born at the hospital?''

''On average, I'd have to say they are healthier.''

Nolan stopped writing for a second. ''Healthier than the babies born in the hospital?''

''You have to remember that Lydia won't touch a case where the mother drinks or has a drug dependency. She refers all those women to me. And rightly so.''

''I see.'' Nolan drew a big fat zero around his notes. Clearly he wasn't getting anywhere. If there was a problem at the center, a problem with Lydia, Ochoa didn't know about it.

''Well, thanks for your time, Doctor.''

"You're welcome. Take care of yourself, Nolan. And of that little niece of yours."

"I will. Thanks."

Nolan hung up the phone, then ran both hands down his face. It seemed his life was filled with puzzles these days. That letter he'd received about The Birth Place. And now Kim. He still couldn't fathom how she'd been able to put a stop on her passion that way, then to trivialize what had happened between them.

If she was so hell-bent on leaving Enchantment, why had she come here in the first place? He had no idea. They'd never discussed her family or her background. So far all the focus had been on Sammy and *his* family.

He needed to get to know this woman better. Which would be hard since apparently she wasn't interested in dating him.

Yet, she'd let him kiss her. And kissed him back. Why? It didn't fit with her "hands off—don't get too close" policy. He didn't buy her "I was just curious" explanation. Was she, like him, affected by an attraction that defied all logic? In other words, was it possible that the inimitable Kim Sherman might actually give in to her base human impulses every now and then?

His phone rang, reminding him that there were only so many hours Sammy was in school and he had a lot of work to accomplish before three-thirty. What was he doing wasting his time thinking about this woman?

As he reached for the receiver, Toni came in with the morning mail. She dropped the pile of envelopes and fliers into the in box on the corner of his desk.

"Just in case you don't already have enough to do," she said.

He frowned at her as he brought the receiver to his ear. The woman could be so cruel. "McKinnon here."

The caller was one of his biggest advertisers who wasn't happy about the rates he'd been offered from the woman who usually dealt with this stuff. As Nolan listened to the man's tirade, he noticed a bit of blue peeking out from the pile in his in box.

Oh man.

He waited for his call to finish—which it did when he offered a special half-page rate for color rather than the usual black-and-white—and pulled the blue envelope from the pile.

Another one.

Same envelope, same handwriting. Hand-delivered again with no stamp and no postmark. What was going on here? Who was writing these things? Nolan tore open the second envelope, hoping for some answers.

AT ELEVEN-THIRTY in the morning Kim's office phone rang. She was expecting a call about the invitations for the fund-raiser. She'd finalized the wording with

Lydia and Parker that morning and planned to meet
with the printer this afternoon.

But Nolan was on the line.

"Want to meet for lunch?"

Oh, Lord, was she tempted. But after what had happened on Tuesday she didn't dare. She'd never have
guessed Nolan McKinnon could kiss like that.

Well, maybe she'd had a hunch.

But she'd had no business confirming it. Falling for
the newspaper editor would be just about the dumbest
thing she could do right now.

"I'm sorry but I'm busy."

"Ah, Kim."

His obvious disappointment should have been a
balm to her ego. But her own regret was too keen for
her to take any pleasure in it.

"I hoped I wouldn't have to resort to bribery. But
would you change your mind if I told you I received
a second letter today?"

Kim's gaze shot immediately to her door, which
was firmly closed. Still she whispered. "About
Lydia?"

"Yes."

Oh, no. With her index finger she pushed back on
her glasses. "Read it to me, Nolan."

"I could do that." He paused a moment. "But will
I?"

"You can't be serious." This was nothing short of
blackmail. But hadn't he admitted as much already?

"The Silver Eagle at noon?"

"Forget it, Nolan. I'm not meeting you. I said I would help you with Sammy, and I'm not backing out on that promise, but lunches alone with you are out."

"Afraid you won't be able to resist me?"

Oh, he was too confident. And too right. "I'm very busy. And I don't usually take a lunch hour."

"Of course you don't. But since the letter indirectly affects the birth center, our meeting could safely come under the classification of work, don't you think? Come on, Kim. It's the only way you'll see the letter."

"Maybe I don't care what's in that letter. It's probably just more trash."

"Probably," he agreed, his tone immodestly cheerful. "But you *do* want to see. So meet me at noon. And order me a cheeseburger if I'm late."

He hung up on her. *The nerve!* Kim banged the receiver back onto the console. No way was she letting him get away with this. Why had she gotten involved with him in the first place?

Sammy. Oh, yes, Sammy.

Kim folded her arms on her desk and let her head drop. The little girl made Kim's situation so much more complicated. Kim hadn't wanted to become too involved, but she knew she was. Right now, she was one of the few people Sammy counted on. Oh, she had her uncle, but he didn't really want her and she knew it. Six-year-olds might be little, but they weren't stupid.

Kim could help Nolan be a better father figure for

Sammy. Hadn't she already taught him a lot? But there was so much more he needed to know.

For Sammy's sake, she couldn't wash her hands of Nolan McKinnon. And that was before any consideration of Lydia. She needed to check out this second letter. And make sure Nolan intended to live up to his promise not to publish unfounded accusations.

Like it or not, she had to meet him for lunch.

The real problem here, of course, was that she did like it. She could tell herself she was meeting him for Sammy's sake. And for Lydia's. But the truth was pounding in her ears at the rate of one hundred and fifty beats per minute.

KIM HAD BEEN to the Silver Eagle a couple of times on her own. The restaurant was named for a beautiful sculpture positioned near the entrance, but it was the framed photographs decorating the walls, all taken by restaurant owner Mitchell Dixon, that most fascinated Kim. There were many shots of the town, spanning almost thirty years. The pictures she loved best were of the desert, especially those with the mountains in the background. They were filled with beautiful color, yet seemed heartbreakingly lonely to her.

A sign just past the entrance invited customers to seat themselves, and so Kim did. She was five minutes late and Nolan still wasn't here. When Mitchell came to take her order, she requested two veggie burgers with salads on the side and iced teas.

The food hadn't yet arrived when Nolan sauntered

in, grinning, his eyes sparkling with triumph when he spotted her. At least she thought it was triumph. He couldn't simply be happy to see her. She noticed several female patrons give him lingering once-overs. Did he notice, too?

"What a surprise." Nolan slid into the seat opposite hers.

"Ha. You didn't leave me any choice."

"Maybe not. But I'm really glad to see you." He reached over the table and put a hand on hers. "You're cold."

"It's just the icy glass." His touch was heaven. She remembered—would never forget—the feel of his hands on her skin and in her hair. Just as she'd always recall the taste of his—

"Two veggie burgers with salad, dressings on the side." Mitchell Dixon arrived with their orders. Kim knew that he was divorced and worked very long hours keeping his restaurant afloat. In the past, she'd felt a certain kinship to the man, even though they hadn't spoken more than a dozen words to each other.

He was lonely, too. Not only did she sense it in his photos, sometimes she was sure she glimpsed the emotion in his eyes, as well. But he always had a smile for his customers.

"Nolan, how's the newspaper business?"

"Just fine, Mitchell."

"Good to hear." He stepped back from the table. "Hope you enjoy your meals."

Nolan watched the man leave, his expression

thoughtful. Then he turned back to Kim, eyebrows raised. "Did he say *veggie* burger?"

Kim popped a sliver of radish into her mouth. "You did ask me to order for you. A burger, as I recall. You didn't specify a *beef* burger, did you?"

He rubbed his chin and conceded the point. "No, I guess I didn't. Just as I didn't ask for fries instead of a salad..."

"Of course not. You're too health conscious. As the guardian of a young girl you know how important it is to eat at least five servings of fruit and vegetables a day."

Oh, she was enjoying this. Maybe too much. But Nolan put up with the kidding and even ate the food she'd ordered for him. When he was done he dug the blue envelope from his jacket pocket and dropped it on the table.

She pushed aside her unfinished meal, knowing she wouldn't want to eat anymore now. First she wiped her hands on her napkin, then she pulled out the piece of stationery.

Dear Editor,
You didn't print my letter in the paper last week. Why not? The people of Enchantment have a right to know. Lydia Kane's birth center should be closed. Tell them now, before more lives are lost.

"Oh, Lord. This one is even worse!" Clearly the author was determined to put an end to the birth center. Which would not only be a tremendous loss to Enchantment—the blow would destroy Lydia.

How could anyone be so cruel? And cowardly. Again the letter was unsigned, with no return address on the envelope.

"I spoke to Dr. Ochoa this morning." Nolan stowed the letter back in his pocket. "He confirmed everything you said about Lydia and all the stats in that report of yours. The Birth Place does appear to be a very safe, responsible establishment. Why would anyone want to sabotage it?"

"I wish I knew. This morning I wondered if the writer might be a disgruntled ex-employee."

"That's a good possibility."

"So I went through the payroll records. We don't have a very high turnover—only a handful of people in the past year. I didn't go back any further than that."

"You wouldn't think someone would hold a grudge longer than a year," Nolan agreed. "What did you come up with?"

"Only three people, but from subsequent letters of recommendation on file, they appear to have left on good terms."

Mitchell Dixon returned to their table, this time offering coffee and dessert. Kim stuck with coffee but Nolan asked for apple pie to go with it. Once Mitchell was out of earshot, Nolan restarted their conversation.

"Let's consider another angle. Even more than the birth center, Lydia appears to be the main target. Could the letters be from a disgruntled family member? Lydia's divorced, isn't she?"

"Yes. But her ex-husband lives in New York City, close to their son, Bradley, and his family. I don't think Lydia hears from any of them very often. I get the impression she isn't close to her son. As for her ex, well, the divorce happened long ago."

"True." Nolan leaned back in his seat, watching her thoughtfully. "You know, about six months ago, when Lydia resigned from the board...?"

Kim tensed.

"The press release stated that Lydia intended to ease into retirement, but I've been around the center a few times and I've noticed Lydia is still putting in pretty long hours. Doesn't seem like semiretirement to me."

"Lydia loves her work too much to slow down."

"What about the granddaughter who took her position on the board? What do we know about her?"

"Devon Grant is a Certified Nurse Midwife in Albuquerque but she almost never visits her grandmother. She comes to town for board meetings and that's it."

As Nolan leaned forward, eyes alert, she realized she'd been too open.

"Is there a problem between Devon and Lydia?"

Kim lowered her gaze to the table, shook her head.

But Nolan had sensed a near hit and wouldn't stop firing his questions.

"Lydia didn't voluntarily quit the board. She was compelled to resign, I'm sure of it. I only wish I knew why." He looked at her, as if he expected her to give him the reason.

"Nolan, I can't discuss this with you."

"No? Well, maybe someone else can. I noticed Jessica Green works part-time in reception. She was a friend of my sister when we were younger. Maybe she—"

"No." She didn't want Nolan grilling the staff—or anyone else. Rumors would really start to fly then. "I'll tell you what I know. But it isn't much."

He waited.

"In the weeks before her resignation, Lydia seemed very tense, very unhappy." Looking back, Kim could pinpoint the beginning of Lydia's downward spiral.

"It was around the time Hope Tanner came to town, searching for the baby she had about—oh, ten years ago." Shortly after her arrival, Hope had become involved with Parker, and the two had recently married.

"Did she find her baby?"

"No, but she found a husband." She smiled, thinking of how happy the new couple appeared every time she saw them together.

"There has to be more to the story."

"Maybe." She'd overheard a conversation between Parker and Lydia once. Hope's baby had been mentioned. But she'd backed away from the open door as soon as she'd realized the conversation was personal. She didn't know details, but she had her suspicions.

"Well, it had to be something serious," Nolan speculated. "And Hope coming back stirred up the pot enough that Lydia felt she had to resign."

Kim had to admit the pieces lined up—all too tidily. But what could Lydia have done? "Whatever the problem was, Nolan, I'm sure Lydia found the best home she could for Hope's baby."

"Maybe she cut a few corners on the adoption."

"If so, I don't see why it would matter to anyone but Hope. And if you're about to suggest *she's* sending the letters…"

"No, I've seen the smile on that woman's face lately. She and Parker are very happy together. I can't believe she's sending any nasty letters."

"Of course not. But if Lydia did cut a few corners on the adoption, as you say, and if this secret letter writer knows it…well, public disclosure could really damage Lydia's reputation. And the reputation of the center."

"Still, a fudged adoption is hardly a reason to call Lydia a baby killer."

"I know. But even false rumors can be hurtful. Lydia can't afford this—especially right now."

"What's so special about now?"

"The birth center's been on precarious financial footing for ages. Typically Lydia goes on a fund-raising rampage and builds a healthy bank account.

Then she extends credit and reduces billings for every client who walks in the door. I've been working on setting some standard policies and procedures in place…''

She saw him struggle not to grin and slapped his hand lightly.

"Standard policies and procedures…go on," he managed to say, choking back a laugh.

"But the future of the center really rests on the fund-raiser Lydia's asked me to organize. It's going to be March nineteenth. So an ugly scandal—even if it's about something that isn't true—could cause a lot of damage. Damage that might be impossible to undo."

She took a sip of her cooling coffee while Nolan dug into his pie. He ate so efficiently, she wondered if he had time to taste the food. When he was done, he set down his fork.

"I'm not looking to destroy a not-for-profit birthing center on the basis of a couple of unsubstantiated letters," he said.

She could have kissed him and was glad the surroundings, and their situation, made such an ill-advised move impossible. "I can't tell you how relieved I am to hear that."

"But I'm still going to nose around a little."

She sighed. "Of course you are."

"I'd like to talk to Lydia."

"Oh, Nolan. Couldn't you please leave her alone? She's been so tired and unhappy lately." Not in public, but whenever she thought no one was looking, her face would crease with worry. "Surely we can find out what's going on without upsetting her further?"

"We?"

"I'll do whatever I can to help. As long as we leave Lydia out of it."

CHAPTER ELEVEN

LATER THAT AFTERNOON, Nolan was racing to finish his summary of the Tuesday-night town council meeting before he had to pick Sammy up from school, when Irene Davidson called.

"I thought you should know I'm back at my house now. I moved out of Mabel's on Sunday night," she told him.

"You're sounding better." Her voice was definitely stronger.

"I feel more like myself. In fact I was thinking I could give you a hand with Sammy. I've really missed her. Is she at school right now?"

"Yes. The bell rings at three-thirty." He checked the time on his computer. In about twenty minutes.

"I could pick her up from school and bring her to my house."

The offer was tempting. But was this too much, too soon?

"I'd love to see Sammy. She used to visit me every Sunday you know. Sometimes I'd have her over Saturday night, too, if Steve and Mary wanted a chance to go out."

The poor woman sounded so sad. Her granddaughter was all she had left.

"Actually, it would be a help if you could pick Sammy up from school."

"Oh, good. I'll make her dinner, too—soft tacos, that's her favorite. And maybe she could stay for a while in the evening? We could watch TV together and play checkers. Sammy loves checkers."

Soft tacos. Checkers. Nolan scribbled down the information about Sammy's preferences for future reference. "You sure this won't be too much for you, Irene?"

"Oh no. We'll have fun."

She sounded so keen to have Sammy. And being able to work through the dinner hour would certainly help him get things under control.

"I usually help some students with the school paper on Thursday evening. Would nine be too late for me to pick her up?"

"Not at all. I'll put her in the spare room. She could stay the night and you could come get her in the morning."

"Maybe next time." Provided everything went all right tonight, which he certainly hoped it would. With Irene's help, looking after Sammy would be so much easier.

"Okay, Irene. I'll phone the school and let them know to expect you."

"Wonderful. I can hardly wait to see my little girl."

WHEN NOLAN CALLED with the news she wouldn't need to baby-sit for him tonight, Kim was disappointed. And that worried her.

She had to face the truth. She wanted to see him again. Their lunch today had only exacerbated the problem. The more she saw of Nolan McKinnon, the more she liked him.

Agreeing to help with his continued investigation had been a risky move on her part. But she didn't see that she had a choice. As long as she stayed involved she could continue to watch out for Lydia's best interests. Of course, whoever was writing those letters was a crank. But if there was something at the bottom of them, some tiny misdemeanor that had somehow become warped into something bigger than it really was, then Kim would be in the perfect position for damage control. She'd protect Lydia and the birth center to the best of her ability.

Which left one question. Who would protect her heart from Nolan McKinnon?

Kim didn't know the answer to that one.

She made herself pasta for dinner, then tried to sit down with a good book. But she couldn't stop wondering how Irene was making out with Sammy. According to Nolan, Steve's mother had been on prescription drugs to control her deep bouts of depression. Was she really capable of looking after her granddaughter on her own?

By seven o'clock Kim was too distracted to enjoy her quiet evening. She decided it couldn't hurt to drive by Irene's house and check on Sammy. She found the address in the phone book. Irene Davidson's house wasn't far from The Birth Place.

Kim felt a little silly fifteen minutes later, standing on the spacious landing in front of the charming, adobe bungalow. What excuse could she possibly give Irene for checking up on her? When Nolan heard about this he was going to be so angry.

But no one answered her knock at the door. Kim rapped her knuckles on the beautiful old door once more, then tried to peer in the front window.

"Oh!" She jumped at the sight of a little face staring out at her.

Sammy.

Kim put a hand to her chest and took a deep breath. "Open the door, Sammy," she mouthed to the little girl. Looking closer, she noticed tears running down Sammy's plump cheeks.

Something was wrong in there.

"Unlock the door, Sammy." She shouted this time, hoping the sound might carry through the single-glass panes. But Sammy remained frozen in place.

Kim ran to the back of the house, checking windows on the way, but they were all closed firmly. A spacious patio led up to wide glass doors off the dining room. Kim pulled back the screen easily. Next she put her hand on the glass frame and gave a quick prayer of thanks when it glided open, too.

"Sammy?" Kim stepped onto the polished tile floor. The room was filled with an antique oak table and huge matching chairs. She slipped through another door and found herself in a big, updated kitchen. The only sign of life here was a spread of taco fixings on the counter—untouched.

"Sammy? It's Kim. Can you hear me, honey?" Kim dashed down the wide hall. Through an arched opening she could see the living room. A second later she noticed Irene Davidson, sprawled facedown on a Navajo rug. Beside her sat Sammy, pulling on her grandmother's limp arm.

Tears poured from the child's eyes. "Is Grandma dead, too?"

IRENE WASN'T DEAD. She'd overdosed on Valium. Kim cradled Sammy in her arms as she called the paramedics, then Nolan at his office. She told him to go to the hospital to meet Irene. After the ambulance arrived, she'd take Sammy to her apartment and wait for him there.

At home, Kim made Sammy rice pudding and gave her a bath. They had no books, so Kim sang the little girl songs until she fell asleep.

An hour later, Nolan showed up. Since the moment she'd found Irene unconscious, Kim had been wondering how Nolan could have been so foolish. Why had he left his niece with a woman he knew was unstable?

But the impulse to lash out at him died when she saw his ashen complexion and weary eyes.

"How's Irene?"

"Fine. Mabel's with her now. Irene claims she just mixed up her dosage. Tomorrow Mabel's going to research rest homes in Taos. She thinks Irene might benefit from a couple of weeks of relaxation and care in a different atmosphere."

"That sounds like a good idea."

"What about Sammy?" With bleary eyes, Nolan scanned the living room beyond the entrance. "Is she okay?"

"She's asleep in my bed right now. The situation was pretty terrifying for her, Nolan. She thought her grandmother was dead." That was as close as Kim could come to accusing him of poor judgment. And even those words caused Nolan to wince.

"Poor kid. What an idiot I was…"

Kim didn't give in to the impulse to pat his shoulder. "How about a cup of tea before you take her home?"

"That would be nice."

He crashed on her sofa while she boiled water. When she came back with two cups of Earl Gray, though, he perked up a little.

"I don't know how to thank you, Kim. If you hadn't gone to Irene's when you did, the two of them would have been stuck there like that for hours."

She couldn't stand to think of it. "Tomorrow, or maybe in a few days, you'll have to explain to Sammy about 911."

He nodded. "I'll add that to my list." A list that

no matter how hard he worked at it, seemed to grow longer, not shorter.

What an unbelievably messed up day. Finally, though, everyone was safe. No thanks to him, Nolan knew. When Sammy hadn't been able to wake her grandmother, she must have been terrified.

"I'm such an ass." He leaned over the mug cradled in his hands. "If Sammy wasn't already scarred for life, she will be now for sure."

"How could you know Irene would make a mistake with her drugs like that?"

He'd expected Kim to tear a strip off him. But here she was, being nicer than he deserved. Her behavior made him wonder about that tough-girl image she had at work. If that wasn't the real Kim Sherman, why did she go to so much effort to give everyone the wrong impression?

"I should have eased Sammy into Irene's life more gradually. Expecting Irene to handle her after school, then for dinner and the evening as well, was just too much. But I was so relieved to be able to concentrate on my work and on the high school kids. I didn't even think to worry if Irene could cope. Thank God, you did."

"I've had some experience with women going through depression. My third foster mother lost her sister to breast cancer shortly before taking me on. I felt as if she'd brought me into her house to take care of her three younger kids, so she could have the luxury of falling apart. She'd start drinking every afternoon, right after lunch. By dinner she'd be passed out on her bed.''

''Your *third* foster mother. How many sets of foster parents did you have?''

Deliberately Kim set down her teacup. ''Four. They were all very nice except for that one. And she wasn't that bad. She was a drunk, but she was a quiet drunk. And her husband was a real sweet guy. After dinner he always made time to play with his kids.''

''How old were you at the time?''

''I stayed with the Handleys for two years—between the ages of twelve and fourteen I guess.''

''Did you tell the social workers about Mrs. Handley's drinking?''

''No. She wasn't horrible. I figured I could always do worse. And Mrs. Handley eventually stopped drinking. Cold turkey, on the day after the second anniversary of her sister's death. About four weeks later I was packing...''

So they used her, and when they didn't need her anymore, they showed her the door. ''Was that hard? Leaving a foster home you'd lived in for years?''

''The first time? Yes. But after that—no.''

''Tell me about the first time.''

Kim shook her head. ''You don't want to hear all this.'' She made a move to collect the dirty cups, but he touched her shoulder to stop her from getting up.

''Yes, I do. Please tell me. What were the first foster parents like?''

Reluctantly Kim settled back into the sofa. ''Wonderful...especially the mother. I guess I was kind of numb when I first went to live with them, but she was patient and kind. I seemed to fit in so easily with that family. My foster parents' two natural children were older, in their teens, and they treated me like a pet. I never stopped missing my mother, but I was definitely happy in that house.''

And yet Kim's expression was achingly sad. ''Why did you leave?''

''My foster dad worked in the oil business. His company transferred him to Calgary, Canada. At the time I didn't understand why I couldn't move with the rest of the family.''

Poor Kim.

''This may sound silly, but I hadn't realized that my foster arrangement wasn't permanent.''

''That doesn't sound silly. It sounds heartbreaking.''

''I was actually one of the lucky kids. Because I wasn't considered a problem child—I achieved good marks at school and behaved myself—I was placed in another home within a month. And I was lucky. The new people were nice, too.''

But he bet that time around she didn't let herself forget her new foster parents weren't her real family.

''Do you stay in touch with any of them?''

''No. My original foster mom tried. But at ten, I already had a fully developed stubborn streak. I refused her calls and never answered letters. Eventually I stopped hearing from her. And, two years later, when it was time to move on again, I hardly felt any sadness at all..."

The chill in Kim's voice was quite deliberate, and suddenly Nolan understood how she could switch from being kind and caring one minute to cold and hard the next. She'd perfected the technique as a child.

"Nolan, why didn't you get along with your mother?"

His mother was a subject he considered off-limits to most of his friends, even Miguel. But given her honest replies to his questions, how could he brush her off?

"I wish I knew the answer to that, Kim. We were never close. When I was a kid, she was more connected to my sister. I didn't mind at the time. I had my dad and we did everything together. Looking back, I've wondered if maybe we did *too much* together. And maybe my mother resented me because of it."

"Complicated." Kim sighed.

"Yeah. But your complicated was harder than my complicated." He was beginning to think he should maybe have given his mother a break. So what if she'd been hard on him at times?

She'd cooked and she'd cleaned for him. Taken care of him when he was sick. She'd *been there*. After a few weeks of looking after Sammy, he thought parents should get more points for just being there.

"What was it like to grow up in the same town all your life?" Kim sounded a little wistful.

"Mostly it was great. I wouldn't still be here if I didn't think so, would I?" He'd enjoyed his stint at university and he'd always be hooked on traveling. But home was here in this small New Mexico town rich in tradition and history.

"You must know just about everyone."

"Oh, the stories I could tell you…"

She sat cross-legged on the sofa, scrunching back to make room for him next to her. "Like what?"

"Well, there's the mystery of the Homecoming Baby. It starts out as a love story but has a pretty tragic end."

"Don't all the best stories? Go on…"

"Thirty years ago Angelina Linden was the most beautiful, privileged girl in Enchantment—"

"Linden? Any relation to Trish at the center?"

"Sisters."

"Really?"

He nodded. "Anyway, Angelina was the wild one. She had a scandalous relationship with the town bad boy—Teague Ellis, or more commonly called 'Tee'. On the night of the annual Homecoming dance they skipped town and were never seen again. Also on that night, a baby was found in the high school bathroom. He was born while boys and girls in suits and formal dresses rocked to Bob Seger and Eric Clapton in the adjacent school gymnasium."

"*Angelina* had a baby in the school bathroom?"

"Apparently. She wrapped the baby in a jacket and just left him there."

"Did the baby survive?"

"Someone, possibly Angelina, called the birth center to alert them to the abandoned child. Lydia Kane rescued him and took him under her wing until an adoption was arranged."

"That poor baby. See the good work Lydia does? That's why we can't let that stupid letter-writer get away with what he's doing."

"Okay. I get your point. Do you want to hear the rest of the story or not?"

"I'll be quiet."

"Fine. We're at the tragic-ending part now. Nobody ever heard from Angelina Linden again after that day. But Tee's body was found several years later... decomposing in an abandoned mine shaft several miles from town."

Kim shivered. "Did Angelina kill him?"

"No one knows."

"Oh, Nolan. I've got goose bumps. Do you think anyone will ever find out what really happened?"

The mystery had always intrigued Nolan, but right now he was more interested in Kim's goose bumps. He wanted to *inspect* those goose bumps. But a whimper from the bedroom brought them both to their feet.

"A bad dream?" Nolan guessed.

"Let me go." Kim forestalled him with a hand on his arm.

Nolan figured he should be the one to check on his

niece, but Sammy would find Kim's presence more comforting than his.

"Okay."

"I'm coming, Sammy. I'm coming."

Nolan waited, not liking the way he felt inside. Never had his incompetence as a substitute parent been more apparent than today. Through the partially open door he heard Kim's calm voice, interspersed with Sammy's sniffling. He picked up the mugs and carried them to her kitchen.

He wasn't surprised to find this room immaculate, too. Just like the living room, just like her office at work. Everything had its place. Kim didn't tolerate junk—and didn't seem fond of little decorative touches like ornaments or flowers or anything.

In fact it was the spotlessness of the counters that drew his attention to the sparkle of something metallic by the telephone. He rinsed out the mugs and left them in the sink, then went to investigate.

He found a pair of earrings, partially obscured by the cord of the telephone. They were delicate, beautiful things. The filigree silver was probably antique, the beautiful stones, swirled with pinks and light purple and gold, seemed rare. He tried to remember if he'd seen Kim wear these earrings, but didn't think he had.

Gently he returned the earrings to the counter, tucking them right up next to the telephone so they couldn't roll onto the floor. Then he went back to the sink to wash and dry the mugs.

Kim still wasn't back, so he dared a peek into the bedroom. Light from the hall spilled in a gentle pool on Sammy's face. The little girl slept peacefully, though her coloring was brighter than usual. Kim sat beside her on the mattress, in the shadows, stroking her hair.

The little girl looked so vulnerable lying there. He felt a flooding sensation in his chest, something he'd never experienced before. He just had to do better for that girl. But how? So far everything he did only seemed to hurt her.

Kim saw him and smiled. She eased off the bed and crept toward him. Taking his hand, she led him back to the living room.

He let out a deep breath. "Do you think she's okay?"

"For now? Yes. Would it be okay if Sammy spent the night? I hate to wake her now that I've just settled her down again."

"But where will you sleep?"

"The couch folds out. I'll be fine."

Nolan knew he ought to object. Looking after Sammy was his job. "You've already done more than enough for one night."

"Seriously, I don't mind."

He knew it was wrong to be tempted. A good uncle would want to be there for his niece. A good uncle wouldn't wish she could be at her grandma Irene's for the night and that he and Kim were alone right now.

He wondered if, under those circumstances, Kim

would let him kiss her again. She certainly wouldn't under *these* circumstances.

"I'll come by for Sammy in the morning. What time do you leave for work?"

CHAPTER TWELVE

THE NEXT MORNING Nolan awoke, determined to do better with Sam. He stopped at the bakery and purchased some assorted muffins, then arrived at Kim's half-an-hour early.

He'd wondered if he might catch Kim in her pajamas and a robe, but she was already dressed for work, her clothing dowdy as usual. Why did she pick such dull colors and unflattering shapes? Was she trying to hide that great body of hers? Because he'd felt the curves under the clothes, he was no longer easily deceived. He longed to kiss her good-morning. But behind her dark-framed glasses, her eyes were only distantly friendly.

He turned, instead, to his niece. Sam had on the same outfit as yesterday, but her T-shirt had been pressed and possibly washed, as well. Her pretty hair was tied up in pigtails and she was seated in front of a plate piled with oatmeal pancakes and fruit.

Wham, he was hit again with his hopeless inadequacy as a caregiver. Sammy never looked this good when *he* got her ready for school. He was never organized enough to manage a hot meal for breakfast, either.

"Want a coffee, Nolan?" Kim had a spare mug in her hand. "I have some made."

She did and it smelled wonderful. "That would be great." He slumped into the chair next to Sammy's. "Did you sleep okay last night, Sam?"

She nodded. "I like Kim's house."

"Great. Your grandmother's okay now. You know that."

"Kim told me."

He wondered if he should talk about what had happened. But Sammy seemed happy and calm and he didn't want to upset her. They'd discuss this later, he decided. Or maybe he could simply apprise Celia of the situation and let her handle it at Sammy's four-o'clock appointment this afternoon.

ANXIOUS ABOUT that appointment, Nolan arrived at the school early to pick up Sammy. He hung around a group of other caregivers waiting for their children, most of them mothers. He listened as they discussed things like "play dates," "class sizes," and the extracurricular activities their children were involved in.

He'd never thought to ask Sammy if she wanted a friend over to play. He'd tried calling Teresa Saramago once, but she'd delivered early and was busy with her new baby. He'd never asked Sammy if she'd like to enroll in swimming lessons, or ballet, either. Good God, what would he do if she said yes? His schedule was already insane. How did single parents manage all this stuff?

Eventually the bell rang and Sammy emerged from the school.

"Hey, Sam. Did you have a good day?"

She nodded.

The drive home only took a few minutes. As Sammy wiggled out of her booster seat, he turned around with a wink.

"I picked you up a little present today. It's in my briefcase. Want to go inside and check it out?"

Again she only nodded, but her eyes did seem to widen a little. Or was he being hopeful?

"We only have time to grab a snack and look at the present, before we leave for an appointment with Celia." He opened the front door of the condo for his niece. "Do you like Celia?"

Sammy's gaze was fixed on his old leather briefcase. "Yes. I like her."

Why could he never get more than a few words out of this kid? They were in the living room now. He passed over the briefcase. "Why don't you take a look in here. I'll grab us a couple of apples."

He'd had business in Taos today and had stopped at the hardware store thinking to get her a soccer ball or maybe a pair of skates. Sammy would benefit from spending more time outdoors.

Then he'd had a second thought. In his opinion sports would be good for Sammy. But Sammy didn't seem to enjoy sports. She liked books.

So he'd headed for the bookstore, instead, and asked the clerk for help picking out a story for a six-year-old girl—something relatively new that she wouldn't have read.

Apples in hand, Nolan headed back to the living room. He found Sammy on the floor, her new picture book in hand. As he watched, she flipped through the first few pages. Then she abruptly lost interest and closed the cover.

No smile. He'd hoped for at least a smile.

"Thanks for the present, Uncle Nolan." She took the apple he offered and followed him out to the Explorer, leaving the new book behind.

She didn't like it. So much for that bright idea.

"DO YOU HAVE A MINUTE?"

Upon hearing the question, Lydia Kane set aside the patient chart she'd been updating. Or trying to update. She was finding it so hard to concentrate these days.

She smiled at Kim Sherman. Anyone else would have knocked, then barged in. But the intensely private accountant stood uncertainly at Lydia's office door, her body language anxious.

"For you, Kim, always. How are things going? Were you able to find a way for Trish to help with the fund-raiser?"

"Um—not yet." Kim brushed at a strand of hair that had escaped the severe bun at the back of her head. "I actually wanted to discuss the guest list."

"Sure. Sit down, please."

Kim perched on the edge of the chair, her knees

pressed together like a schoolgirl's. "My question is about Devon. Since she's on the board, I assume you want her invited?"

Hearing her granddaughter's name gave her heart a flutter, but Lydia did her best to keep her voice steady and pleasant. "Absolutely. All the board members should be included."

"I thought so. Would it be best to send the invitation to the hospital where she works? Or her home address?"

Lydia put a hand to her pendant and longed for the calm to descend as it usually did when she fingered the smooth rose-colored stone.

"I only ask because this is a social function. I thought it might be nice to send the invitation to Devon's personal residence as I've done for the other board members. The only problem is I don't have that address in my database." Kim straightened her eyeglasses nervously. "Maybe I should forward the invitation to the hospital…" She started to rise from her chair, but Lydia waved a hand.

"No. You're quite right. Let's send the address to Devon at home. She lives…" Words escaped her as she gave in to another wave of sadness. She had Devon's address, but she'd never been invited to visit.

Kim was looking at her sympathetically. "I can get it later."

Lydia pushed away from her desk and went to close the door. "No. Let's do this now. But first I want to tell you something. I don't talk about my family with many people. But I think maybe you'd benefit from hearing a little of my history.''

She was surprised to see how interested Kim appeared and was encouraged to go on. ''I was about your age when I started my midwifery training. Since the age of sixteen, I'd known what I wanted to do with my life. But I was sidelined by my marriage, and soon after, the birth of first my son, then my daughter. They were both very young when I began to attend home births with a wonderful woman who ran a birth center in the Taos area.''

Lydia went back to her chair. Kim was still listening intently. The young woman was always so serious. But Lydia had been serious at that age, too. She remembered how focused she'd been in her late twenties and early thirties.

''My dream was to open a similar birth center here in Enchantment. It took me years to turn my vision into reality.''

''You're a true inspiration.''

''I'm afraid my children wouldn't agree. Nor would my ex-husband. You see when a woman has a great dream, a real passion, her family can suffer. This is a truth I have never been able to reconcile in my own mind. I loved my children, Kim. I still do. But they resented the hours I spent at work. And so did my husband.''

''I'm so sorry.''

''So am I. Sometimes I wonder if I made the wrong decision. I've helped to bring thousands of children into this world. But in the process, I lost my own family.''

''Oh, but surely...''

''The last time I saw my son was five years ago. My daughter I usually manage to visit once a year. But the bond between us is fragile at best. I'd hoped with Devon...''

She touched the pendant again. Her talisman. Some days her only comfort was knowing that this piece of jewelry would one day be her daughter's, then Devon's. That much of herself and her history, at least, would be passed on.

Coming out of her reverie, Lydia noticed that Kim seemed unduly upset. ''I only tell you this so that you can see what happens when a woman concentrates too hard on her career at the expense of her personal life. This is a mistake I feel would be a travesty for you to make, as well.

''And as for the invitation...'' Lydia filled her lungs with air, forced a smile. ''By all means, send Devon's invitation to her home. I'll copy out the address for you. But I'm sure she'll send her regrets. Devon always shows up for business meetings, but I doubt she'll see the fund-raiser as an obligation requiring her presence.''

''Maybe she'll surprise you.''

''Perhaps.'' Without much hope, Lydia jotted down the address, then passed the slip of paper to Kim. As she did so, her hand trembled a little. Lydia hated the sign of weakness, which she'd noticed cropping up more and more lately. Was it age? Or stress?

Kim must have observed the tremor, too, because she frowned. "Are you sure you're okay, Lydia? I know you've been very upset since Mary Davidson's death."

Was that when her life had gone from bad to worse? Lydia could hardly pinpoint the events anymore. The decision to arrange a secret, private adoption for Hope Tanner's baby, the subsequent estrangement with Devon, Hope's return to town, then Mary's disastrous labor and finally, as if she didn't have enough worries, enough stress…the letters.

They were locked in the third drawer of her desk, those vile messages all written on the same pretty blue stationery.

Should she show Kim? She longed to share the burden with *someone*. But Kim already had enough on her plate.

"I'm fine, dear. Just fine. But thanks very much for asking."

LEAVING LYDIA'S OFFICE, Kim had the unsettling hunch that some new problem had been troubling the older woman. Had others in the center noticed the new worry lines around Lydia's mouth, or the slight shakiness of her still strong, capable hands? If only Lydia trusted Kim enough to confide in her, Kim would do anything possible to help.

As she detoured to get a coffee, Kim realized that

of course she was the last person someone like Lydia would turn to. Lydia wanted Devon. Would the young woman accept the invitation to the fund-raiser? Kim was tempted to add a handwritten note to the envelope. *Please come to Enchantment. Your grandmother needs you.*

But the estrangement between Lydia and Devon wasn't really her business. Even though both women were her blood relatives.

At the coffee machine, Kim refilled her mug and added a dash of milk. If she hurried, she could print off the labels for the invitations tonight. The invitations themselves would be available on Monday, so she could stuff envelopes Monday night at home.

Maybe I should invite Trish and Celia Brice over to help. As soon as the idea popped into her head, Kim disregarded it. She could manage very well on her own. No sense making friends this late in her stay.

Thinking of friends, though, reminded her of Devon. In her few brief conversations with the woman, she'd wondered what it would be like to get to know her better. They were cousins, after all.

Cousins. The very concept was almost scary. Having a cousin was the closest Kim could ever come to a sister or brother. But the reality of the matter was that she had no family at all. When she left Enchantment she would never see Lydia or Devon again. And no one would be any wiser.

Rounding the corner to her office, the sight of Nolan by her office door caused Kim to stop short, sloshing coffee over the edge of her mug. "Darn!"

Nolan dashed forward to offer a napkin from a fast-food joint—something he must have had in his pocket.

"Here, let me clean that up for you."

He touched her elbow and she jerked back again, spilling yet more hot coffee on her hand. "Ouch!"

Nolan grasped her wrist and held it steady. "Calm down, Kim. Gosh you're jittery today." He blotted off her hand, then the mug, all the while standing so close his broad shoulders seemed to bar out the rest of the world.

"Nolan…" She avoided his face by staring at the top button of his shirt.

"Kim?" He inched closer, lowered his head. "You okay?"

She nodded, thinking there was no sense talking since her pounding heart would block out all sound anyway. Lord, but he looked good. Why did she react like a schoolgirl with a crush, every time she saw him?

"Here, let me." He pried the mug from her fingers. "I'll put this on your desk for you."

Suddenly aware how silly and clumsy she must look, Kim glanced around. Parker's office door was open, but he seemed engrossed in a telephone conversation. Relieved, she followed Nolan, regrouping as she walked.

He'd caught her by surprise, that was the problem.

Why did he keep showing up with no advance warning? Was he investigating those letters again?

"What are you doing here?" she demanded once she was safely on her own turf. She settled behind her desk. The extra distance between them made her feel safer. With exaggerated movements, Nolan placed her coffee mug on the coaster by her phone.

"Sammy has another appointment with Celia. I thought I'd drop by and say hi."

Kim opened the side drawer where she kept a container of dampened wipes. She cleaned first her hand, then the side of her mug, giving her emotions time to level off.

"Did you get another letter today?"

"No. Why?"

"I just came from a meeting with Lydia. She's so stressed, Nolan, it's the first time I've thought she was beginning to look her age." She *couldn't* let news of these letters get out. No way would Lydia be able to cope with one more thing gone wrong.

"Well, maybe our secretive letter-writer has had his or her thrill. Maybe there won't be any more letters."

"Wouldn't that be wonderful?" But she could tell Nolan didn't really believe this was likely. Neither did she. The letters would continue until Nolan printed something in the paper. Or until they found the person responsible and exposed him as the troublemaker he was.

"How's Sammy? Is she still upset about what happened yesterday?"

Nolan sank into the empty chair by her desk. "Not that I can tell. I drove Irene to a rest home in Taos today. As for Sammy, I'm hoping she'll talk to Celia about the episode at today's appointment."

"That would be good," Kim agreed. Sammy probably had questions and anxieties about her grandmother that needed to be addressed. Celia would know the right things to say. But if Nolan and Sammy were ever going to forge a relationship, they needed to learn to communicate with each other, too.

As if he could read her thoughts, Nolan leaned forward with a confession. "I've tried to connect with her, Kim, I really have. But I just can't seem to give her what she needs."

He seemed distressed about something in specific. "What happened now?"

"I wanted to get her a gift. Something she would really enjoy. So I bought her a book. Sammy loves books, right? But she didn't like the one I bought her. Or, more likely, she didn't like it *because* I gave it to her."

"Oh, Nolan. Don't take Sammy's rejection so personally."

"The bookseller helped me choose a story a girl Sammy's age ought to like. But what do I know." He sank back into his chair. "I should have bought her a soccer ball."

He reminded Kim of a dejected kid, but Kim didn't dare allow herself a smile.

"Just give yourself some time. You haven't had Sammy very long."

"Almost three weeks. Not that I'm counting."

"I hope not. She's going to be under your charge for at least twelve years."

He groaned. "Some criminals get life sentences shorter than that."

"Oh, Nolan. It's not that bad, surely. She's such a sweet girl. And she needs you. She really does."

"I wish I could believe that. But I can't help wondering what my sister was thinking when she made out her will. Why did she pick me to be Sammy's guardian?"

Kim shook her head. When would Nolan figure out the answer to that question? She already had.

"So how was the session today?" Nolan asked.

Celia Brice had asked him to stop for a moment to chat. Sammy had run down to the reception area to play with a toy that had caught her eye earlier.

"Not bad, Nolan. That episode with Sammy's grandmother was very unfortunate. Poor Sammy still isn't sure her grandmother is alive. I'd take her for a visit as soon as possible."

"I'm not sure Irene is up to it." He explained about the rest home in Taos.

"Well, have Sammy write her a letter then. Hopefully Irene will be able to correspond back."

"That's a good idea. Anything else?"

Celia smiled kindly. "Don't worry so much.

Sammy is going to be fine. She grew up loved and well cared for. All she needs is a little extra patience and kindness.''

Patience and kindness. He hoped he could manage that.

''I think it would be a good idea if we continued these sessions for a few more weeks.''

''I agree. It's a big relief to me, knowing she has you to talk to.'' After a brief discussion about fees, Nolan went downstairs to find Sam. On their way out the front door, they almost bumped into Mitchell Dixon. Nolan put out a hand to avoid a collision.

''Hey there, Mitchell.''

The restaurant owner seemed startled to be recognized. ''Nolan.'' His gaze dropped. ''This must be your niece.''

As Nolan introduced Sammy, he noticed Trish Linden watching the three of them. *Something's up.* He remembered that Mitchell Dixon had been talking to Trish the last time Nolan had spotted him at the center.

But before he could frame a question for Mitchell, the older man said goodbye and hurried from the center, head bowed as if he didn't want anyone else to see him.

''Ready to go home, Sam? It's Friday night. How about we get us some pizza?''

''Sure.''

Nolan took her hand again and wondered if this was what all his Fridays were going to be like from now on. Pizza and movie, him and Sam. If only he could add a woman to the mix it wouldn't be such a bad deal. Marriage had never appealed to him much before. Now it was starting to look like a brilliant idea.

Or maybe it wasn't because of Sammy that the idea suddenly had so much attraction. Maybe it was meeting Kim Sherman. Because when Nolan pictured a woman in his world, hers was the face he saw.

Fading sunlight hit him in the eyes as he stepped out the front door. With it came an amazing realization. He was falling in love.

Disturbed, and a little excited, too, he swooped Sammy into his arms and positioned her up on his shoulders.

"Want a piggyback ride, Sam?"

She laughed and clung to his hair, which hurt, but he didn't mind. Hearing the first joyous sound he could remember passing through his niece's lips was well worth the pain.

He was falling in love. Really, truly falling in love, for the first time in his life. He laughed, too, the sound mingling with Sammy's giggles.

He'd never guessed love would make him feel so happy, so carefree, so buoyant.

He decided not to worry about the fact that Kim didn't want to date him. Or that her plan was to leave Enchantment in a month or two. Those were obstacles, but he could deal with them. He *would* deal with them.

Starting tomorrow.

CHAPTER THIRTEEN

SATURDAY MORNING Kim lingered for an uncharacteristically long time in her robe and pajamas. Her apartment was so quiet she could almost hear the snow falling outside, accumulating on the edge of her window and the railing that framed her small four-by-ten-foot balcony. A cup of coffee in hand, Kim leaned her head against the cold pane of glass and gazed down Sage Street.

In its new white coat of snow, the town of Enchantment certainly lived up to its name today. The boughs of the pine trees were scalloped with white. Kim imagined tiny fairies skipping from one dazzling snow crystal to the next. It was a setting suited to the Snow Queen herself. In a word—magic.

Kim sighed, and moved away from the window. Outside might be a winter wonderland, but her apartment was dull as ever and that was exactly the way she felt, too. The fund-raiser was a little over a month away. After that, she would be leaving. Already she feared she'd stayed too long.

On the kitchen counter were copies of the résumé she'd updated last week. Kim glanced over the one-page summary of her educational background and working history. Strange how a life could be summarized so tidily.

If she wanted to have a job lined up for when she returned to Denver, she needed to start sending this out. She refilled her coffee, then grabbed the résumé and headed for the computer in the bedroom. After connecting to the Internet, she called up the *Denver Post,* then went to the Classifieds. Clicking on the Careers icon led her to Accounting/Bookkeeping positions.

A list of forty possibilities came up on her screen, the first a position with the agency she'd worked at last—one that provided temporary accounting services. She paused, wondering if she should apply again. Her record had been exemplary, and she knew they'd take her in a flash.

But rather than working for a series of different companies, perhaps she should try to settle in to one place. The thought caused a flurry of anxieties. What if the other employees didn't like her? It wasn't bad being the outsider for a short period of time. But if her position was permanent, that would be a whole different matter.

Kim continued scrolling. Another job opportunity popped out at her. "Accountant/Bookkeeper: accounting degree required. Great opportunity for detail-oriented individual."

The ad sounded tailor-made for her. She moved the mouse to the "Place on My Job Lists" button. Just after she'd persuaded herself to click the mouse, her phone rang.

With several swift moves of her fingers, she closed the Internet connection, then raced to the counter, catching the call before the third ring.

"Hello?"

"Kim? It's Nolan here."

She leaned on the counter and closed her eyes. *Nolan.* "Do you need a baby-sitter?"

"As a matter of fact, I do. Sorry for the late notice, but could you possibly be here in an hour? Something's come up."

An hour? She still hadn't showered, but if she hurried… "Sure. No problem."

"Oh, and Kim, do you have a warm ski jacket and mitts? I think Sammy will definitely want to play in all this new snow today."

"Yes." She'd brought all her ski gear with her, had it stored in the big front closet. She made arrangements to meet Nolan at his home by ten o'clock. As she hung up, she chided herself, too late, for being so available, so *accommodating.*

She hoped Nolan would believe she was eager to see Sammy. Which she was, of course.

Kim rushed to get ready—showering, dressing, drying her hair in minutes. To prove to herself that she wasn't out to impress Nolan, she wore a severe ponytail and only a little gloss on her lips for makeup. After digging out a warm jacket, mitts, ear band and boots from her closet, she was ready to go.

She found Nolan outside his condo, loading a set of skis onto the roof rack of his Explorer. She wondered about his plans, specifically whether there might be a woman involved.

He looked terrific in black snow pants and a matching jacket with gold trim. Dark sunglasses set off his thick, sandy hair and the firm lines of his strong jaw. She noticed he hadn't shaved that morning, which only added to his appeal in her opinion.

Her knees felt weak as she approached him. To compensate, she stiffened her voice. "You're going skiing, obviously."

He spared her a quick smile. "So are you. And Sammy. Here she comes now."

The little girl, bundled in a purple one-piece snowsuit, trundled out the front door at that moment. She waved and smiled. "Kim! I'm going to learn to ski today!"

"Are you, sweetheart?" Kim opened her arms for a big hug. As her arms squished through the insulating layers of cloth and fiber, Kim glanced quizzically at Nolan.

"But I thought you needed me to baby-sit?"

"Would you have come if I'd invited you for a day of skiing?"

She took a step backward. "You tricked me."

"I did." And he seemed totally unrepentant. "Come on, hop in the front seat. Sammy, I'll help strap you into your booster."

Kim stood her ground. This wasn't right. She

couldn't spend the entire day in Nolan McKinnon's company. It wasn't *safe*.

Then Sammy asked if *Kim* could strap her in, and Kim realized she really was trapped, unless she was willing to disappoint the little girl.

"Sure, Sammy." She leaned through the open door and assisted her into the plastic seat. In her winter gear Sammy was about double her usual size, and the strap had to be adjusted.

"I'm glad you're here." Sammy looked like a cherub with her face framed by the fake fur trim of her toque. "I'm a bit scared."

"It'll be fun," Kim promised. "The bunny hill is very gentle." She snapped the seat belt into place, then backed out of the car and shut the door. Glaring at Nolan, who'd stepped up beside her, she muttered, "This is really dirty pool."

"All's fair in love and war…" he murmured in reply, touching the small of her back as he guided her toward the passenger door.

Love? Even through the cloth of his gloves and her jacket, Kim's body burned at the contact.

Acting the perfect gentlemen—even though he'd just proved he was anything but—Nolan opened the door for her and made sure she was seated comfortably before closing it again, then dashing back to the driver's side.

He'd started the engine earlier, so the heating vents were already blowing out warm air. "I thought we'd go to Angel Fire. That's nice and close."

"Fine." Kim sighed. She couldn't believe she'd been so neatly maneuvered. Using Sammy hadn't been fair. But now that she was committed, she had to admit a day on the ski hill held a lot of appeal. "Would you mind stopping at my apartment? I might as well bring my gear along."

"You have skis?"

"Yes, I have skis. We have mountains in Colorado, too, you know. Perhaps you've heard of Vail? Or Boulder? Or Snowmass…?"

"Well, the first one sounds sort of familiar."

He gave her a grin, so infectious it was impossible not to grin back. She covered her mouth with her mittened hand and turned to face out the passenger window. The second he parked in front of her apartment, she had her hand on the door handle.

"Make sure you come back, okay?" Nolan called after her as she raced out the door. "*Sammy* and I will be waiting for you. Won't we, Sammy?"

As if she'd needed the reminder. Slightly breathless from taking the stairs to the second story so quickly, Kim gathered her boards, poles and boots awkwardly in her arms. The person who invented a convenient way to carry all this gear was going to make a fortune.

She locked up the place again, then took the stairs, slowly this time. Nolan met her at the front door and whisked the skis and poles from her hands. "Put the boots in the back. I'll load these on the roof rack."

Ten minutes later they were on Paseo de Sierra, on their way out of town, and within the hour they were actually on the ski hill. Showing a patience Kim hadn't seen in him before, Nolan helped Sammy into her boots and her skis.

"I know it feels weird now," he said. "But when you're gliding down your first hill, you're going to feel like an eagle, Sammy. You'll see."

Kim stood back and framed the two of them—uncle and niece—in the lens of the one-use camera she'd purchased in the gift shop while Nolan stood in line to pay for their ski passes. She clicked one picture, then another.

"We have to capture Sammy's first time on skis, Nolan," she said in response to the questioning look he shot her.

"Right. Good thinking."

He gave her a nod of approval, but she could tell he was wishing he'd thought to bring his own camera. She was beginning to know Nolan, to understand how he thought. Right now he would be giving himself a lecture about pictures and photo albums. She couldn't resist sliding up to the duo and putting a hand on his arm.

"Where did Sammy get all this gear if she's never been skiing before?"

"We bought it yesterday," Sammy said, adjusting her goggles. "Uncle Nolan bought me *everything.*"

"Most of it secondhand," Nolan added.

"Lucky girl." Kim smiled and tugged gently on the pom-pom at the end of Sammy's toque. "You look perfect. Are you ready to give the hill a try?"

Sammy nodded, and Kim glanced at Nolan for confirmation. "Have you enrolled her in lessons?"

"I want to teach her," he replied. "If you prefer to do your own thing, you could meet us back at the lodge for lunch."

"No thanks. I'll help, too."

Between them, Kim and Nolan pulled Sammy up the hill a short distance, then, each holding one of her hands, let her experience the gentle slide back down.

"I want to go faster," was Sammy's verdict.

Over the little girl's head, Kim and Nolan grinned at each other. "I think she's ready for the Handle Tow," Nolan said.

Sammy proved to be a fast learner, easily mastering the "pizza" stop and soon moving on to gentle turns. After lunch, they took her up Dream Catcher and that's when the real fun began.

Sammy couldn't get enough. No sooner was she down than she headed for the lift lineup again. For the first time since she'd lost her parents, she looked happy and healthy. Her eyes sparkled, her cheeks glowed.

"I love skiing," she told Kim when they were traveling up the lift together.

"Me, too."

"My daddy didn't like to ski. Mommy wanted to teach me, but we never had time."

"No? I bet your parents would be really proud to see how well you're doing."

Sammy nodded, her expression suddenly sad. Kim

worried she'd said the wrong thing. But it was only natural for Sammy to feel blue occasionally, she reasoned to herself.

At the top of the lift, they waited for Nolan, who was on the next chair. "Race you down," he challenged Sammy.

"Okay!" She took off, flashing a grin at them, before facing down the hill as she'd been taught.

For a second Nolan lingered beside Kim. Nolan's gaze was trained on the little girl. Kim watched Nolan.

"She's a real firecracker, isn't she?"

"Do I detect a note of pride in your voice?" Kim teased.

His smile held a trace of embarrassment. "It's funny the feeling I get when I'm watching her sometimes. Like someone's taken an air pump and started filling my chest. I want to cry and I want to smile at the same time. Isn't that the strangest thing?"

Kim understood. She put a hand on his shoulder. "You're falling in love with her, Nolan."

She felt his shoulder stiffen and immediately dropped her hand. He caught it up and held it. Squeezed it.

"I am falling in love, Kim. You're right about that."

She couldn't read a thing in his eyes, thanks to the double barrier of their sunglasses. But his smile was unbearably tender.

Swallowing her own silly emotions, Kim gestured down the hill. "Better catch up to her."

Nolan's gaze followed hers. Sammy was halfway down, carefully sculpting the wide turns they'd taught her that morning.

"Right," he said. "Come with me."

Then, leaving her no choice, he tugged on her hand and for a few seconds they skied together. The hill was so gentle, they didn't need to turn. Still, Kim experienced the same rush she usually felt on a double black diamond run.

Nolan. Lord, he was such a fine-looking man. And a good man, too. As they approached Sammy, he swooped down to grasp her left hand, leaving the right one for Kim. Once they had the little girl firmly under control, they pointed their ski tips straight down the hill.

"Tuck in a little, Sammy," Nolan shouted over the rushing wind. "You'll go faster."

"Whee, this is fun!"

Sammy showed no fear as they raced down the mountain. The three of them an undefeatable team.

THEY STOPPED for burgers on the way home. By the time Kim had helped Sammy to shower and the little girl had enjoyed a mug of her uncle's hot chocolate, Sammy couldn't keep her eyes open any longer. She fell asleep on the couch, with her head on a pillow on Nolan's lap and Kim tickling the soles of her feet.

"Poor thing is wiped." Nolan switched off the Disney movie they'd begun to watch. "Hang on a second while I tuck her in."

While he was out of the room, Kim tidied the room then washed the mugs. As soon as Nolan reappeared, she dried her hands.

"I guess my baby-sitting duties are over for the evening."

Nolan didn't look pleased. He came up beside her and took her hands in his. "I'll pay time and a half if you stay a little longer."

She couldn't look at him, especially not when he was this close. "Not a good idea."

"You keep saying that. Why are you fighting what's between us? I meant what I said on the ski hill this afternoon. I *am* falling in love. And I'm not talking about the parental kind of love. Not where you're concerned."

The various romantic entanglements of her past had not prepared Kim for any of the feelings that were confusing and befuddling her at this moment. Logically she knew what her next move should be, but body and soul had different opinions.

Mobilizing her courage, she tipped her head up and met his gaze full on. His expression took her breath. He was completely focused on her, as if she was all that mattered to him.

She was so tempted to give in. To tell him she felt the same way. To kiss him again. Yes, that was what she wanted. To kiss him again.

But hadn't she already decided that was one mistake she wouldn't repeat?

"I *have* to go home, Nolan."

"Aren't you having a good time? I don't understand."

"Yes, you do. I already told you I won't be staying in Enchantment much longer. In fact, when you called this morning, I was looking at career opportunities in the paper."

That brought him up short. "Where?"

"Denver."

"That's where you grew up?"

"And went to university. And worked my first two years out of school."

"Is someone waiting for you there? Is that the problem?"

"No. That's not it." She only wished it was. She had no one in Colorado, other than her old university roommate and her husband, who were Kim's closest friends. She'd lived all her life in Denver but she felt like she belonged in Enchantment.

"Is it too much to ask for one simple reason why you won't stay?"

For a moment she considered telling him the whole story. How she'd saved money to hire a private investigator. How he'd tracked down her grandmother to this town. How she'd used Nolan's paper, the *Bulletin,* to find a job here so she could learn a little about her roots.

But she knew telling him wouldn't solve anything.

He wouldn't understand. He'd think her connection to Lydia was all the more reason for her to stay. He wouldn't understand that Lydia might be embarrassed, or worse, angry at being reminded of the past. That her very job might be placed in jeopardy.

"I don't have to explain myself to you." She knew she sounded hard, but that was probably for the best. Let him believe she was callous. It would be easier for both of them that way.

"Is that right?"

He glared at her, as if he hoped to see something different in her eyes, but she kept her expression as stern as her voice had been.

"Okay," he said finally. "I get the message. You want to go home? Then go." He turned his back to her. Opened the fridge for a beer. After few tense, silent seconds, she left.

NOLAN HEARD the front door close after Kim. He twisted the cap off his beer, trying to convince himself that he really was thirsty.

The evening was so still he even heard the sound of her car driving away.

He tossed back some beer, hoping to fill the empty space that had suddenly developed in the middle of his abdomen. How was it possible to feel so lonely in his own home?

Why was he falling for Kim Sherman?

He couldn't figure it out. Why couldn't he have fallen in love with the delightful Celia Brice? The sweet and conscientious Connie Eckland? Or any of his past flames for that matter?

Any woman in the world would have made a better choice than the perfect ice maiden, Kim Sherman. She must have been putting on an act the night he'd kissed her. Because that wasn't the real her at all. She was cold and hard, and he and Sammy were going to be much better off without her.

CHAPTER FOURTEEN

TWO WEEKS WENT BY before Nolan received a call from the rest home in Taos. Irene Davidson was anxious to return to Enchantment. Could he please come and get her?

According to the nurse, Irene wasn't ready to be living on her own, but Mabel was willing to have her stay again, so that seemed the perfect solution for now.

Since it was Sunday and Kim wasn't at work, Nolan phoned to ask if she would baby-sit Sammy while he drove to Taos.

"That's fine, Nolan. Why don't you drop her off with her ski gear? We'll go to Angel Fire for the day."

Sammy had turned into a fanatic for the sport, and he knew she'd be thrilled to hit the slopes again. "Thanks, Kim."

"You're welcome."

The stiff, formal exchange was typical of the few times they'd spoken since their last disastrous parting. The only times he saw Kim now were the brief moments before and after she baby-sat Sam on Tuesday and Thursday evenings.

They hadn't even met to discuss the anonymous letters—mainly because they'd stopped coming. Kim was relieved about that, and he ought to be, too. But deep down, he felt cheated. He still wanted to know who'd sent them. And why.

A good excuse to see Kim again wouldn't hurt. His decision not to invest any more emotional energy into the prickly accountant hadn't proved very sound. True he wasn't seeing her much. But he couldn't stop thinking about her. Even *dreaming* about her.

All in all, Nolan was in a prickly mood himself as he drove back to Enchantment with a delicate-looking Irene in the passenger seat beside him. He made an effort to be cheerful, however, as he asked how she was doing. Her mumbled response made it clear this was one of her down days.

"Well, not much is new in Enchantment since you left... Oh, Sammy's taken up skiing. You'll have to come out with us one day so you can see for yourself. She's a real little daredevil on the hills."

"That's nice."

Nolan was concerned by Irene's despondency. At Mabel's, Irene showed a brief moment of animation as she greeted her old friend and neighbor. But after a few minutes of conversation, she excused herself.

"I'm sorry, Mabel. I see you've made us a lovely lunch, but I'd like to lie down for a minute."

"You go right ahead, dear. Your room's all ready for you."

Nolan carried in her suitcase, then returned to the

living room, where Mabel had spread out an assort-
ment of sandwiches and a fruit plate. Irene hadn't
touched any of it.

"No sense wasting this food." Mabel waved a
hand for him to sit. "Please help yourself, Nolan. Can
I offer you a cup of tea?"

Since Kim and Sam wouldn't be home from the ski
hill for a couple more hours, Nolan saw no reason not
to enjoy the homemade sandwiches. Mabel had cut
neat triangles of bread spread with tuna salad and curried chicken. He piled his plate with several of each,
then added slices of pineapple and cantaloupe.

"Your sandwiches are delicious, Mabel. Thanks a
lot. And thanks, too, for having Irene again."

"My pleasure."

Mabel poured them each a cup of tea before settling
into an ornately carved, antique-looking chair. She
was wearing a dress and had her gray hair tightly
curled. Because it was Sunday, Nolan supposed. Normally Mabel wandered around in her gardening duds.

"I don't know what you think," he said between
mouthfuls, "but Irene doesn't look that great to me.
She barely said a word on the drive down here. She
doesn't even seem interested in Sammy."

Mabel shook her head sadly. "It must be awful to
lose a child. And I know Irene was so looking forward
to the new grandchild, as well. She was certain it
would be a boy and she hoped Steve and Mary would
name him after her father."

The baby had been a boy, and he'd been buried

with the name Irene wanted. Which was all very cold comfort, indeed.

"She still has a granddaughter." And it wasn't just for selfish reasons that Nolan wished Irene would take more interest in Sammy. It would help the little girl to have her grandmother back in her life—Sammy needed every bit of continuity he could provide her.

At least Irene had replied to the letter he'd helped Sammy write to her. So she *must* have some good days, too.

"Eventually, Nolan, Irene will be very grateful to have both Sammy and you. We'll just take things one step at a time. If I can get her taking walks, that will be a start."

Nolan helped himself to one more sandwich. The curried chicken was his favorite. "You're a good friend, Mabel."

She smiled warmly. "And an old one, too. Irene and I have lived on the same street for more years than I'd care to tell you, young man."

Idly he wondered how many years. Mabel was around retirement age. And she'd spent all of her life here in Enchantment. She'd probably rival his newspaper archives for information about the past.

"Did you know Lydia Kane when you were growing up, Mabel?"

"Sure. She was about eight years older than me, but she did date my eldest brother, Richard, for a few years. They were quite 'hot and heavy' during their high school years. Being the usual pesky baby sister,

I would follow them around and make a real nuisance of myself. I believe I ended up seeing more than either of them could have imagined.''

Mabel raised her eyebrows and gave him a naughty smile.

''But Lydia and your brother didn't end up together?''

''No, they broke up the Christmas of their sophomore year. Would you like some more tea?''

Before he had a chance to reply, she'd refilled his cup.

''I meant to phone you to tell you how much I enjoyed your last editorial.''

He'd come down against the latest proposed skiing development—Angel's Gate—by the owners of the existing Angel Fire resort where he'd taken Sammy. Much as Nolan enjoyed skiing, he didn't think the environmental implications of developing yet more wilderness could be ignored. Nolan suspected Mabel was setting him up for a lengthy conversation about the particular flora involved in this project.

It was a diversionary attempt he did not intend to fall for. He guessed the subject of Lydia and Richard's breakup was a delicate one—which in those days had usually meant...

''Am I right in guessing that Lydia became pregnant while she was dating your brother?''

Mabel's teacup wobbled on her saucer.

''I'm sorry if you find my bluntness rude. I do appreciate your hospitality, Mabel. Especially where

Irene is concerned. But my question isn't based on idle curiosity.''

''No?'' Her hands were steady again, the focus of her aging brown eyes sharp.

''I'm sorry I'm not at liberty to tell you the details, but I've been doing a little investigating into Lydia's past.''

''I can only imagine you would find good things. That woman is amazing, in my humble opinion. Especially when you consider the hardships she had to overcome in her youth. Her mother died when she was quite young, you see, and her father was extremely strict.''

''So he probably wasn't very sympathetic when he found out his unmarried daughter was pregnant.''

His persistence paid off, as it often did.

''This happened so long ago... I guess it won't really matter if I tell you. Besides, these sorts of teenage travesties aren't considered as scandalous as they once were.''

Nolan waited.

''Yes, Lydia did become pregnant, and you're right, her father was furious. He sent Lydia to stay with his sister in Denver. Our family was told that the child would be given up for adoption. But there were rumors otherwise...''

Nolan didn't follow. ''What rumors? That she kept the baby?''

''No. That she'd...gotten rid of it.''

''Abortion?''

Mabel nodded. "In those days it was considered a very ugly word indeed. But the speed with which Lydia returned home and resumed her life generated those types of questions."

Baby killer. The phrase from the anonymous letters popped into Nolan's brain. Could this alleged abortion be what his letter writer had been referring to? "Did your brother ever ask Lydia if she terminated her pregnancy?"

"No. Lydia's father had forbidden them from seeing each other again. Richard tried to write, but he was almost positive Lydia's father destroyed the letters. At any rate, he never received a reply."

What a story. Nolan set his empty plate on the table and downed his tea in several long swallows. Was it possible that this event had triggered the letters he'd been receiving?

But if Lydia *had* undergone an abortion, it had been over fifty years ago. Why would someone bring up the old rumors now?

ON MONDAY Kim processed billings for the previous week and followed up on delinquent accounts. She was pleased to note that the percentage of overdue receivables had dropped steadily since her first day on the job. For the past month or so the rate had stabilized, indicating she'd done all she could for the birth center. With her new systems and procedures—all spelled out in a carefully organized manual—her replacement should have no trouble maintaining financial viability.

That knowledge was a comfort to Kim. She liked knowing that she had been able to help her grandmother. After the fund-raiser—little more than two weeks away now—the center's bank account would be robust. And Kim would be able to leave with a clear conscience.

She'd finally mailed off some résumés last week. She hadn't heard anything yet, but didn't expect to for at least a week. If she received any nibbles, she'd be free to attend interviews in Denver in early April.

The timing was perfect. If only she could control her emotions as easily. Knowing that in three weeks' time she'd be living in Denver once more made her depressed.

She'd worked so hard not to get attached to this place, or to the people who lived here. Yet it had happened anyway. The same way it had with her foster families—even though she'd *told* herself she didn't care.

No matter how hard she tried not to, she'd *missed* those families when she left them. She'd even missed the foster mother who drank too much and given her so much work to do. The kids had been sweet. One little girl had been the same age as Sammy....

No. She wouldn't think about that. Looking back was always a mistake. Why could she never learn that simple lesson? She had to be strong. All her life she'd had to be strong and nothing had changed.

A soft tapping sounded on her closed office door.

"Yes?" On Monday Sammy met Celia at the center at four o'clock. Half-expecting Nolan to saunter in, Kim was disappointed to see Parker Reynolds.

The birth center's chief administrator stepped into her office. "Kim, I saw the receivables report on my desk this morning. You're doing a great job. Lydia and I were just saying last week how lucky we were to find you."

Kim didn't comment.

"Anyway," Parker soldiered on, "on an unrelated matter, Hope and I are planning to have a few people from the center over on Friday night. Just a casual get-together. It would be great if you—"

"Sorry." Kim made a point of not smiling in return. "Thanks for the invitation, but I'm afraid I can't make it Friday."

"If we switched to Sat—"

"Saturday's out, too. I'll be spending most of the weekend working on the fund-raiser." Almost as soon as the words were out, she realized her mistake.

"Is there something we could do to help? We could turn the party into a work bee."

"No, really, it's fine. I have everything under control." Kim was getting desperate for him to leave. Why did everyone in this center have to be so damn nice? How could she be expected to just pack up and leave when—

"Kim, are you all right?" Parker stepped closer. "You look a little upset."

Kim adjusted her glasses and forced a hard smile. "I'm very well, thank you, Parker. Just rather busy at the moment, that's all." She went to her bookcase and picked out the fund-raiser binder. She glanced back at her boss. "Is there anything else?"

"No, I guess not." Reluctantly he turned away, closing the door behind him.

Kim sat at her desk, letting out a sigh that felt heavier than the binder she held in her hands. She turned to her master list. For each major task, a separate tabbed section contained all relevant details for invitations, venue, food, program, decorations, miscellaneous.

First she turned to the invitation list. This morning's mail had brought a flood of RSVPs, and she needed to note who was coming and who was not. Opening the mail, making a series of checks and crosses, was satisfying work. At the end she had eighty confirmed guests. So far Devon wasn't one of them. Lydia's granddaughter hadn't yet replied to the invitation, but there was still time.

Making a note to follow up any "no replies" at the end of the week, Kim flipped to another section of the binder.

AFTER DROPPING SAMMY OFF for her appointment with Celia, Nolan contemplated going out for a coffee. The smell of peach tea in this place was enough to make a guy nauseous. But then he encountered Lydia Kane in the hallway.

"Nolan!" She'd been rushing like mad, but she stopped suddenly as if nothing in her world could be more important than saying hello to him. "How's little Sammy doing?"

"Better, I think." He told her about the skiing, which thrilled Lydia to no end.

"Fresh air and exercise. Nolan, I couldn't have prescribed a better tonic for that little girl. Good for you for thinking of it."

She sure knew how to make a guy feel good about himself. But then Nolan thought about Sammy's weird reading habits and his self-satisfaction ebbed. Neither he nor Celia had been able to figure out his niece's strange behavior where books were concerned.

"Is Kim still doing the occasional baby-sitting for you?"

"Every Tuesday and Thursday night and sometimes more," he admitted. "I don't know what I'd do without her." But if she was serious about leaving Enchantment—and she clearly was—he'd soon have to figure something out. If only Irene could pull herself together by then.

"I'm sure helping the two of you is very good for Kim, as well." Lydia fingered her pendant as she spoke. "In my opinion Kim spends far too much time on her own. Everyone at the center has tried to draw her out, but only you and Sammy seem to have had any success."

As Lydia dropped the pendant, he noticed the unusual pink stone. Embedded in the swirling pattern was the outline of a mother and child. Something about the colors and texture struck him as familiar.

"Will we see you at the fund-raiser on the nineteenth? After all, you were born here."

He'd received an invitation but had assumed it was so he could cover the event for the paper. "My mother delivered here?"

Lydia smiled. "That's right. Both you and Mary. I do hope you'll be able to come. It would mean so much to me." She patted his arm and smiled warmly. "Now I must be going. I have patients waiting. Take care, Nolan."

He stared after her, his mind replaying their conversation and pausing at the highlights. Lydia thought he was doing a good job with Sammy. He and Mary had been *born* here. Lydia's pendant reminded him of…

The answer hit him suddenly and he knew who he needed to see. His cup of coffee would have to wait.

WHILE JOTTING NOTES neatly in the Program section of the fund-raiser binder, Kim's hands froze at the sound of another knock on her door. Was Parker going to try again to convince her to attend his party?

But this time it *was* Nolan. She was so overwhelmed she dropped the binder with a thud onto her desk, triggering the spring mechanism on the rings. Papers spilled everywhere.

"Oh, no!" Every time he came to her office, something went wrong. Why was she so clumsy?

"Let me help."

She frowned, not wanting him to touch the papers. "Please, no. I'll do it. I know where everything belongs." As she sorted through the mess, realigning pages, she noticed him close her office door before sitting down to watch her. What was he up to?

He certainly *looked* good. Today he had on his leather jacket and jeans, an outfit he'd worn many times before in her company. An outfit she couldn't imagine ever getting tired of seeing on his lanky, athletic body.

She waited for her respiratory system to calm down a little before attempting conversation. "Is Sammy with Celia?"

"Yup."

"Is she okay?"

"Pretty much."

Apparently he wasn't here to talk about his niece. "How about Irene?"

"Fine, as far as I know."

"Well, that's good." She waited, but he offered nothing. Only kept staring as if he'd never seen a woman in a gray cardigan and glasses before. Kim had no illusions; she knew she looked far from glamorous. So what could possibly explain Nolan's presence in her office?

"You received another letter." It was so obvious this should have been her first guess.

But Nolan shook his head. "No. There haven't

been any more letters. I think we've heard the last from our little troublemaker.''

Could he be right? Kim wanted desperately to think so.

''And I may have found out what was behind the letters in the first place.''

''Really?'' Kim closed the binder and set it aside. Leaning forward, hands folded in front of her, she waited for the details.

''When I dropped Irene off at Mabel's on Sunday, Mabel shared some details about Lydia's past. It appears she may have had an abortion when she was sixteen.''

''What?'' Kim's back went rigid.

''Apparently Lydia was dating Mabel's brother at the time. When Lydia became pregnant, her father sent her to Denver.''

Kim had a hard time processing what he was saying. ''Could you say that again?'' When Nolan did, she couldn't contain a small buzz of excitement. If this was true, then Mabel's brother was her grandfather. Mabel would be her…great-aunt.

Oh, Lord, she couldn't believe it. She'd wondered if she might learn more about her background here. But discovering who her grandfather had been…she hadn't expected as much as that.

''Kim? Are you all right?''

Nolan was the second man to ask her that question this afternoon. She was becoming far too open with her emotions. Struggling to contain herself, she nodded, trying to seem impatient.

"Of course, I'm all right, Nolan. I'm just trying to figure out why you'd think anyone would be interested in something that happened all those years ago."

"Yeah, I admit that's a hole in my theory. Still, it would be something if it were true, wouldn't it? The head of the local birth center getting an abortion when she was younger."

"I don't believe that story for a minute," Kim said firmly. "You don't have any documented proof, do you?" She felt safe asking the question, because there was no way he could have. Lydia had delivered that baby when she was sixteen. That baby had been Kim's mother.

"No, I don't have proof. But the possibility is worth looking into. If I didn't have Sammy, I'd go to Denver and check this out myself. As it is, I've asked a university buddy to find Mabel's brother for me and see if he confirms the story."

Kim realized she shouldn't have prodded him. "Nolan, whatever Lydia went through back then doesn't matter now. I can't believe the person who wrote those letters is referring to *that*."

"What are they referring to, then? I haven't been able to come up with anything else."

"That's because the accusations are complete fabrications. And since the letters have stopped, I don't understand why you're even interested anymore."

"Is that right?" Nolan leaned back into his chair, the picture of ease.

"Just drop it, okay? You have bigger problems to worry about."

"Well, maybe you're right about that." Slowly Nolan rose from the chair. She expected him to leave, but before he reached the door, he turned back with one more question. "By the way, there's something I'd like to ask you."

Kim's internal warning system went on full alert. Carefully she got up and slid the fund-raiser binder into position in her bookcase. "Yes?" she asked calmly.

"When I was at your apartment, I noticed a pair of earrings by your phone."

Earrings? Oh, Lord. She remembered finding them under the phone when she'd been cleaning a few weeks ago. He must have seen them that night she'd invited him in for tea.

"That pink-colored stone is very pretty. What's it called?"

Kim's throat felt very dry. "Rose onyx."

Nolan nodded thoughtfully. "I thought so. Do you know that mineral is very rare? In fact, the only place I know where you can find it is in the wainscoting of the Colorado state capitol."

"I d-didn't know that. The earrings were my mother's. I have no idea where she got them." Kim glanced down at her desk as she uttered what she knew was a lie.

Her mother had told her the story often. When she was twenty-one, her adopted mother had given her the earrings. She'd told her that they'd belonged to her birth mother, who had wanted her to have the special jewelry as a keepsake. The story had been one of Kim's favorite bedtime tales when she was little.

"Is that right?" Nolan appeared to accept her version of events at face value. "Well, maybe you should be careful where you leave them. I think they might be quite valuable."

CHAPTER FIFTEEN

ON THURSDAY NIGHT, Kim arrived at Nolan's as usual to baby-sit. Sammy was eating her dinner, so she sat at the table with the little girl and leafed through that week's edition of the *Bulletin*. A quick scan assured her Nolan was keeping his word and hadn't printed any of those ridiculous letters about Lydia.

About to turn the page, she was stopped by Sammy's finger as the little girl pointed to the bold-lettered heading.

"What does that say?"

"'Letters to the Editor,'" she read.

"Who writes the letters?"

"People who read the paper, Sammy. People who live in Enchantment and have questions, or problems, or concerns." Insane wackos trying to make themselves look important by vilifying others. Kim was still tense from the quick conversation she'd had with Nolan as they passed in the front entrance.

"Could you stay a few minutes after I get home?" he'd asked. Lately she'd been out of the door only seconds after he came in. "Something came up today. We need to talk."

Kim was certain what had come up was another blue envelope. She'd known it was too good to be true that the letters had stopped. So what had their anonymous author written this time? She dreaded finding out.

"I'm done." Sammy set down her fork.

"Okay. Let's put your dishes in the dishwasher, then we can play." Kim had already trained Sammy to place cutlery in the basket, and now she did so while Kim rinsed her plate and glass. With that chore taken care of, Kim followed the little girl upstairs.

"How about we work on a puzzle tonight?" she suggested. Sammy had several, as well as a variety of easy board games. Surely they could find something to do other than—

"I want to look at my books."

Every day Sammy brought a pile home from the school library. "She's got quite a reputation with the school librarian," Nolan had told her. Kim could well imagine.

"Wouldn't you like to do something else for a change?"

Sammy ignored the question. She picked up the pile of books and settled them in her lap. Reluctantly Kim sat next to her on the floor.

"Okay. What do we have today?"

Sammy went through the usual process of examining the cover carefully, then passing the book to Kim. After the first couple of pages she became bored.

"I don't like that one."

"Sammy, give it a chance. I think it's a lovely story." Kim read on, but Sammy showed lackluster interest.

After an hour of reading it was time for Sammy's bath. Tonight Kim used a dryer on Sammy's hair, then when it was just damp, she fashioned French braids.

"I hope these will still be nice in the morning," she said. "If not, your hair will have pretty waves at least."

"Thanks, Kim." Sammy gave her a big hug. "I like you. I wish I could live with you always."

"Oh, Sammy." Kim held tightly to the little girl and closed her eyes. She'd never imagined herself with a family. For a moment she let herself feel how sweet it would be to have a girl like Sammy. To take care of her and love her and know the feeling would never have to end.

"If you had an extra bedroom, could I come and stay with you?"

Kim knew she ought to tell the little girl about her plans to move. But she just couldn't. "Nolan is your uncle, Sammy. Your mother's brother. He's your real family. I'm just a friend."

Sammy's bottom lip began to quiver and Kim felt awful.

"Of course, I'm a very good friend. And I do love you. You're a wonderful little girl. Should we put on some sleepy music then I'll tuck you in?"

Sammy had a collection of lullaby tapes. She selected one and Kim put the music on softly, then turned out the lights and shut the blinds.

"Don't go, Kim."

"I'll stay for a few minutes." She sat on the edge of the bed and brushed her fingers softly over Sammy's hair. The little girl looked up at her with big, trusting eyes and Kim's insides tumbled. Leaving this child was not going to be easy.

Ten minutes later, Sammy was asleep. Kim went downstairs and read the rest of the paper, concentrating on the articles Nolan had written—articles that highlighted the differences between the two of them.

Nolan knew about everything that was going on in Enchantment. He was totally connected to his community and devoted to its best interests. Whether the task involved starting a drop-in center for teens, helping students with a high school paper, or just doing his job covering local events, Nolan was always ready to step up to the plate.

Whereas she had never felt a part of any neighborhood she'd lived in. She avoided people. Until this fund-raising event, she'd never been involved in a community project of any sort.

If she needed any evidence that they were totally wrong for each other, those facts alone ought to be enough. Kim folded the newspaper and put it on the coffee table in the family room.

She was tired after the long day at work and dispirited about the situation with Sammy. Had she been wrong to let the little girl get so attached to her? Her plan had been to help Sammy and Nolan form a bond. But apparently that plan had backfired. A bond had been formed all right. But between herself and Sammy.

Kim yawned and checked the time. The news would be starting in about five minutes. She'd just picked up the remote control to turn on the television when she heard the front door open, then footsteps in the hall.

Nolan walked in carrying coffee in disposable cups and a brown paper bag. "I bought us a snack," he said, setting down the food on the counter. "How was your night with Sammy?"

His energy filled the air around her. Suddenly she was not nearly as tired as she had been moments ago. She joined him in the kitchen.

"Sammy and I had a nice evening." She decided not to tell him that his niece had asked to live with her. "How about you?"

"Those kids are amazing." He shook his head and grinned. "The stories they come up with." He passed her a cup then offered her the open bag of goodies. "Honey-dipped or Boston cream?"

She chose the less messy doughnut. Nolan scooped out the other, which he demolished in two bites over the kitchen sink.

She couldn't wait any longer. "I take it you received another letter?"

Using a napkin, he brushed doughnut crumbs and cream filling from his mouth. "Afraid so. It was in the mail this morning. Just like the others, it seems to have been written right after the paper was delivered.'' He dug a too-familiar-looking blue envelope from his pocket and dropped it on the counter.

Kim rinsed her hands then opened it. She read out loud.

"Dear Editor,
I'm very disappointed in you. I thought you cared about the people of Enchantment. How can you stand by and let this baby killer continue to spread her poison throughout our community? I urge you to do something before that ridiculous fund-raiser. This is your last chance."

At the end, she went back and read it all again, silently this time. Then again.

"The other letters weren't like this. This sounds *threatening…"*

Nolan took a sip of his coffee. "I agree. I had lunch with Miguel today and put him on the alert. Not much the cops can do, I'm afraid. Talk about a vague threat.''

They stared at each other across the kitchen counter. In his eyes she saw more than her own alarm. She saw a hint of fascination.

On some level, he was getting off on this, she realized. She could almost hear his journalistic instincts humming. Up until this point she'd considered Nolan her ally to the cause. But they weren't on the same side at all.

She wanted to protect Lydia.

Nolan wanted a story.

"This is great stuff as far as you're concerned, isn't it?" She waved the letter at him. "I'll bet you were hoping he would write again. That way you'd get an interesting newspaper article. You don't care about Lydia or the birth center."

"Kim." He sounded angry but calm. "I admit I'm challenged by the puzzle. And sure I want to get to the bottom of it, and I definitely will write an article if it's warranted. But I don't want anything bad to happen any more than you do."

Kim realized she'd been unfair. She was lashing out at Nolan, instead of the real cause of the problem. "Who is writing these damn letters?" She examined the envelope carefully, but as before it offered no clues.

"It's a long shot, but I checked out Mabel's brother. Richard's in Houston, a retired geologist, living with his wife of thirty-odd years. I don't think he can be behind any of this."

Her grandfather. Kim held back the impulse to ask for more information. At the moment she needed to concentrate on her grandmother and her reputation.

"The letters have all been hand delivered sometime between Wednesday evening and Thursday morning—right?"

He nodded.

"What if we sat outside your building and watched?"

"I've considered the same thing. And I even tried to do it for an hour or so yesterday afternoon. But there are just too many people, Kim. My office is on the main street of town. Several hundred people walk past every day. It would be nothing for one of them to drop the envelope into the mail slot without anyone noticing."

The shock of the latest letter was wearing off and Kim had begun to feel tired again. And discouraged. "You're right," she admitted. "But it makes me feel so helpless. I want some answers."

"Me, too. But you want to know something that interests me almost more than the question of who's behind these letters?" Nolan leaned over the counter, close enough for her to touch.

She saw the keen interest in his eyes and guessed she didn't want to know the answer to his question. But he didn't wait for an invitation to tell her.

"I want to know why you care." He touched her hand. "You've made a point of not getting involved with *anyone* in this town, yet you're going out of your way to protect a woman you've known for less than a year."

Kim backed away, beyond his reach. "I've already explained—"

"You've explained nothing. Don't give me that mumbo jumbo about all the good Lydia does for the community. Lots of people contribute to the welfare of Enchantment. Some people even think that I—the lowly newspaper editor you clearly have no interest in—help make this town a better place to live. But you don't care about me, do you?''

While he'd been talking, Nolan had circled the counter. He caught up to her, backing her against the oven. Now they stood inches apart, close enough to hear each other's breathing.

Kim didn't know what she wanted more. To flee this place and Nolan's too insightful questions. Or to kiss him.

''Tell me your connection to Lydia,'' Nolan said softly. He placed an arm on either side of her, gripping the counter, trapping her.

She cast her gaze downward, following the line of his legs to the floor. ''I want to go home.''

''Do you really?'' He touched her chin, lifted her face. The slow grin he gave her was filled with sexual invitation. ''I think maybe you want something else, Kim.''

Deliberately he lowered his mouth to hers, giving her a chance to turn away if she wanted. But of course she didn't. Couldn't. The second it took for their lips to meet seemed like an eternity. And like a starving animal, she welcomed his kiss, gripping his shoulders, pulling him closer.

But Nolan didn't cooperate. Every time she leaned forward, he moved back, keeping the distance between them constant. Close enough for their lips to touch, but not for a real, intense kiss.

His resistance frustrated her. Puzzled her. She stepped back with a sigh. "What's the matter?"

"I want the truth, Kim. And I want to hear it from you."

Allowing herself the luxury of holding his face between her two hands, Kim scrutinized him. The confident light in his eyes, the ironic twist of his mouth, the stubborn cast of his jaw.

Was it possible he'd figured out the truth? Or was he just trying to trick her?

"I don't know what you want from me."

His hands were on her waist now. He tightened his grip and his lips narrowed with a touch of bitterness. "You won't make this easy, will you? All right, let me ask you a direct question. Those earrings you got from your mother...are you aware they're part of a matching set?"

Kim gasped. How could he know? Of course, he'd seen her earrings on the counter, and Lydia always wore her pendant. Nolan was a very observant man. Way too observant.

"Are you going to answer my question?"

Why was he putting her through this? If he knew the truth, he could just say so. Why play these games? Did it give him some perverse feeling of power over her?

"Kim, please. Are the earrings part of a matching set?"

"Yes, damn it. They are."

"Thank you." He smiled grimly. "And, by my calculation, that makes Lydia somehow related to you. Is that right?''

Oh, he was a beast. He *did* know. But what he couldn't possibly understand was how hard this was for her. She'd told no one the truth. No one.

''God, you're making me squeeze out every word, aren't you? Just give me one more and we'll be finished. I need to hear it from you. Tell me, Kim, tell me. What relation is Lydia Kane to you? Lydia Kane is your...''

''Grandmother.'' She spat the word at him, unable to take the pressure anymore. Yet, as soon as she'd confessed the relationship, her resentment faded. She collapsed her head against Nolan's chest and felt his arms encircle her.

''Lydia Kane is my grandmother, Nolan. But you have to swear never to tell her.''

CHAPTER SIXTEEN

NOLAN COULD HARDLY BELIEVE Kim had finally admitted the truth. "You know, the way you keep a secret, you should join the CIA."

Kim barely smiled at his joke.

"Come on, let's sit down." He led her to the sofa. "I'm sorry I was hard on you." He sat next to her, his arm still wrapped around her shoulders. "I know you're fragile under that tough shell of yours. But I had to break through somehow, Kim."

"Why?"

Because I love you. He didn't think she was ready for the truth. "You've made a habit of holding people at arm's length. But it isn't healthy. You've got to let the odd person in now and then."

"Sammy…"

"Sammy's a child. You need friends, Kim. And you need family. Why not tell Lydia the truth about who you are?"

"You don't understand."

He could feel all the old tension returning to her slight body. Maybe he'd pushed a fraction too far.

"My mother's birth was Lydia's biggest mistake. Why would Lydia want to be reminded of that?"

"I'm sure Lydia considered getting pregnant at sixteen a mistake. But I doubt she'd look at your mother as a mistake. Or you."

Kim didn't even contemplate the possibility that he might be right. "The truth would embarrass her. And it would make her look bad to the board of directors. Trust me on this. Telling Lydia who I really am would be a disaster."

"How can you be sure? She might be delighted to discover she has an unexpected granddaughter."

"If she wanted to find us she could have. But she didn't."

"Are you sure she didn't try?"

Kim shook her head. "Please keep this secret of mine."

"Don't worry. It's not my secret to tell. But you might be happier—"

"No."

Well, that was definite. "Why did you come to Enchantment if you aren't willing to identify yourself to Lydia?"

"I wanted to get to know her. To see what kind of people I came from."

"And that's really enough for you?"

"It's more than I had before. Nolan, I'm so proud to have someone like Lydia as my grandmother. Seeing what she's accomplished with her life makes me believe I can do whatever I want with my own."

"That's a good thing. But what *do* you want?"

"I haven't figured that part out yet," she confessed.

He touched her hair. Wisps had worked free from the bun she wore. He located a pin and tugged it out. More strands fell free. He pulled at another pin and another. Soon Kim's blond hair tangled in sexy waves around her pretty face.

"Do you think you're going to find the answer in Denver?" Carefully he removed her glasses and set them on the table with the pins. He touched the side of her face, then let his hand slide down her long, slender neck.

"I—I don't know."

He tilted his head slightly to the right. Lowered his head an inch, then backed up. "Kim?"

She nodded, her eyes huge, her lips parted.

Again he lowered his head, but he didn't stop until his mouth was on hers. And this time, he didn't pull back when she ignited passionately in his arms.

He kissed her, over and over, all the time thinking, *What you want isn't in Denver, sweetheart. It's right here in Enchantment with me.*

FRIDAY NIGHT, Nolan ordered in pizza and Kim joined him and Sammy for a video. Later, once Sammy was in bed, they ended up kissing on Nolan's sofa. Kim knew she was behaving irresponsibly. She just couldn't help herself.

Saturday she baby-sat so Nolan could volunteer at the teen center. On Sunday, the three of them went skiing. Then on Monday, Nolan turned up, unexpectedly, to take Kim for lunch at the diner. They laughed about Sammy's antics on the hill that weekend. When Nolan's leg brushed against Kim's under the table, she didn't move away. On Tuesday, Nolan arrived at her office again at noon.

"How about we go to my place for lunch?" he asked.

She knew what he was really asking. With Sammy in school they'd have some real privacy for a change. But did she want to take advantage of it?

She didn't wonder long. "I'll get my coat."

Only when they stood in the entrance of his condo did she experience another moment of doubt. Making love with Nolan would definitely complicate their relationship.

Nolan opened the door for her. When they were inside, behind the locked door, he admitted that the situation wasn't ideal. "Kim, I would have liked to take you out for a beautiful meal. I would have enjoyed spending hours seducing you."

As he spoke, he shucked his jacket. Next off was her coat, then the pins in her hair, her glasses.

"But?" Despite her reservations, she felt breathless and…happy. Yes, she was truly happy for one of the few times in her life. Nolan was already working on the buttons of her cardigan. As his hands brushed over her breasts, her nipples tingled with pleasure.

"But Irene isn't well enough to baby-sit yet and so I figured this was our best option. Kim, we've got forty-five minutes." He pushed the cardigan off her shoulders and dropped it to the floor. "An hour if you're willing to be a little late."

He reached around her to unfasten the button of her skirt. Gravity did the rest.

"Oh, sweetheart," Nolan said, then dragged her to him for a kiss.

Kim was already desperate for him when their lips met. She'd been desperate for him since their first kiss and the passion had only built since then.

She kissed him as if she were trying to devour him, and he groaned with satisfaction. "You have no idea how many times I've dreamed of this moment." Nolan was ripping off his own shirt and unzipping his jeans. He couldn't shed his clothing fast enough for Kim. His body was strong, lean and everything she wanted at that moment.

Only forty-five minutes. She didn't see how it could possibly be long enough. They held hands and laughed as they raced up the stairs. For a moment Kim was touched to see how tidy his room was…he'd even made the bed that morning.

For her.

"You're so beautiful."

She was glad he thought so. They tumbled onto the bed, disposing of the last barriers of cotton and lace that stood between them. And half an hour later, Kim realized that an hour with Nolan wouldn't be enough, nor would a day or a week or a year.

I love him.

Her efforts to remain detached hadn't worked. She was as involved with this man as a woman could be.

"TONI, COULD YOU BRING the morning mail into my office please?" It was Thursday and Nolan had been so busy, he'd forgotten about the possibility of another letter. The weekly edition had come out yesterday morning. According to the established pattern, that meant he could expect another blue envelope today.

He wasn't sure if he wanted one, or not.

Kim would be upset, especially since the fundraiser was one week away. And he didn't want her upset. They had plans for another lunchtime rendezvous at his place today.

But the journalist in him couldn't help but hope that this time he'd find the clue that would allow him to unravel this whole mess. He laughed at himself, knowing part of his motivation was to be a hero to Kim. But what if he discovered that the sender of the letters had a legitimate grievance against Lydia?

He wouldn't be her hero then.

"Not much today," Toni said, tossing a small bundle into his in box.

"Thanks, Toni." Nolan's heart pounded heavily as he saw a blue envelope. Covering it was another interesting piece of mail. A letter-size envelope with the paper's address printed in childlike block letters.

He set aside the blue envelope and opened the other

first. The single sheet of paper contained a message from a kid, all right.

> *Dear Editor,*
> *Can you help me please? I want to live with Kim.*
> *Please let me live with Kim.*
> *Sammy*

Nolan sank back into his chair. Damn, what a kid. There wasn't a spelling mistake anywhere. She'd copied the address correctly, even known to put a stamp on the right-hand corner. Of course, he'd shown her how to do all that when he'd helped her write to her grandmother.

He felt oddly proud of her, even as a dull pain crept like fog through his body.

He knew he'd made mistakes with his niece. Knew, too, that her connection to Kim was much more solid than the one she had with him. But he'd thought he'd been doing okay. Since the skiing he'd actually hoped there might be light at the end of the tunnel.

But obviously Sammy didn't think so. She was *really* unhappy with him. She wanted to live with Kim, which wouldn't be a bad idea, if he could be included in the package.

Could he?

Of course, he *could.* He, alone, couldn't stop Kim from returning to Denver. But maybe he and Sammy, together...

Nolan rubbed his suddenly-damp palms against his

jeans. He loved Kim, but they hadn't known each other all that long. Shouldn't he wait a month or two before taking such a drastic step?

Right away he knew the answer. He didn't have a month. All he had was one week until she tendered her resignation at The Birth Place. If he waited, he could lose her. He had to act fast. He had to act *now*.

Nolan checked the time and wondered if he could drive to Taos and back before lunch. Then he shoved both letters into his jacket pocket and told Toni to take care of business until he returned.

He grinned on his way out the door. Perhaps the next time he saw Toni he'd have an announcement to make. And Kim would have something to wear on the fourth finger of her left hand.

AT NOON Kim checked the bottom of Nolan's mailbox and found the key he'd told her about. She unlocked his front door, wondering why he'd asked her to meet him here this time instead of picking her up at her office as usual.

The warm air welcomed her as she stomped snow from her shoes. She closed the door behind her, then realized she could hear music.

"Nolan?"

No reply, even though his Explorer had been parked out front. She hung her jacket in the closet and left her damp shoes to dry on the rubber mat by the door. With stockinged feet, she padded through the front room to the kitchen. In the arched opening between kitchen and family room, she paused. What was that she smelled? Flowers?

At the foot of the stairs she saw them. Red roses, still in bud, strewn in a path on the floor. She smiled.

Nolan had a romantic streak. Who'd have guessed?

She collected the flowers as she traveled up the stairs, careful not to prick her fingers on the thorns. She had a bundle of at least two dozen by the time she reached the open bedroom door.

Nolan was sitting on the bed in his jeans and bare feet. He held out his hands, and she dropped the flowers in a heap on the floor to join him.

"What's up?"

"I wanted to surprise you." He reached over to the bedside table where two glasses of fizzing champagne were poured and waiting.

Kim felt the first stirring of concern. "Nolan, I can't drink at noon. I won't be able to concentrate when I go back to work."

"Would that be so terrible?" He pressed one glass into her hand, then tapped his flute to hers. "To us, Kim. Are you willing to drink to that?"

Maybe one sip. She allowed herself that much. Nolan smiled, then pressed his lips to hers. She wrapped her free arm around his neck. Did he have any idea how much she treasured these illicit meetings of theirs? She could barely sleep at night for remembering every tiny detail and exquisite pleasure they shared together. She didn't need champagne to get high. All she needed was to make love to him.

But he was pulling back.

"Just one second, okay, Kim? There's something I need to ask you."

She'd thought there was something different about him. Now she realized he was nervous. *Of course, it was Thursday....*

But this was something else. Something personal. The first thought to hit her was *he's bored with me.* But a man didn't buy roses and champagne for a woman he was planning to dump.

A crazy possibility occurred to her, but she knew she couldn't be right. She knew it until she saw him put his hand behind his back, then bring out a small velvet box.

"Kim, will you marry me?"

In panic, she took another sip of champagne, then a gulp. He was waiting for an answer. But she couldn't believe she'd heard him right.

"Kim? I love you. You know that, right?"

Oh, and she loved him. But marriage. She couldn't. Not if it meant staying in Enchantment and, of course, with his business, it would.

Except...wouldn't it be lovely if she *could* stay? For a moment she saw a life for herself that was impossibly happy and beautiful.

"Nolan, we haven't known each other very long."

He grasped her wrist and held on tightly. "I know, Kim. But it's been long enough for me to realize what I want. And that's you."

His sincerity was almost her undoing. She couldn't

believe he would really go to all this effort for *her*. The flowers, the champagne…the ring.

She gasped as he opened the box to show her. "Oh, it's so beautiful."

"Put it on, Kim…" He took the glass flute from her hand and set it on the bedside table. Then he kissed her, gently, as if he truly *cherished* her. Oh, she wanted to give in to this exquisite moment. She wanted to say yes and to put on the ring and to make love with this man. She let him pull her close and hold her to his chest as he fell back onto the bed. Their legs tangled, as he kissed her on the mouth, on the neck, behind her ear.

"Say yes, sweetheart," he pleaded, the enticing warmth of his breath on her skin.

She closed her eyes. She wanted him so badly…and that scared her. She rolled away from him, then realized she was crushing his jacket. As she shifted her weight to pull it out from under herself, she saw the corner of an envelope in the breast pocket. Her gaze flashed back to him. "Why didn't you tell me?"

Nolan shook his head. "I had other things on my mind."

Other things like her. Excitement swirled with fear as she realized she wanted to accept his proposal. Putting off the dizzying temptation, she pulled the envelope from his pocket.

"Can I read it?"

"Go ahead."

"But—what's this?"

She'd pulled out the envelope from his niece at the same time. Nolan sighed. Those damn letters. He should have left them in the office. He'd been sure Kim had been about to accept his proposal until she'd been distracted by them. "Go ahead and read them both."

He stepped over the pile of roses in order to turn on the lights. Kim was on the bed, her skirt high on her thighs, her cardigan twisted and her hair unruly. They should be making love right now, but she was focused on Sammy's simple letter.

"Oh, the poor girl." She pressed the sheet of paper to her chest. "The other day she asked me about letters to the editor. I can't believe she actually wrote this on her own."

"Yeah. She's an amazing kid all right." He stayed near the doorway, not trusting himself to get any closer to Kim. He wasn't sure if he wanted to strangle her or try to kiss her again. Neither option seemed particularly smart at the moment.

A light of comprehension sparked in Kim's eyes. "Is this why you asked me…"

"No," he said quickly. But when she nodded and slowly refolded the letter, he knew she didn't believe him. And he realized his small window of opportunity was gone. She thought he was proposing to make Sammy happy. To make his life easier. She wasn't going to say yes.

As his excitement cratered, it occurred to him that

she might be making the smart choice. They *hadn't* known each other very long. If he didn't have Sammy, would he have been willing to propose marriage so soon?

The ache in his chest gave him the answer. Yes, he would have.

She had the blue envelope in her hand now. "It isn't opened."

He shrugged. As he'd already said, he'd had other matters on his mind. He put the velvet box in a drawer and imagined the embarrassment of having to take it back. What a fool he'd been to think she might consider scrapping her precious plans and staying in Enchantment with him and Sam.

Eyes on the piece of blue stationery, Kim edged off the bed, tugging on her hemline. He turned his head deliberately. He wished she could have been half as interested in his proposal as she was in that damn letter. She read aloud.

"You've left me no choice. The fund-raiser is in one week. I guess I'll have to take care of Lydia Kane on my own—"

"Oh, no! This is scary."

Despite his bruised ego—that's what the tender aching in his chest had to be—Nolan shared her concern. The first two letters had been rantings. The third had been somewhat threatening, though not to Lydia personally. But this—

He held out his hand to see the letter for himself and swore. "I know you didn't want to scare Lydia, but I don't think we have a choice anymore."

She looked at him solemnly, then nodded. "You're right. I'll go speak to her right now."

"And I'll talk to Miguel again. He'll want this letter, eventually, but maybe you should take it with you when you see Lydia. Otherwise, she might not take the threat seriously."

Kim took the piece of paper from his fingers, without meeting his gaze. "Thanks, Nolan."

She didn't say anything about his proposal. Just turned and left. Nolan sat on his bed and stared into space for a good half an hour before he finally picked up the phone and called the police station.

CHAPTER SEVENTEEN

KIM PASSED Parker's open door purposefully, merely nodding as he called out a greeting. At Lydia's office, she paused. Lydia sat behind her desk, writing furiously. At Kim's knock, she called out a pleasant "Come in, please."

Just the sight of her grandmother made Kim feel dangerously emotional. She pretended to admire a collage of baby pictures on one of the walls as she struggled to control the unexpected urge to cry. She hadn't had time to think over Nolan's proposal and what she had lost by walking out on him this afternoon.

Lydia's safety was more important. She would deal with the rest later.

Swiveling, she forced a polite smile. "Lydia, I'm sorry to disturb you, but something important has come up."

"Anytime, Kim. You know that."

Lydia dropped her pen and waved Kim into a chair. She had on her long gray dress today, and as always, the rose-colored pendant.

"You like my necklace? I've seen you notice it

before. Here.'' Lydia pulled the chain over her head.
"Take a closer look."

Kim wanted to touch the pendant so badly she was
almost afraid to give in to the need. But she couldn't
be rude to Lydia. "It is beautiful." She knew she
shouldn't, but she stroked the rose onyx, almost wor-
shipfully.

As she handed it back, she slipped in a quick in-
quiry. "Where did you get it?" As soon as the question had been uttered, Kim felt the heat rise in her
cheeks.

"It's a family heirloom. The set was handed down
to me from my mother when she passed away."

"Set?" Kim was amazed at the artful innocence in
her voice.

"Yes, there are matching earrings, but I don't own
them anymore."

A hint of a question showed in Lydia's wise, silver
eyes, and Kim realized she'd better change the subject.

"First let me tell you the good news," she said,
forcing animation into her voice. "I received a reply
from your granddaughter this morning. It seems
Devon will be coming to the fund-raiser after all."

"That *is* good news. Now, something tells me the
other matter you want to discuss won't be so pleasant."

"It isn't." Kim had no idea how to broach the subject of the anonymous letters. She didn't want to add

to Lydia's burden. But the older woman had to be forewarned.

"For about five weeks, Nolan McKinnon has been receiving some strange mail at the *Arroyo County Bulletin*. He showed the letters to me, and we both thought they were the work of some poor, sick individual. But the tone of the letters is becoming more threatening and we decided we'd better tell you about them. Here's the most recent one."

Kim passed over the blue envelope. Lydia's complexion turned quite pale.

"I know," Kim said, "it's so crazy. Let me get you some water." Kim jumped out of her seat to go to the water cooler. She came back with a tumbler and handed it to the midwife. Lydia was still staring at the letter, mesmerized.

"I wonder what he means when he says he intends to take care of the problem?" she mused.

"No idea," Kim admitted. "But I do think you should be careful. Who knows what crazy things this guy is capable of?"

It occurred to her, suddenly, that Lydia didn't seem all that shocked. "These letters aren't a total surprise to you, are they?"

For a moment Lydia regarded her cautiously. Then she gave a slight nod. "Quite right, Kim. I'm not at all surprised. Let me show you why."

From a pocket in her dress she pulled out a small brass key then used it to unlock the third drawer of her desk. She removed a packet of letters. Kim recognized the stationery.

"You've been receiving them, too."

"I have. The letters—four in total—have all been hand delivered to the center. Feel free to read them."

As Lydia drank her water, Kim leafed through the pile of correspondence. She noted the familiar handwriting, the lack of a signature line. As she skimmed the content, one phrase kept popping up: baby killer.

"Whoever is writing these nasty things wants me to give up my career at the center," Lydia said calmly. "Well, I won't. I've already had to resign my position on the board. And that's been difficult enough to do."

"Have you shown these to anyone?" Kim stacked them back into a neat pile.

"No."

Kim gathered her nerve. "Do you have any idea why anyone would call you a baby killer?"

For the first time, Lydia showed a trace of weakness as her bottom lip trembled. "No. Unless they're referring to Steve and Mary's baby."

"But that wasn't your fault," Kim reminded her firmly. "Look, it's just not right for someone to terrorize you like this. I think we should go to the police."

"Oh, I don't want to bother them. I can't believe I'm in any real danger."

"We can't take that chance. Come on, Lydia. Let's do it now."

The older woman hesitated.

"Please, Lydia." She realized Lydia would never act out of concern for her own well-being. But maybe for The Birth Place. "You know the fund-raiser is coming up. Bad publicity could kill the donations."

Lydia stroked her pendant with her thumb. After a few seconds, she nodded. "Maybe you're right, Kim. I *will* take those letters to the police. Are you sure you don't mind coming with me?"

THE POLICE STATION was on Paseo de Sierra, just down from Nolan's office. Kim made a determined effort not to glance at the gold lettering on the *Arroyo County Bulletin* window as she drove past searching for a parking space.

"There's a spot," Lydia directed. She was sitting impossibly erect in the front seat of Kim's Camry. Perched carefully on her lap was her tapestry bag containing the letters.

Kim snagged the prime parking space, right in front of the civic complex to which the police station was attached. Inside, they were directed to Sergeant Miguel Eiden, a black-haired cop in his early-thirties. Kim had seen the striking-looking man on the streets, but had never met him.

Lydia had, though, and she took care of introductions.

"What seems to be the problem, ladies?" Having waited for them both to take a seat in the small, utilitarian office, Miguel pulled out a chair for himself.

"This." Lydia dropped the package of letters in front of him, then sat patiently while he leafed through them.

"Very interesting," he said when he was done. "Nolan's been getting similar letters at the *Bulletin*. Do you by chance remember when you received these?"

"I copied the dates on the back of the envelopes."

Miguel smiled. "That'll help."

Kim felt compelled to add, "And here's the latest letter sent to the *Bulletin*. Nolan received it just today."

Miguel scanned the short message. "Yeah, he called about an hour ago and told me the gist of it."

"Does the guy sound dangerous to you?" Kim asked, anxiously.

"It's always hard to say with quacks like this. I'm glad you've brought this to our attention. If you don't mind, we'll keep these and start a file. In the meantime," he turned to Lydia, "it would be wise for you to take more precautions than usual." He gave her a list of situations she should avoid, then assured her he would keep an eye on The Birth Place and her home.

"What we usually see in these cases is that the person writing the letters eventually loses interest. We'll hope that's what happens this time, too."

KIM DROVE LYDIA BACK to the birth center, then followed her home, waiting until her grandmother was safely inside before driving off. It was now five minutes to six, time to head to Nolan's to baby-sit. His condo was only a short drive away and once there she sat in her car for long moments regarding the familiar front door.

It was hard not to compare the way she felt right now with her emotions as she'd driven up to this address at noon today. She'd been so looking forward to her hour with Nolan, never guessing this was the day their relationship would go up in smoke.

Kim turned off the ignition and pocketed her keys as she made her way up the sidewalk. The door opened when she was still several feet away. He stepped out on the landing and closed the door behind him.

He had on the same jeans and shirt as earlier, but his eyes looked about ten years older, and his mouth was set in a grim line. Kim paused, remembering how excited and happy he'd seemed just hours ago. She hurt, badly, knowing he'd never look at her that way again.

"I'm assuming you still need me to baby-sit tonight?"

The bones in Nolan's jaw stood out in sharp relief as he regarded her. After a few seconds, he rubbed his chin, then shook his head. "I'm in the process of finding another baby-sitter."

"But tonight?"

"That's my problem, isn't it?"

He wasn't looking at her, but past her, and Kim didn't like the way that made her feel. But what right did she have to complain? Their relationship was over. It had been inevitable.

"I gave the letter to Miguel Eiden."

"Yeah. He called and told me."

She decided Nolan deserved to know the rest. "Lydia has also been receiving threatening letters at the center."

For the first time, Nolan focused on her. "Has she told anyone?"

"Just me. We took them to the police station, too, but I don't think there's much they can do."

"At least Lydia's on her guard."

"Yes. And I've convinced her to phone me if she needs to go out for a late-night delivery. I don't want her traveling alone after dark."

Nolan frowned. "It might not be smart for you to be driving around after dark, either. Maybe you should tell her to phone *me*."

"What about Sammy? You can't just leave her to provide an escort for Lydia."

"Right. Sammy." Nolan seemed annoyed at himself for forgetting.

Now that they were on the topic, though, Kim couldn't stop herself from asking, "Can I say hi to her?"

Nolan's expression grew hard again. "I'm not sure that's a good idea given that you're only in town for another couple of weeks. I've always found that a clean break is best."

Maybe so. But was he thinking of Sammy's best interests? Or his own?

WELL, THAT PROVED IT, Nolan thought, slipping back inside his house. The woman had a mineral deposit in the place where her heart ought to be. He couldn't believe she'd shown up at his door, only hours after ignoring his marriage proposal.

"Was that Kim?"

Sammy appeared, a little waif in red overalls and a white shirt. He was reminded of her letter to the editor and his sense of failure deepened. What was he going to do with her? Especially now that Kim wasn't a member of his backup team. Actually Kim hadn't just been a member. She'd *been* his backup team. He couldn't cope without her.

But he had to.

"Kim can't baby-sit tonight, Sam."

Her face began to crumble. Tears would be next. Nolan thought fast.

"You know what?" He bent to her level. "You're a member of a newspaper family now. I think it's time you learned how to put a paper together. Why don't you come to the office with me?"

He caught her attention with the offer.

"You'll show me how to make a real newspaper?"

He nodded. "The high school kids do it all the time. If you want, we could print off a paper just for you. You could hand it out to your friends at school. Do you have any drawings here?"

Sammy nodded. "I have a bunch of stuff in my backpack. Stuff I made at school." She dipped her head shyly. "I was supposed to give it to you."

Nolan made another mental note: *Check backpack after she gets home from school.* "That sounds just fine, Sam. Grab your backpack and we'll get going." Another great idea occurred to him. "We'll order pizza delivered to the office for dinner."

"Sweet!"

To Nolan's surprise, the evening went well. The high school kids were great with Sammy. They helped her write an "editorial" for her paper and one of the guys drew her a comic strip.

Best was the expression of awe on Sammy's face when she held the final product in her hand. "I made a real newspaper, Uncle Nolan."

"That's right. You can show your friends tomorrow." He hustled the high school students out about an hour earlier than normal, but still Sammy was exhausted by the time they reached home.

He helped her brush her teeth and, once she was in pajamas, returned to her room to tuck her in.

"I got all the black ink off my hands." She held up her palms for him to inspect.

"Looks good, but let me check your face. You had some ink on that, too." But she'd scrubbed it clean. Looking at his niece, Nolan felt the flooding sensation he'd experienced before. God, but she was so adorable.

"Why are you looking at me like that?"

"'Cause you're such a cutie."

"Do I look like my mom?"

Nolan considered the question. When he'd first taken Sammy in, all he'd seen were the similarities to his sister and brother-in-law. Now, none of them seemed as obvious. "You have some of your mom in you. And some of your dad, too. But mostly you just look like Sammy to me. And you know what?" He drew her covers up to her chin.

"What?"

"That's a good thing." He kissed her forehead. "Want a story?"

She yawned, then nodded. Watching her, Nolan realized how exhausted he was, too.

"How about if I just tell you one instead of reading a book?" He cast his memory back to his childhood. "Once upon a time there was a magical raspberry patch in the middle of a deep, dark forest."

"Uncle Nolan!" Sammy sprang up in her bed. "How do you know that story?"

"Your mother told it to me. She was always making up tales when we were kids."

Sammy's eyes were huge. "I thought they were in a book. But I couldn't find it."

Was that why she'd been plowing through the school library, as well as her own collection? Nolan pressed a hand to his forehead and blinked rapidly. He'd been so worried she was becoming neurotic or something. And all the poor kid had been doing was trying to find her mother's stories.

"You're in luck, Sam, because I think I've got most of them memorized." At least he hoped he did. Mary must have told them to him a hundred times when they were little.

Sammy snuggled back down next to him. "Tell me the one about..."

NOLAN MANAGED to make it through the tale with only a few corrections from a sleepy Sammy. By the time he announced, "And that is the very end of the story...until tomorrow," which was the way Mary had always ended for the night, Sammy was fast asleep.

Nolan watched her for a while. "Samantha Lynn," he whispered, "you *are* a real beauty." He brushed a wisp of hair off her forehead, then pressed another kiss in its place.

Heavy emotion—Kim had been right, it was love— welled inside him again. He thought back on his life with his sister. She'd been five years his senior and when they were little, she'd been a mother hen. Later, they'd become pals. Like Sammy, they'd loved skiing, been real daredevils, too.

It wasn't until their mother became sick that the trouble started. Mary had been angry at him for not spending more time at the nursing home. Now he was prepared to admit she'd been right.

So his mom had given him a hard time growing up. She'd still been his mother. He should have given more back to her. And mended fences with Mary before it had been too late.

Now he could see only one way to make up for his mistakes. And his generous sister had given it to him. She'd placed her child in his care and he was suddenly so very, very grateful that she had.

CHAPTER EIGHTEEN

WHEN SHE WAS GROWING UP, Kim had found it impossible to sleep the first few nights in a new foster home. She was reminded of those long, lonely hours on Thursday evening as she lay in her bed and gazed out at the moon. At age six she'd had conversations with the moon, even pretending that the moon was her mother.

A silly little game, but she'd taken real comfort from it. Comfort she couldn't find tonight, no matter how many cups of tea she brewed, books she tried to read, television programs she attempted to lose herself in.

All she could think about was Nolan. The contrast between his expression when he'd been proposing to her, and the hardness in his eyes when she'd stopped by to see if he wanted her to baby-sit.

He hated her now. And she, who tried not to care what anyone thought about her, cared about that.

Kim finally found relief with the morning light. She dozed for an hour before dawn, then got up to take a shower and get ready for work.

She decided to put Nolan out of her mind. He was a completed chapter, like all the foster families she'd left behind. For her last days in Enchantment she would focus on keeping Lydia safe and ensuring the fund-raiser was a big success. To her great chagrin, she realized that these were two goals she could no longer attain without help.

Usually she entered the birth center through the back door, going past the birthing rooms and straight to the administrative area. Today she came in the main entrance. Trish was already at the reception desk, adding fresh water to a vase of daisies.

"Morning, Kim."

Her smile seemed strained, and Kim couldn't blame her. She'd spurned many kind offers from Trish in the time she'd worked here.

"Trish, I need to speak to as many members of our staff as possible today at noon. Do you think you could organize a meeting for me?"

The middle-aged woman ran a hand over her Venice snow globe. "I'd be glad to, Kim."

"Twelve o'clock, upstairs in the storage area." She started down the hall toward administration, then turned back. "Oh—and keep this from Lydia. I don't want her at the meeting." She'd only fuss and insist all the trouble wasn't necessary.

But Kim was very afraid that it was.

KIM SLIPPED UPSTAIRS five minutes before twelve. She'd prepared handouts for everyone and had a floor plan of the Legion Hall mapped out on a large chart that she taped to the wall. As people filed upstairs, she kept her gaze lowered on her pages. At twelve, sharp, she glanced up.

Parker was there, leaning an elbow against a metal file cabinet. Trish and Jessica from the front office had pulled up a couple of metal chairs along with several of the midwives, including Katherine Collins and Gina Vaughn. Even Celia Brice, sitting cross-legged on the floor, had made it.

"Thank you for coming." She walked to the door and closed it firmly, then returned to her place next to the wall where she'd taped her drawing. "As you all know, the Mother and Child Reunion is scheduled to take place next Thursday evening."

Everyone nodded.

"All the plans have been made and everything is in order." She paused, uncertain whether she'd heard someone from the back mutter "Of course," after her sentence. She cleared her throat. "Except for one potential difficulty."

Eyebrows raised at this. There was no doubt she had their attention.

"For the past five weeks someone has been sending threatening letters to Lydia Kane." As she made the announcement, Kim watched faces sharply, observing surprised and shocked expressions. Nolan had wondered if the person sending the missives might be a birth center employee. Judging from the reactions she saw today, Kim didn't think so.

She described the general nature of the letters and

explained how she and Lydia had gone to the police station last night.

"Good for you, Kim," Parker commented. "That was the smart thing to do."

Kim felt a pang of guilt. Parker was always quick to compliment his employees. But would he be so pleased with her if he knew she intended to tender her resignation next Friday? Though she wasn't the most popular of employees, finding a replacement with the right qualifications wouldn't be easy for her boss.

"Unfortunately, the police aren't able to do that much to help," she said. "They're increasing patrols around here and Lydia's home and I intend to ask them to watch the Legion closely on the night of our event."

Heads nodded, in concurrence with her plan.

"However, you know the size of our police force. At best we can expect to have one officer doing sporadic patrols. That's why it's up to all of us to be extra vigilant in the days to come, leading up to the fund-raiser. Here's a list of precautions I'd like you all to take. As for the night of the fund-raiser, we'll need to take turns monitoring the various entrance points of the Legion Hall..."

MUNCHING ON A PITA POCKET stuffed with veggies and cream cheese, Lydia strolled down the hallway, heading for the photocopier in the administrative wing. Her thoughts were focused on the young expectant mother she'd met with that morning. The poor child was only seventeen. Her plight brought back so many memories.

Lydia inserted a page into the copier, then pressed the green button. Usually at lunchtime a group assembled around the coffeemaker and microwave in here. Where was everyone?

Gathering her papers, Lydia checked Parker's office, then Kim's. Both were empty. She walked down the corridor that led to the birthing rooms, then back past her own office and the exam rooms. Finally at the stairwell, she heard the murmur of voices.

She trod up the stairs lightly, following the sound of conversation to one of the storage rooms. Peering in the small glass panel at the top of the door, she saw that the staff were crowded into the room, all listening to…Kim Sherman.

Imagine that. They must be discussing final preparations for the fund-raiser.

Lydia smiled to herself with satisfaction. The thorny accountant was finally learning to work as a member of a team. Her little plan had worked.

KIM SPENT HER WEEKEND reviewing every detail of the fund-raiser. At the staff meeting, Celia Brice had browbeaten her, in a very charming manner, into appointing a decorating committee. The five women met at the Sunflower Café for smoothies and wraps on Sunday—and as much as Kim had fought against sharing responsibility, she had to admit the four other women came up with some great ideas. And the extra hands would definitely be helpful on Thursday when they would have only a few hours to prepare the hall for the event.

At the office on Monday, Kim immersed herself in work. She wanted everything in order when she departed. During her lunch hour, she composed a letter of resignation, which she sealed in an envelope and placed in the top drawer of her desk, all ready for the morning after the fund-raiser.

She'd received a reply to one of her queries and had a job interview booked in Denver for the first week of April.

All this progress should have brought her piece of mind, but Kim couldn't stop thinking about Sammy…and Nolan. She did her best not to recall the magical lunch hours she and Nolan had spent together in his bed. Or the fun all three of them had experienced on the ski hills. Most of all she tried not to remember the expression on Nolan's face when he'd presented her with that ring.

Oh, God. For someone who was trying not to remember, she was doing a pretty pathetic job of it. Kim pressed her hands against her eyes, wishing there was some way to clear the mental screen inside her head.

Coffee. Maybe coffee would help. Kim grabbed her mug, then headed for the pot out by the photocopier. On her way back, she encountered Mitchell Dixon, a large envelope in his hand.

''Have you seen Trish?'' he asked.

"Isn't she at reception?"

"I didn't see her."

"Well, she won't be back here by Lydia's office. Come with me, I'll help you find her."

The older man hung back. "I don't want to trouble you."

"It isn't any trouble, Mitchell. She was probably in the back room updating charts when you walked in and you missed her." She took his arm and led him to reception. Sure enough Trish stood behind the counter, jotting down a new appointment.

Kim left Mitchell waiting to attract Trish's attention, then headed back to her office. On the way, she spotted a man and a little girl. It was Nolan and Sammy. She checked her watch. Monday at four. Of course, they were waiting for Sammy's appointment with Celia.

Kim tried to hurry past without being noticed.

"Kim!"

Sammy's delighted voice compelled her to stop. Carefully balancing her mug of coffee, Kim gave the little girl a one-armed hug. "How are you doing, sweetie?"

"Pretty good. I made a newspaper with Uncle Nolan. Would you like a copy?"

"She insists on carrying them in her backpack and distributing them to everyone she knows." Nolan sounded proud and apologetic at the same time.

Kim exclaimed over Sammy's newspaper. What really impressed her though, was Sammy herself. The little girl seemed more animated today. And she was much more open with her uncle, including him in her conversation and even taking his hand when Celia came down the stairs to call them up.

"Bye, Kim!" The little girl turned to wave.

"Bye, Sammy!" She could hardly get out the words as she watched the two of them walk away. This might be the last she saw of the little girl. The very idea made her long to cry again—a feeling she'd been having all too often these past few weeks.

She meant to return to her office, but was still there when Nolan came down the stairs about three minutes later. He stopped abruptly when he saw her.

"What is it, Kim?"

His expression was guarded, but maybe not quite as hard as the last time she'd seen him.

"Sorry, I was just…that is, I'm amazed by how well Sammy is doing. Congratulations, Nolan. You really must be doing a good job with her."

"Well, thanks." He glanced toward the exit, and she was afraid he would just keep walking. But then he put a casual hand on the wall and added, "We had a bit of a breakthrough the other day. I found out why she's been so obsessed with books."

"Really?"

He nodded. "She was trying to find the stories her mom used to tell her. Only they weren't in any book. They were Mary's. She made them up when we were kids."

"Oh, good heavens. Do you remember any of them?"

"Mostly. And the details I forget, Sammy fills in."

"That's wonderful, Nolan." She couldn't think of anything else to say, but still she stood there, feeling like an idiot because all she really wanted was to be with him and that was impossible.

Nolan was the one who turned away first. "Good luck with the fund-raiser Thursday night."

"Will you be there?" She'd received his RSVP, but she had to ask anyway.

"You bet. I'll be covering the event for the *Bulletin*. I'll be sure to give you a nice write-up."

Before she could thank him, he was gone.

NOLAN COULDN'T CLING to his wounded-pride theory any longer. Seeing Kim again, even for those short minutes, had proved that much.

He still loved her. God, how he loved her. Thanks to Sammy, he had finally remembered what it felt like to love another human being so much that you cared for them more than yourself.

At one time he'd felt that way about his dad and his sister, too. Maybe he'd even had those feelings for his mother, if he'd let himself admit it. Since that big fight he and Mary had at their mother's funeral, he'd blocked a lot of this out.

But now his emotions had returned with a vengeance. All due to one little six-year-old girl.

And a woman he knew he'd never replace. For all

her apparent indifference, Kim was the woman he loved. And in her eyes, he was sure he'd seen reason to hope. Her heart wasn't built of stone. It was encased in ice. And ice would melt if the temperature was high enough.

WEDNESDAY MORNING Nolan poured a mixture of oat circles, rice crisps and corn bran into a bowl and added milk.

"Here you go, Sam." He added a glass of juice with a multivitamin on the side.

"Thanks, Uncle Nolan." Sammy squirmed up on the stool, then spread out the morning paper so she could read while she ate.

What a picture she made, Nolan thought proudly, watching the six-year-old focus on the weekly paper that had been delivered that morning. His gut tightened as she flipped impatiently to the editorial page. Deliberately he turned back to the counter and began arranging slices of apple over the peanut-butter layer he'd already spread on whole-wheat bread. Inspiration struck him.

"Say, Sam, would you like mini-marshmallows in your sandwich today?"

She glanced up from the paper. "Hmm. Marshmallows are good. But maybe put them on the side, please."

"No problem." He wrapped the sandwich and a handful of marshmallows into separate packages, added a container of yogurt and there it was. Lunch. He was getting pretty good at this, he had to admit.

He checked Sammy's progress with the paper, then couldn't stop himself from asking, "See anything interesting in there today, Sam?"

Just at that moment her little finger pointed at the first letter to the editor. He watched her eyes open big and round.

"Uncle Nolan!"

"What?" With nonchalance, he moved closer.

"My letter. My letter's in your newspaper."

And there it was, just as he'd received it:

Dear Editor,
Can you help me please? I want to live with Kim.
Please let me live with Kim.
Sammy

"Well, look at that. That's some letter, Sam. Can you read me the editor's answer?"

The little girl studied the words.

"Dear Sammy,
Thank you for your letter."

She smiled a little, then carried on.

"I'm sorry you can't live with Kim. But I love you, Sammy. Can you give me another try? I promise to work really hard to make a nice home for you."

She frowned, then glanced up at him. "It's signed by the editor."

"That's right. I'm the editor, Sam. You knew that, right?"

She shook her head no, her eyes wide. "I thought the editor was like Dear Abby. My mom used to read Dear Abby all the time."

Nolan put a hand over his smile. "Well, the editor of the *Arroyo County Bulletin* is me, Sam."

"Oh." She glanced back at the paper. He watched as she read his letter over again. Finally she smiled shyly. "You want me to keep living here with you?"

"I really do, Sam. I love you, Samantha Lynn."

Her bottom lip trembled. "I love you, too."

The words were powerful. He lifted her out of her chair and brought her to him for a big hug. It amazed him that after all she'd been through, she could be so generous. But then, maybe she sensed the same thing that he did.

They were family. They belonged together.

AT TEN MINUTES AFTER TWELVE, Kim pulled out a sandwich and the newspaper she'd brought from home. She unwrapped the cheese bun she'd stuffed with cranberry chutney, lettuce and smoked turkey, then folded the paper in half to make it easier to read. A leisurely perusal of the *Arroyo County Bulletin* had once been a highlight of her week.

Now, however, it was pure torture. She hadn't made it halfway through the first article, commemorating the death of a local octogenarian, before tears began to gather.

Not for the woman who had passed away, but for the man who'd written the article. Nolan had a way with words that made her feel he was in the room talking to her. His intelligence, his good humor and basic decency were woven into his stories along with facts and interview quotes.

In a way, she'd fallen in love with him before she'd even met him. Now, reading his words made her long for his company.

Kim unfolded the paper and flipped to another page. Out of habit, her gaze dropped to the letters to the editor section. As she scanned the assorted contributions, on the alert for anything touching the subject of Lydia or the birth center, her attention was caught by a short, simple letter.

I want to live with Kim. She put a hand to her heart. Nolan had printed Sammy's letter. How like him not to worry about how he would look to the community at large.

Next, she read his response to Sammy's letter, and now the tears flooded her eyes. They were going to make it work, Sammy and Nolan, she just knew they were. That had been her goal from the beginning—to help them form a bond.

But now that she'd been successful, why did she feel so miserable?

CHAPTER NINETEEN

THE MORNING OF THE FUND-RAISER, Trish Linden was almost as keyed up as Kim. Together they fussed over the particulars for the evening. While Kim checked in with the caterers and briefed the various speakers on their responsibilities, Trish kept rushing into her office with details she was certain Kim would have forgotten.

"Flowers!" she exclaimed during one of these impromptu visits. "Kim, did you remember to order flowers?"

"Of course." Kim ticked off the item on her clipboard. "They'll be delivered to the hall at five o'clock." She wished she could go to the Legion now and start organizing, but the town seniors played cribbage and canasta on Thursday afternoons. She wouldn't have access to the building until four o'clock.

Even calm, unflappable Lydia wasn't impervious to the commotion. She'd worn a beautiful silk caftan to work and had taken pains French-braiding her luxurious gray hair. Every time Kim passed her in the halls, she gave the impression of looking in the distance…down the hall, out a window, toward the door.

Kim knew she was hoping Devon would arrive early from Albuquerque and drop by the birth center.

Finally, it was four. Huddled in her coat against the cool winter breeze, Kim hurried to the parking lot, thankful that at least the March day was sunny. A storm would have made the high, mountainous roads treacherous for their out-of-town guests.

In two hours Kim, along with the other members of the decorating committee, managed to transform the utilitarian hall into an inviting, beautiful stage for the Mother and Child Reunion. They ran banners of baby photos around the hall—Trish had found one for almost all the guests who'd been born in The Birth Place. Silver- and gold-colored helium balloons, crisp white tablecloths and sparkling silver candle center-pieces managed to seem elegant and inviting at the same time. The flowers—white calla lilies and sprays of baby's breath—provided the perfect finishing touch.

Birth center staff had been asked to arrive early, with their escorts. Kim stationed them in pairs at each of the building's entrances to make sure no uninvited guests gained access to the building. She, herself, manned the main door. As people began to arrive, she checked off the names from her list. No way was any-one crashing this party.

By seven-fifteen, the large hall was buzzing with laughter and conversation, and Kim knew her evening was well on the road to being a great success.

"Congratulations, Kim. What a turnout."

Kim had been steeling herself for the moment when Nolan would arrive. She'd gone so far as to prepare herself for the possibility that he might bring a date. But he walked in the front door alone. He wore a charcoal-colored suit for the occasion, and a tie and shirt both in gray silk. He looked…incredible.

"Thanks."

"I see you haven't had time to get yourself a drink."

"That's fine. I'm really too busy."

He ignored her protests and five minutes later returned with a glass of white wine. "Let's drink to a night of generous donations." Nolan touched her glass with his. Even as he took that first sip, though, he kept his gaze on her.

She swallowed a mouthful of wine, feeling self-conscious about her off-the-shoulder neckline. Tonight she'd given in to vanity and curled her hair and worn a pretty dress. She'd even put on contact lenses and high heels.

But Nolan was looking at her strangely. "Is something wrong with my dress?"

"The dress is fine. It's not your gray cardigan, of course, but it's not bad."

She bit her lip at the silly comment. Her old sweater was hideous. That he could even *pretend* to be fond of it…

Well, it was touching.

Too touching.

Buck up, Kim. She *would not* get teary about such a little thing. "Where's Sammy tonight?"

"Toni Perez invited her for a sleepover."

The name sounded familiar. "Does she work at the Bulletin?"

"Actually she's my right-hand man. She's also one of the few people in town who was neither born at The Birth Place, nor gave birth in it. So when she heard of my baby-sitting predicament, she generously offered to help me out."

"Irene Davidson is here," Kim noted. "Is she doing better, then?"

"I think so. She has a doctor's appointment next week. She's hoping to get the green light to return to her home."

Kim ticked off Mitchell Dixon's name as he entered the hall. What was his connection to The Birth Place, she wondered? Trish had added his name to the guest list, but he was a few years too old to have been born here. Did he and his ex-wife have any children?

She might have asked Mitchell, but she was painfully aware of Nolan still standing at her side. Like an escort or something.

"Well, thanks again for the wine," she said, thinking to release him from whatever perceived obligation held him there.

But instead of joining the party, he began chatting about an article he was working on. Kim was happy to listen to the sound of his voice, even though she felt too keyed up to take in any meaning. By ten minutes to eight Kim decided it was time to lock the front doors.

Anxiously she checked her spreadsheet. "I have to find Parker. He needs to be at the front podium in ten minutes."

Nolan's continued presence at her side, while stimulating in more ways than one, was making her nervous.

"Excuse me," she said, attempting to brush past him. Unfortunately, her graceful exit was spoiled when she slipped and had to lunge forward to prevent a fall.

"You, okay?" Nolan steadied her. "I see I was wise to bring you white wine instead of red."

A few drops of her drink had splashed onto her black silk. The marks would disappear when the liquid dried. Why did she again feel on the verge of tears?

"I'm fine, Nolan. You don't need to keep holding me."

"Now, that's a matter of opinion." Still he obliged her by removing his hand, and then disappearing into the throng of guests.

Kim knew it was foolish to stare after him. She wasn't here as a guest—she had duties to perform. Cocktails from seven until eight were to be followed by a sit-down dinner. Parker would be providing the opening comments; Lydia's speech would come later, followed by a tribute from a former client.

Ashleigh Logan, the host of a popular talk show

about babies, had delivered her own son at The Birth Place last year. Although her busy schedule prevented her from attending the fund-raiser, she'd insisted on sending a special video greeting to be played at the festivities. The cassette had been forwarded along with a very generous donation from Ashleigh's wealthy husband, Greg Glazier. Apparently he was very happy with his new wife and their young son.

The presentations were to be concluded with a gentle reminder from Parker that a donation to The Birth Place was a wonderful way of ensuring the future health and happiness of the mothers and babies of Enchantment.

The program, Kim hoped, would run like clockwork. Only where was Parker? She'd seen him arrive with Hope earlier, but now the couple had become lost in the crowd.

"Good evening, ladies and gentlemen."

The familiar voice traveling over the sound system erased her worries. She should have known she could count on Parker. Circulating through the crowd, she encouraged guests to select a spot to sit.

A few minutes later, Parker called for quiet, then delivered his opening remarks. Kim didn't hear a word he uttered. From her spot in a far back corner, she located Nolan, sitting at a table about twenty feet ahead of her. From that moment on, she avoided glancing in his direction.

Lydia and Devon were both at the head table, Parker's currently empty chair between them. The other five members of the board of directors, along with the rest of the birth center staff, had mingled with invited guests as per her request. At a table on the opposite side of the room from Nolan, Kim spotted Irene Davidson and her neighbor, Mabel.

"And now," Parker's voice rose as he neared the end of his speech, "I'd like to introduce Lydia Kane, the woman whose vision created The Birth Place. Lydia, won't you please—"

"Baby killer!"

Kim glanced around the room, stunned. Irene Davidson stood at her table and shrieked again, *"Lydia Kane is a baby killer!"*

Kim's gaze collided with Nolan's as the familiar phrase brought them both to the same deduction.

"Lydia Kane is a dangerous woman. Don't anyone here listen to a word she says."

Guests stared in wonder as the well-dressed, respectable-looking matron made her way determinedly to the front of the room. Nolan leaped to his feet to follow and Kim wasn't far behind.

Unfortunately, the crowded tables and chairs made for slow progress. Irene, whose table had been near the front of the room, was soon at the podium.

Kim pulled out her cell phone and dialed the local police station.

"Let me have that microphone, young man."

Parker stepped back at Irene's command but wasn't prepared to have the older woman forcibly yank the microphone from his hands. He signaled to Kim, who was already insisting that an officer be sent to the Legion Hall immediately.

She was told that a constable had been cruising the area and would be at the door within a few minutes.

"I'm here to demand Lydia Kane's immediate resignation from The Birth Place." Irene's cheeks were burning with color, and her eyes flashed with unleashed passion as she faced the crowd of stunned onlookers.

Poor Lydia, sitting on public display at her place of honor, took the verbal attack in silence. Yet even from a distance Kim could spot a sudden tremor in her proudly held head.

Why was this happening? Kim blamed herself. But how could she have guessed Irene Davidson would be the guilty party? The poor woman had been so sick lately…

"I want everyone in this room to know this." Irene slammed her fist on the podium. "Lydia Kane killed my daughter-in-law. And she killed my grandson, too. If it wasn't for her, my Steve would still be alive—"

Her voice broke at this point, but spying Nolan, who was almost upon her, fueled her determination.

"And that's not all. Lydia Kane killed her own baby when she was just sixteen years old. She went to Denver and had an abortion. Tell them the truth, Lydia. Admit it!"

Finally Nolan reached the stage. He pulled the microphone from her hands and immediately scooped the woman into his arms as she fainted. A local cop, one Kim didn't recognize, burst into the room at that point. Nolan signaled for his help, and together they carried Irene out of the room.

Expecting chaos to erupt at that point, Kim was stunned by the sudden quiet that fell over the crowd. The guests stared blankly at each other—and at Lydia, who sat, motionless, at her place at the head table.

Kim felt as if a knife had been shoved into her own heart. Poor Lydia didn't deserve any of this. And the fund-raiser... In five brutal minutes Irene Davidson had turned it into a total and crushing failure.

Who would give The Birth Place any money after this? And how could Lydia—still sitting tall, her face frozen into a shocked expression—face any of these people again?

At that instant, Kim saw there was only one thing to do.

"Could I have your attention for a minute, please." In the hushed room everyone heard her. The crowd remained quiet as she made her way to the front and collected the microphone from the floor where it had fallen.

"I apologize for the unexpected interruption to our program," she said quickly. "I think we all feel badly for Irene Davidson and her terrible losses. But Lydia Kane certainly bears no responsibility for the death of Mary Davidson. Her actions were commended by Dr. Ochoa at the Arroyo County Hospital. I see he's here tonight."

She nodded at the doctor and was relieved when he

acknowledged her comment by standing and bowing gallantly in Lydia's direction.

"If you have any concerns about Lydia Kane's competency as a midwife, I'm sure he'll be pleased to set your mind at rest."

A slow murmur of conversation started as the initial shock wore off. Kim could tell people accepted her explanation as correct. But it wouldn't be enough, she knew. She had to dispel *all* the ugly rumors that Irene Davidson had planted in their minds.

"As for the accusation made by Irene tonight that Lydia Kane had an abortion when she was sixteen…"

Immediately the buzz of light conversation died off. All heads turned in her direction once more including, Kim noticed, Lydia's. A movement from one of the back doors caught her attention and she saw Nolan standing there, listening, too.

"It's true that Lydia Kane became pregnant when she was only sixteen. But I'm the living proof that she did not have an abortion. You see, my mother, Eliza Ann, was Lydia's daughter. And I'm her granddaughter."

CHAPTER TWENTY

KIM IS MY GRANDDAUGHTER. For several moments after Kim's announcement, Lydia couldn't breathe. And it seemed as if the others in the room couldn't, either.

Then the preternatural quiet exploded in applause. Some guests stood, others cheered. Parker rescued the microphone from Kim, who had begun to tremble so wildly she could barely stand. Nolan McKinnon stepped forward to help her off the stage.

Lydia wanted to run after them. In fact, she was pushing back her chair when she sensed someone watching her. She glanced over at Devon.

Oh no. Devon, her beautiful Devon. Lydia reached out a hand, but her granddaughter avoided the touch.

"Well, Lydia."

Devon's voice, tight with restrained anger and hurt, claimed her full attention.

"Yet another secret from your past. You are so full of surprises."

Fury boiled in Devon's normally cool gray eyes. Eyes just like her grandmother's…and, come to think of it, like Kim's, as well. The glasses Kim always wore had camouflaged the similarity.

"Devon, darling, I know this must be a shock."

Lydia held out her hand again, beseeching her grand-daughter to withhold judgment.

But Devon was young. And strong willed. And idealistic. She turned away as if the merest touch from Lydia was offensive. "Does Mom know you had a baby when you were a teenager?"

"No," Lydia had to admit. "This happened years before your mother was born." And there'd never been occasion to raise the subject, though the baby she'd given up for adoption had often been in Lydia's thoughts.

But she'd never tried to find her. She hadn't done such a great job with the children she'd kept. Why stir up painful feelings in the one she'd given away?

Now she looked at her granddaughter and wondered if she'd ever regain her trust and respect. How did she manage to make mistake after mistake where the people she loved most were concerned? The muscles in her chest tightened with the pressure of all those errors from her past. She could well imagine how poor Devon felt. To her, choices were black-and-white, wrong and right.

At sixteen Lydia had learned the world wasn't that simple. Her father had browbeaten her into giving her baby up for adoption. She'd consoled herself with the hope that her child would have a better chance at happiness with a real family and a mature mother.

Whether she'd made the right choice, she'd probably never know.

She longed to try and explain all this to Devon, but

knew it would have to wait for another time. Tonight, another young woman needed her more. Kim Sherman's unexpected announcement had probably saved The Birth Place fund-raiser. But Lydia knew it had come at great personal cost.

She needed to speak to Kim.

UNDERSTANDING THAT KIM WOULD crave privacy, Nolan whisked her into a small office at the back of the hall. She followed him meekly, her body still not fully under her control. Nolan recognized shock when he saw it. He took off his jacket and covered her bare shoulders.

"Sit down, Kim," he urged gently.

She did as he asked, moving robotically, her gaze vacant. God, but she'd been brave to go up on the stage and tell the truth, not just to Lydia, but to a crowd of her co-workers and strangers, as well. This past week he'd been pretty angry with her for shutting him out, but all those negative feelings melted in the face of her current distress.

He sat next to her, took her hand and rubbed it briskly. "That was a very courageous thing you just did."

No response.

"I realize you didn't want Lydia to know who you really are. I'm not sure I understand *why*, though." Kim's hands were ice-cold and her face was so…blank. What thoughts were racing through her mind right now? Or was she still too numb to think?

He was just beginning to realize how complicated this woman he'd fallen in love with was. But that was okay, because he had a lifetime to devote to figuring her out. If she'd only give him the chance.

"Kim—" he placed an arm around her shoulders "—it's going to be okay."

A new voice came from the doorway. Lydia Kane's. "Nolan is right, Kim. Everything is going to be okay." She entered the room bringing her trademark combination of kindness and authority.

Kim responded immediately. Her muscles stiffened, her eyes widened. "I can't talk to her." She buried her face against Nolan's chest. He circled his arms around her protectively.

"Maybe it's too soon," he said to Lydia. But the older woman shook her head.

"Kim, I'm sorry. I'm an old woman and I've learned there are certain moments in life that should never be put off."

Slowly Kim pulled out of Nolan's embrace.

"I should have known the first time I saw you." Lydia regarded the young woman with new perspective. "Those eyes are a dead giveaway. How did I miss the similarity to Devon?"

"Tell Lydia about the earrings," Nolan urged. Then wondered if he should have kept silent when Kim didn't respond.

But Lydia's interest had been piqued. "Do you own them, Kim? I always wondered if they'd been passed down as I asked. I thought maybe your mother…"

Finally Kim began to show normal signs of responsiveness. Her shoulders relaxed, her eyes focused. "My mother died a long time ago. The earrings were saved for me, though. I have them with me. I don't know why." She opened the clasp of her little black purse and pulled out the jewelry.

Lydia held out her hands, and Kim passed the earrings over.

"I never thought I'd see these again. How sad about your mother. Though, it's strange, I don't feel surprised to hear about her death. It's almost as if a part of me already knew."

Lydia held the tiny stones next to her pendant. Clearly all three stones had been mined from the same vein, the coloration and patterns of movement were so similar.

"I wanted to wear them tonight," Kim admitted, "but I couldn't risk you seeing them, so I put them in my purse, instead."

"Would you try them on now?" Lydia asked gently. "For me?"

Kim had already proved how much she would do for her grandmother. But her fingers were trembling too much to work the delicate silver clasps. And so were Lydia's.

That left Nolan. Touching Kim's smooth skin, smelling her perfume, brushing his face against her hair, were vivid reminders to him of how fragile this woman was. Her toughness was such an act. An act she'd come damn close to perfecting.

"Beautiful." Lydia smiled fondly at the young woman in front of her. "Those earrings might have been made for you, Kim, they suit you so perfectly."

Kim put a hand tentatively to one of the stones.

"I hope you'll wear them often," Lydia continued. "I can't believe this is happening. Perhaps one of you should pinch me. You're my *granddaughter*. Oh, Kim, this is one of the happiest days of my life."

Kim blinked back tears, but Lydia let her own fall freely. Nolan realized that much as he wanted to stay by Kim's side, these two women needed to be alone for a few minutes.

"Let me know if you need me," he murmured to Kim.

She heard his words and felt the cool air waft in from the hall as he departed. But all she could truly concentrate on was Lydia's last statement.

"Did you say you're *happy?*"

"But of course. Do you know how often I wondered about your mother? Whether she'd ever married. Whether she had children herself. Oh, there's so much you need to tell me, Kim. So much I need to tell you."

Then, as if she could no longer resist the urge, she hugged her. And as Kim felt those strong arms reach around her back, something that had been clutched tightly inside her heart for many, many years was released.

"Oh, Grandmother."

"My darling girl. Now that we've found each other, I don't want to ever let you go."

And that was exactly how Kim felt, too.

"Looks like we're the last ones out."

Parker sounded—and looked—tired as he handed the last batch of donation checks to Kim. She added them to the rest, then locked her briefcase. She hadn't had time to run any totals, of course, but The Birth Place's financial future had never looked brighter.

"Here's your coat, Kim." Parker helped her on with it, then slid into his own jacket. "Do you have the key?"

"Right here." After they stepped outside, she locked the doors and Parker checked them just to be sure. The wind had died down through the course of the evening and the outside air felt almost warm. Above, stars blazed in the New Mexico sky.

"What a great evening." She inhaled deeply.

"It sure was. Thanks to you."

She'd been referring to the weather, but Parker's compliment was all about the donations that had flooded in that night, with promises of more to be mailed in the next week or so.

"I'm just glad that we won't have to worry about money so much."

"Not for the next few months anyway," Parker joked. "Let me walk you to your car. I don't like the idea of you wandering around with all those checks in your briefcase."

From out of the darkness came another male voice. "Neither do I. I'll provide the escort tonight, if that's okay with Kim."

As her eyes adjusted to the low light, Kim made out Nolan perched on the hood of her Camry. He'd changed out of his suit and was wearing jeans and his old leather jacket.

"Fine with me," Parker said. "Have a good night, you two. And Kim? If you want to sleep in a little tomorrow, be my guest. I know I'm going to." Whistling cheerfully, he walked off, obviously pleased at the idea of returning home to his wife who had left earlier to relieve their teenage baby-sitter.

Kim was left standing in front of Nolan, her briefcase in one hand, her purse in the other.

"Sleeping in and going to work late sounds like pretty wild behavior," he teased. "Do you think you're capable?"

She smiled. Yesterday, she wouldn't have been. Today—who knew? A lot of things had changed for her in the space of a very short period of time.

She had lunch planned with Lydia for tomorrow. Her grandmother had made it very clear that Kim was family now. Family. And Mabel had made a tentative overture, as well. She'd talked about introducing Kim to her brother Richard the next time he visited Enchantment.

Kim wondered if anyone could understand how much this all meant to her.

"Where have you been?" she asked. After he'd

slipped out to let her and Lydia talk in private, she hadn't spotted him again.

"At the hospital." Nolan patted the Camry's hood for her to join him. After a slight hesitation, she hiked up her skirt and let him pull her up.

"Is Irene okay?"

"They've admitted her for the night, but I think come morning I'll be driving her back to the rest home in Taos." Nolan's face showed his worry. "I'm so sorry she caused you all this trouble and grief. I feel responsible."

"But Nolan, you had no way of knowing…"

"Still, with Steve and Mary gone, it's up to me to look out for her. I spoke to Mabel tonight. We figure she must have delivered those letters when she went for her walks. Remember how we didn't receive any when she was in Taos for those two weeks?"

"Right." It was still so hard for Kim to believe that frail Irene Davidson was capable of such maliciousness. The poor woman had been totally twisted by her grief.

"Mabel feels bad, as well," Nolan continued. "She'd told Irene the old gossip about Lydia and her teenage pregnancy. But try not to blame Mabel, Kim. She and Irene have been friends a long time. I'm sure she felt Irene was someone she could trust. And before all this happened, she probably was."

"I'm just glad it's over. I'm not blaming anyone."

"Want to hear something funny? At one point I suspected Mitchell Dixon of sending the letters. I couldn't understand why he kept hanging out at the birth center.''

Thinking of kind, hardworking Mitchell, Kim had to smile. ''And did you get your answer tonight?''

Nolan nodded ruefully. ''He trailed Trish Linden like a lovesick puppy.''

''Yes. He uses any excuse to see her. He often brings his photos by under the pretext of seeking her opinion. But all he really wants is to be near her.''

Nolan took her hand, squeezed her fingers. ''I can relate.''

Pure happiness, brighter than the stars, exploded in Kim's heart. Nolan's touch. The intimate tone of his voice. It was all too much.

''When I asked you to marry me, Kim, it wasn't because of Sammy.''

She hadn't needed him to tell her. Just seeing the way he was looking at her now, and remembering how gentle and patient he'd been with her tonight, told her his emotions were true—just like hers for him.

''I know, Nolan. You and Sammy are fine on your own. I saw it on Monday when you showed up for the appointment with Celia. She trusts you now.''

''Yeah, she does. And I think she loves me, too. The way I've come to love her. She's quite a kid, Kim.''

''She sure is.'' The urge to hug him was so strong. Two months ago Nolan had been the quintessential bachelor. But he'd overcome his own problems in order to be there for his niece. And now he was taking responsibility for Irene, too. Nolan had proven himself loyal, kindhearted and strong.

"Kim." He put her hand against his T-shirt, so she could feel his heart beating. "I asked you to marry me because I love you. If you still feel you have to leave Enchantment, then I guess you do. But when you go, I want you to know what you're leaving behind."

With his other hand he circled her shoulders, making it impossible for her to look at anything but him. Not that she cared.

"I fell in love with you before I even moved here," she admitted.

"What?"

"I had a subscription to the *Bulletin*. I loved your editorials."

"Kim, I still have the ring. It's in my pocket. I hoped that after what happened tonight you might have second thoughts."

And she had. But Nolan didn't give her a chance to voice them. He lowered his head and kissed her and, after a few seconds, she forgot about everything except this man she loved and the way he made her feel.

As if she was the most important woman in the world.

It was a marvelous feeling.

SHE WASN'T LEAVING Enchantment after all. By the time Nolan had driven her home, by the time she'd hidden the checks from her briefcase in the freezer, by the time they'd laughed and cried, made love and cuddled, Kim knew this one fact for certainty.

Lying in Nolan's arms, wearing his ring and her grandmother's earrings, Kim made plans while her fiancé slept. Tomorrow she would go into the office and destroy her letter of resignation. She'd phone the director of personnel who had offered her a job interview and cancel the appointment.

Then she'd have lunch with her grandmother. Maybe Lydia would be able to persuade Devon to join them. Kim was very hopeful that over time Devon might come to like her.

Later, she'd have dinner with Nolan and Sammy. Together they'd tell the little girl their news. Kim was sure she'd be delighted. And she'd make such an adorable flower girl.

The wedding would take place that summer, she and Nolan had decided. They'd talked for a long time after they'd made love. For Sammy's sake, they wouldn't rush anything. But in a year, or maybe two, the little girl might be happy to welcome a new child into her life.

Kim stared out the window and remembered being a little girl and dreaming of a family of her own.

As of tonight, she had it. A grandmother, a husband, a child.

No, she wouldn't be leaving Enchantment. Not ever.

*Please turn the page for
an excerpt from Kathleen O'Brien's*
THE HOMECOMING BABY—
*the fifth title in
Harlequin Superromance's*
THE BIRTH PLACE *series.*

Watch for it next month.

CHAPTER ONE

"I'M PATRICK TORRANCE. Were you looking for me?"

The other man's handshake was firm. "Yes, sir, I was. Your secretary said you'd be here. I'm Don Frost. Frost Investigations."

Patrick nodded, his attention sharpening. He'd hired Frost Investigations two weeks ago, but all their business had been conducted via e-mail, snail mail and secretaries. He suddenly realized he'd done that deliberately. He hadn't wanted to think of a real live human being prying into his background, unearthing the sordid details of his adoption.

It wasn't that Patrick thought it shameful to be adopted. The embarrassment was more from being seen to care. It was pathetic, somehow, to yearn for a reunion with people who had abandoned you decades ago.

Not that Patrick longed for anything of the sort. If he craved anything, it was merely information. Julian Torrance wasn't his father, thank God, but someone was. And Patrick had a right to know who.

Don Frost was squatting now, scratching the ears of a black-eyed mutt who had come by for an introduction. The dog was licking his wrist, and the investigator appeared to be enjoying the experience.

Patrick waited for Don to finish, fighting back a prick of impatience.

He had left instructions that he was to be informed the minute the firm had unearthed anything concrete—but he'd expected a call or e-mail. He wondered what it meant that Don Frost had felt the need to show up personally.

"It's nice to meet you, Don," he said. He put on his best professional poker face. "What brings you here? I assume you have news?"

Don paused. "I think I do," he said, and it was clear he was choosing his words carefully. "Is there somewhere we could go? Maybe sit down? Anywhere a little more private?"

Patrick considered his options. He knew the owners of this estate casually, but not well enough to confiscate their living room for a private meeting. Down by the waterfront was a rather pretentious Greek Folly. It was a ridiculous thing—but it had the benefit of being cold down there, and windy. They'd probably have the place to themselves.

"Come with me," he said. Don Frost nodded and followed without question.

When they reached the Folly, which was close enough to the pounding ocean surf to prevent them from being overheard, Patrick turned to the other man. Time to get to the point.

But the investigator still seemed uncomfortable. He

dug his hands in his pockets and chewed on the inside of his cheek for a long minute before beginning.

"Okay," he said. "Here it is. In this kind of investigation I usually mail the results to my clients, just the names and the dates and enough documentation to establish the facts. Ordinarily it's all pretty neat and tidy."

Patrick leaned against one smooth marble column and smiled. "But this investigation, I gather, was not quite so tidy."

Don met his gaze. "No, it wasn't." He sat down on the curving marble seat. "At first it was fine. I traced the adoption itself fairly easily, to a small town in New Mexico. A town called Enchantment."

Patrick smiled again. "How quaint."

The investigator didn't return the smile. "Yes, sir. But the investigation got a little more complicated from there. You see, the accompanying paperwork doesn't include the full complement of information, and several relevant particulars, items of significance pertaining—"

Patrick's hand twitched. "For God's sake, Frost. You sound like my lawyer, who thinks he gets paid by the syllable. Why don't you cut to the chase?"

The investigator hesitated. But he didn't need to be so miserable. Patrick thought he knew where this was heading.

"Let me make it easier for you," Patrick interjected. "Something's missing on the birth certificate, right? There's a blank where the father's name should be?''

The man nodded. ''Yes, that's right. It's not at all unusual in these cases. Frankly, the name on that particular line is 'Unknown' more often than not. But this birth certificate…'' He cleared his throat. ''This one—''

Patrick waited. It really was cold out here. The ocean breezes whipped thorough his wool-blend jacket as if it were made of gauze.

''This birth certificate?'' he prompted.

The other man squared his shoulders. Down to business.

''This birth certificate doesn't name the father. But it also doesn't name the mother. On this one, both parents are simply listed as 'unknown.'''

Both parents? How? Patrick felt the sudden need to sit down, too. But he overcame it. When you grew up as Julian Torrance's son, you learned early never to show the least sign of weakness.

''How is that possible, Mr. Frost?''

''Well, naturally I wanted to know that myself. I've been looking into it for the past week. I had hoped to find out something that would make the news a little more—'' His gaze slid to the side. ''A little more tidy.''

''But?''

''But I'm afraid this story just isn't tidy. That's why I came myself. I thought I should, in case you had questions.''

"I have nothing but questions," Patrick said. "You aren't providing much of anything but riddles. Surely when a woman delivers a baby, she has to give the hospital her name."

"She does if she goes to a hospital. This mother didn't. In this particular case, the mother delivered the baby herself. The baby was subsequently found and sent to the local birthing center. The adoption was formalized from there."

The baby was subsequently found...

Patrick sat down. He had no choice.

"I'm listening," he said. "Just go ahead and tell me everything."

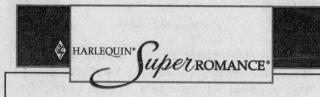

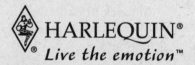

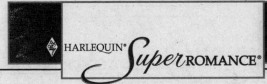

Koomera Crossing

**Welcome to Koomera Crossing,
a town hidden deep in the Australian Outback.
Let renowned romance novelist Margaret Way
take you there. Let her introduce you to
the people of Koomera Crossing.
Let her tell you their secrets....**

Watch for

Home to Eden,

**available from Harlequin Superromance
in February 2004.**

And don't miss the other Koomera Crossing books:

Sarah's Baby
(Harlequin Superromance #1111, February 2003)

Runaway Wife
(Harlequin Romance, October 2003)

Outback Bridegroom
(Harlequin Romance, November 2003)

Outback Surrender
(Harlequin Romance, December 2003)

HARLEQUIN *Super*ROMANCE®

THE BIRTH PLACE

Enchantment, New Mexico, is home to The Birth Place, a maternity clinic run by the formidable Lydia Kane. The clinic was started years ago—to make sure the people of this secluded mountain town had a safe place to deliver their babies.

But some births are shrouded in secrecy and shame. What happens when a few of those secrets return to haunt The Birth Place?

January 2004

The Homecoming Baby (#1176)
by Kathleen O'Brien

Patrick Torrance is shocked to discover he's adopted. But that's nothing compared to what he feels when he finds out the details of his birth. He's Enchantment's so-called Homecoming Baby—born and abandoned in the girls' room during a high school dance. There are rumors about his parents, and he's determined to find out the truth. Even if he has to use some of Enchantment's residents to get the answers he wants.

Watch for the conclusion to THE BIRTH PLACE:

February 2004,

The Midwife and the Lawman (#1182)
by Marisa Carroll

Available wherever Harlequin Superromance books are sold.

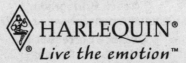

HARLEQUIN®
Live the emotion™

Visit us at www.eHarlequin.com

HSRHCB

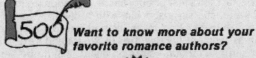

HARLEQUIN *Super*ROMANCE®

The Rancher's Bride
by Barbara McMahon
(Superromance #1179)

9 MONTHS LATER

On sale January 2004

Brianna Dawson needs to change her life. And for a Madison Avenue ad exec, life doesn't get more different than a cattle ranch in Wyoming. Which is why she gets in her car and drives for a week to accept the proposal of a cowboy she met once a long time ago. What Brianna doesn't know is that the marriage of convenience comes with a serious stipulation—a child by the end of the year.

Getting Married Again
by Melinda Curtis
(Superromance #1187)

On sale February 2004

To Lexie, Jackson's first priority has always been his job. Eight months ago, she surprised him with a divorce—and a final invitation into her bed. Now Jackson has returned from a foreign assignment fighting fires in Russia and Lexie's got a bigger surprise for him—she's pregnant. Will he be here for her this time, just when she needs him the most?

Available wherever Harlequin books are sold.

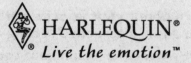

HARLEQUIN®
Live the emotion™

Forrester Square
LEGACIES. LIES. LOVE.

Award-winning author Day Leclaire
brings a highly emotional and
exciting reunion romance story to
Forrester Square in December...

KEEPING FAITH
by
Day Leclaire

Faith Marshall's dream of a "white-picket" life with
Ethan Dunn disappeared—along with her husband—
when she discovered that he was really a dangerous
mercenary. With Ethan missing in action, Faith found
herself alone, pregnant and struggling to survive.
Now, years later, Ethan turns up alive. Will a family
reunion be possible after so much deception?

Forrester Square...
Legacies. Lies. Love.

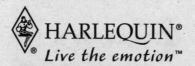

HARLEQUIN®
Live the emotion™

Visit us at www.forrestersquare.com   PHFS5

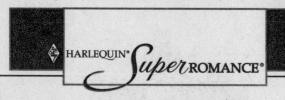

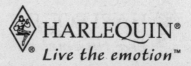